All the Silent Voices

by

Elena Mikalsen

This is a work of fiction. Names, characters, places, and incidents are either the product of the author's imagination or are used fictitiously, and any resemblance to actual persons living or dead, business establishments, events, or locales, is entirely coincidental.

All the Silent Voices

Contact Information: info@thewildrosepress.com

Cover Art by *Diana Carlile*

The Wild Rose Press, Inc.
PO Box 708
Adams Basin, NY 14410-0708
Visit us at www.thewildrosepress.com

Publishing History
First Mainstream Thriller Edition, 2019
Print ISBN 978-1-5092-2889-8
Digital ISBN 978-1-5092-2890-4

Published in the United States of America

I'm gripped by terror, icicles spreading through me and freezing my entire body as I stare into the face of Richard Stolar. His hair is still dirty blond and cropped short. He is wearing a designer black suit, crisp white shirt, and an ugly purple tie.

"Yes, Aidan's been telling me about your latest product campaign. And I've been very impressed with the portfolios I've seen. Your department runs very efficiently." Richard stretches his hand toward me. "It's a pleasure. We need to talk new sales strategy ideas. We are about to bring a breakthrough drug on the market, and I'll need your skills."

Aidan is pushing me toward Richard, and I will my face to contort into a smile and my hand to shake his. I'm terrified of feeling the touch of his skin on mine. My mouth is dry as a desert. I try to focus my eyes on something besides his face, but then all I can see is his ugly purple tie.

Does he recognize me?

Praise for Elena Mikalsen and…

WRAPPED IN THE STARS:

"An intelligent and beautifully crafted story that proves the power of love while illuminating the historical struggles of women in medicine."

~Kelli Estes, author

"A unique and charming work. Endearing characters and the plot is bewitching."

~Fleeta Cunningham, author

"A richly detailed journey. A tale of aspirations and familial pressures, of serendipity and the choices we make, *WRAPPED IN THE STARS* thoughtfully explores how we can take control of our lives."

~Amanda Stauffer, author

THE HOUSE BY THE CYPRESS TREES:

"A romantic tale about the restorative potential of travel… The author presents believable characters with complex interior lives."

~Kirkus Review

"Set in a sun-soaked Italy, *The House by the Cypress Trees* is a treat for the senses. Beautiful food, wine, and romance, along with a gorgeous setting, make this novel hard to put down!"

~Sarahlyn Bruck, bestselling author

Dedication

The world is full of silent voices;
Those whose voices have been taken away
by abuse, fear, and evil,
Those who have been terrified into silence,
Those who haven't had their day in court,
Those who have suffered in pain
and who hide in the shadows
instead of walking proudly
and greeting their future with joy.

One day, I believe you will find your strength
and let your voices roar.

This story is for you.

Acknowledgements

I owe my entire writing career to the writers of the Women's Fiction Writers Association. More specifically to Martha Sessums, Michele Montgomery, and Jennifer Labadie Fromke, my fantastic critique partners who provided invaluable feedback.

A huge thank you to my incredible daughter, Emily, who was an inspiration for Sophie and came up with some of the great ideas for how Sophie could help her mom with her revenge plans. My dear brother-in-law, Edward, provided some great help with understanding how pharma companies operate.

Thank you to my husband, who is the kindest and the most supportive partner any woman could wish for and who, of course, was the inspiration for Aidan. Not only did David inspire this character, he also spent many hours explaining to me the ins and outs of the financial world he lives in and the particulars of business meetings, insider trading, and financial deals I would need to understand.

Even though Emma's story is fictional, all events were carefully researched and have happened at various universities, businesses, workplaces around the country. As I finished writing this story, #MeToo movement was gathering speed and women began to tell their stories. But many women, like Emma, still felt their stories could never be heard. They were not famous, were too frightened, their attackers too powerful, and their voices were silenced. I hope this book gives them some hope.

I hear you. I believe you. And I hope my readers will, as well.

Twenty-one years ago…

He means to kill me—I see it in his eyes.

The pain from the blow travels with lightning speed from my jaw to my brain. I cover my face and turn away as his fists land again and again. I must make it back up the steps. The stairway door is only a few steps away. There are people on the other side. Someone will help me.

I'm not prepared for the next shot he takes. As I fall back down the steps, all hope I reach the door is lost. The breath rushes out of me with a whoosh as my side hits the landing. I wonder if my best choice is to stop breathing altogether. I pretend I'm dead. Will that stop him? The cement floor is cold. I'm terrified I'll shiver and show him I'm still alive.

My stomach lurches suddenly as the scent of stale urine reaches my nostrils. I must not vomit. There is a taste of blood in my mouth. I open my swollen lips and let it pour out, the warm puddle forming by my cheek. Why is this happening to me?

It's quiet for a second, and I open my eyes. The gray wall in front of me—covered in graffiti—sways. I feel his heavy weight on top of me. My neck burns from the heat of his breath. No one is coming to help.

I will survive, and I won't let him get away with this.

Chapter 1

The Potomac River runs wild from the mountains of the Potomac Highlands and into the Chesapeake Bay. As it reaches the Great Falls suburb, just north of Washington, D.C., the river builds up speed and force until it crushes over jagged rocks in a series of rapids and waterfalls.

Years ago, Aidan and I found a perfect red-brick house here, hidden by tall trees, hanging to the edge of a hill. From all our windows, we can hear the calming sounds of the rushing water as the river curves around the bank. It's been a happy home to us and our daughter, Sophie.

I walk to the river with my dog almost every day after work, but there will be no time today. It's Aidan's birthday, and there is a long to-do list. As I get up this morning, I briefly open the window, listen to the river, and inhale the icy wetness of the November air.

"Honey, thank you for the coffee," I say in the direction of the bathroom.

Aidan, forever attentive, placed a steaming cup on my nightstand as I slept. I take a careful sip before I close the window with regret.

"Brr, it's cold in here. Come warm me up." Aidan comes out of the bathroom, wraps his arms around my waist, and pulls me in against him.

He is already dressed and freshly shaved; his neck

smells divine of the new cologne I gave him last week.

"How do you manage to look so handsome this early in the morning?" I ask. I wrap my arms around his neck and raise myself on tiptoes to reach that sensitive spot he likes me to kiss behind his ear. "I love you," I whisper.

He runs a hand along the side of my left breast. "If only I had time," he says in a husky voice. His lips are warm on mine when he kisses me.

"Make time." I want him to stay and hold me for a while longer. I crave his touch. "It's your birthday, after all. We can start celebrating now." I unbuckle his belt and slide my hand down.

He moans but pulls away. "I'm sorry. I have to go. Early meeting with John."

My mind switches its focus. "About the sale?"

"I'm afraid so," he says, fixing his shirt and pants.

"So there's no way to save the company? We're going to be Eli Lilly now?"

"You sit in the same meetings; you know the trouble we're in. If John doesn't sell, D&P will go bankrupt."

"Poor John."

"Poor John? Sweetheart, we might lose our jobs."

"Well, of course I'm thinking about us. But it was his life's work to build this company." I follow him to the hallway. "And I love working for D&P. You know what I mean. John has principles."

"Well, that's why we're still here, right?" He picks up his briefcase. "Let's just hope there are growth opportunities for both of us next. I'm sure we'll be developing large-scale projects for Eli Lilly."

I straighten his tie and kiss him again. "If they let

us keep our jobs. Take John out for lunch or something. But come home early. I have surprises."

"You do?" He smiles. He loves when I go all out for his birthday.

"Just remember to come home early," I reply, winking.

Against our better judgment, Aidan and I work for the same pharmaceutical company, Davis & Parsons. He was promoted to Vice President of Finance three years ago and has been working overtime ever since. As a Marketing Director, I don't keep such long hours, but I do travel a great deal. So we miss each other. And I get very little time with our daughter, Sophie, who leaves for NYU this summer. But today I'm lucky—I can make time for them both.

When Aidan leaves, I peek at my phone. It's still too early to wake Sophie. The quiet in the house is eerie. I unload the dishwasher just to hear noise. I feed the dog, shower, and get dressed. Yet time stands still. I tiptoe upstairs and peek into Sophie's room. I know every corner of the still purple-and-sparkle room, although she doesn't allow me inside as much anymore. On the bed, all that's visible is a mess of limbs and blankets. A voice in my head whispers that I should be a good mother and let my teenager sleep in, but I silence it. I mean—she's been waking me up her entire childhood. Can't I do it just this one time?

I lift the blanket and find a tiny unoccupied spot to cozy into. Sophie's body immediately wraps around me. She'll be mad at me later for this moment. I watch her sleeping face in the light that seeps through the opening in her curtains. The freckles form a triangle on her cheeks and forehead. The golden-brown hair falls softly around her face. I used to have brown hair just like hers, with streaks of gold throughout.

"Mom, are you staring at me again?" Her voice is barely a whisper, and her eyes are still closed.

"I'm allowed to stare at you all I want." I ping her nose lightly, then kiss her forehead. "You are so beautiful."

"What time is it?" she asks, as she opens her eyes and yawns.

"It's still very early. You can keep on sleeping."

"I'm up." She sits up and stretches.

"Sorry, I was lonely."

"I knew you wouldn't let me sleep. You always make such a big fuss about Dad's birthday. So are we shopping all day?"

"Part of the day. We have to bake the cheesecake, too."

She rises slowly and begins to dress. "Can't we just buy a cake like normal people, at the bakery?"

"We could, but it's tradition."

"That's right." She laughs. "He fell in love with you over a cheesecake."

"Not quite. He ordered a cheesecake from the deli I worked at. I went to deliver it to his office, and we crashed into each other by the elevator—"

"And he followed you and started talking to you and invited you for coffee, and you talked for another six hours. Yeah, I know the story." She rolls her eyes.

"Sorry I'm boring you." I raise my brows.

"Is the story true, though? Did he fall in love with you just like that? And did you feel it that instant? Did you know?"

I scramble out of her bed and find her glasses on

the nightstand to hand to her. “Baby, I still remember the look in your father’s eyes when we first met. I knew right then that I was meant to marry him.”

“You are so stereotypical.” She rolls her eyes again. We head to the kitchen, and I pour two bowls of milk as Sophie gets cereal out of the pantry. I reach for my cold bowl with both hands but, as I turn, my hip hits the edge of the kitchen counter. I stumble and try to set the bowl of milk down, but it drops clumsily. Its contents spill all over the counter and drown my phone.

“Crap!”

My phone is soaked. Sophie picks it up with two fingers as it drips white liquid all over the floor. I run to the pantry, grab the jar of rice, and plunge the phone into it.

Sophie shakes her head. “Mom, you know that never works.”

I glare at her, then pull the phone out.

“It’s never coming back. Get a new one. You were due for an upgrade anyway.”

“My phone is perfectly fine,” I say.

“It’s a techno dinosaur.” She raises her brows.

“We’ll need to add a stop at the wireless store to our list.”

“How about you go to the mall and get a new phone and Dad’s presents, and I’ll drive to the grocery store and get all the stuff for the cheesecake?”

“Are you sure? All the Thanksgiving shoppers are there. You might need a bodyguard.”

“I’ll text Jenna to come with me. She has grandparents visiting. She’ll love to get out of the house.”

“Is this what you’d do if your grandmother

visited?"

"I like my grandmother. It's you who doesn't like her."

"I like my mother just fine," I grumble.

As Sophie leaves with a grocery list, I check over my to-do list. Cheesecake, presents. Now I add "pick up new phone" as well. Once the cheesecake is finished, Sophie and I will get dressed, and we'll wait for Aidan to arrive so we can drive him to a restaurant where a dozen of his friends will be waiting to surprise him.

The roads are slippery as I drive, and the traffic is agony. Today is not working out as planned at all. Changes unnerve me. I need organization and order to my life. I thrive on schedules, timelines, and careful planning.

"I need a new phone," I say to the smiling salesperson when I finally arrive at the wireless store, fumbling with my purse as I try to find the dead one.

"Of course." He smiles. "Can I show you our best-selling models?"

"I just want the same one I had," I groan.

He looks up my account on his tablet, his fingers moving fast. "Great news, you're eligible for an upgrade."

His voice is salesman-sweet, he stands too close to me, and he reeks of cheap cologne. Too late, as the nausea arrives, I remember that I skipped breakfast.

"No, thanks, I just want my old phone back," I say through my teeth, breathing slowly.

"Apple doesn't make this version anymore. I apologize."

"Fine, I'll upgrade. Just give me whatever you can set up the fastest. I'm in a hurry."

He glares at me but brings out a box. *He* is not in a hurry and, obviously, ignores my cues. A painful hour later, my new iPhone is booted up and buzzing with texts from Aidan. As I'm ready to check out, the device rings.

"I'm sorry, my phone died a while ago. I spilled milk on it," I explain to Aidan.

"What? Listen, I was trying to reach you about my meeting with John. It's done. He signed the deal."

"What?" My heart skips a beat. "But how come he only shared this with you? Shouldn't all of the senior team know about this?"

"They do know, except for you and Dana since you were both out today. He asked me to break the news to you."

I swallow the disappointment of finding out secondhand. "So—we're Eli Lilly now?"

"It's not Eli Lilly. It's this company I'm not familiar with. But John is very happy about it. Avias Global. The new president will be in any minute for a tour and a meeting."

"It's someone unknown? And it's happening this quickly?"

"Yes. Today."

"Do I need to be there? I should really come in."

"No, no, enjoy your day off. It's fine."

"Are we going to lose our jobs?" I whisper.

"I don't know." He's silent for a moment. "There's a lot of uncertainty at this point, but I think we are safe. D&P is merging with Avias; it's not being completely taken over. John will sit on the board of directors. He is asking me to have dinner with him and the new president tonight. He had me get on a video call with the guy already. I like him, and I believe we might get along."

"This came out of nowhere."

"I know. Are you okay if I go out tonight? I'm sorry about the birthday dinner. I know you planned something nice, but I really need to be there for this."

I lean back against the sales counter. The surprise party. Dozens of phone calls to make. The deposit for the restaurant. The pain in my temples is severe, and my stomach is doing somersaults.

"Sure. Go. It's not a big deal. We'll celebrate another day."

"Thanks for understanding." He sounds more cheerful now. "This president, Richard Stolar, does seem like a nice guy. You'll like him too. You know, he went to Westview for his undergrad, just like you? Studied science. Does the name ring a bell? I know you had a large campus, but you might recognize him."

The salesman hands me my bag of accessories, but I stand frozen.

"What did you…say his name was?" I struggle to pronounce the words. My tongue feels swollen and unresponsive. I have to be positive; it can't be that name, the one I've tried to forget for twenty-one years. The name that only comes to me in my nightmares.

"Richard. Richard Stolar."

He says other words after, but I can't hear. Everything around me sways in a sickening rhythm and, as I struggle to hold on to something—anything—my head hits the edge of the counter and I land in the muddy puddle surrounding my boots.

He found me.

Chapter 2

There is a light blinding me, and I attempt to turn away but can't. Loud noise is all around. A hard surface is under my back. What's going on?

"What's your name, miss? Can you tell us your name?"

Why does someone need my name?

"Katie. It's Katie." My mouth is dry, and it's difficult to speak. My head throbs. I just want to be left alone.

Where the hell am I?

"Says here you are Emma Shephard."

The voice is familiar. I open my eyes and manage to sit up and look around. I remember now where I am. The wireless store, where I appear to be a source of entertainment for a crowd of salespeople staring at me.

"Ms. Shephard, you hit your head. Just stay right there. We've called the ambulance," a tall, grumpy-looking man informs me.

"And who are you?" I ask, holding onto my head.

"I'm the manager of this store. Sergio Ramirez."

"Where is my phone?" And then it hits me. "I don't need an ambulance. Call them back. Tell them I'm fine." I try to get up to prove my point, and the man who sold me my phone rushes to hold me up and help me into a chair.

"I don't need anyone's help. Let me go." I try to

throw him off, but his hands are firm under my arms. "Hey, you are hurting me!"

"Ms. Shephard, we really need you to sit down. You fainted, and you look very pale," the manager says, his face distraught. Honestly, I think he is the one looking very pale.

"Don't worry, Mr. Ramirez, I'm not going to sue this store because I fell here. Just give me some water, please, and then I'll go home."

"We can't give you water until the ambulance gets here," he says.

"Oh, for God's sake, do you need me to sign something that says I release you from liability? I just want to go home."

As I contemplate my escape, the lights begin to flash outside, the doors slam open, and I see paramedics walk in. I moan in annoyance. And then I remember—Aidan's birthday. I need to get out of here. Now.

"I'm fine. I'm really fine," I tell the paramedics in my calmest voice.

"Don't worry, we're just going to check you out," a short paramedic with a braid says, kneeling next to me.

"I appreciate it, but I really don't need to be checked out. I haven't eaten anything today, and I get hypoglycemic." I hope this takes care of it.

"Have you fainted before?" she asks.

"I have. And I have a great family doc who'll be happy to see me today. But mainly I just need to eat something."

"Wendy, we need to take her to the ER. It's Wednesday before Thanksgiving. She can't get in with any doctor." Her partner wraps a blood pressure cuff around my arm, while Wendy gets my pulse oxygen reading.

"Oh, no, my doctor is a friend, and I know for certain that she's still working. I'll definitely see her this afternoon," I assure them.

And then I spot the tall figure of my husband rushing through the doors, his face full of horror as he spots the ambulance and the paramedics crouched in front of me.

"Aidan, how did you find me?"

He kisses the top of my head. "One of these guys picked up the phone and told me you fainted." He turns to the paramedics. "How is she?"

"She's in shock and refuses medical attention. I recommend we take her to University for a scan." Wendy says, getting up and facing my husband.

"No." I shake my head. "Aidan, I'm not going to the hospital. Do you have any idea how much a ride in an ambulance costs these days?"

"Sweetheart, you need to get checked. You hit your head." Aidan's voice is quiet but firm.

"I don't have a concussion," I argue with the entire crowd around me. "Listen, my memory is perfect, and I'm not disoriented. My name is Emma Shephard, I was born on July 20th, 1977." I point at Aidan. "This is my husband Aidan Shephard. Today is Aidan's birthday, and it's November twenty-second. I live at Three Maple Grove Street, in Virginia. You want me to do some math?"

Aidan laughs. "All right, I think she's fine. I'll drive her straight home. I'll take her to the hospital if she feels sick later."

"I strongly advise for her to be at least seen by a family doctor," says Wendy.

"Fine, I'll call my doctor. Will you let me go then?" I look frantically for my phone and the salesperson hands it to me.

As I hold the phone, I suddenly remember why I fainted, and my fingers can't seem to put in the passcode. *No, no, no!* But I can't think about it right now. I must get out of here, get rid of everybody, stop the head from throbbing.

Aidan takes the phone from my hands, and I hear him talking to a receptionist. He turns to the paramedics. "I'm taking her to see Dr. Woods right now."

"All right, just sign here that you decline the transport to the ER." Wendy hands Aidan a clipboard. The EMTs give my husband some instructions and finally leave.

My husband wraps his arms around me and lifts me off the chair. "Can you stand up and walk? Do you want me to carry you?"

"I'm all right," I say.

But I'm not all right. How did Richard find me? How is this possible? I try very hard not to sway. Everything spins, and the nausea is back. I need to think straight; I can't be sick right now. I must figure out what to do. Do I tell Aidan? How do I tell him? I know there are words somewhere in my mind, but they are slipping through, and I can't grasp them.

"I'm so sorry about this, Aidan. Go back to work. I can make it to Lori's."

"Are you serious? You can't drive."

"I'm perfectly fine." I lift my arms up to show him how steady I am, but the world spins, and he catches me mid-fall.

"That's enough. Let's go." He puts my arm around his shoulder and walks me to his car. I shiver, but whether it's from the freezing wind outside or from fear, I don't know.

"I forgot my bag," I say feebly when I'm seated.

"I have it." He hands it to me, followed by a pack of tissues he takes out of his glove compartment.

I pull down the mirror. My face is covered in smudges of dirt. I start wiping. Of course Aidan would have tissues in his car. Always prepared. He wouldn't have anything embarrassing happen to him, ever. I clean my face, then try to wipe the muddy stains off my coat. His Audi is new. The leather on the seats still has that nauseating smell. He'd hate it if I got mud on it.

"Don't worry about it," he says and starts driving.

It's tense in the car. How do I tell him about Richard? What are the right words?

"How's your head?"

Maybe that's a good start. "It's not too bad. I'll be fine. I just forgot to have breakfast, that's all. I was about to, but I spilled milk on my phone, and then I needed to come get a new one." I know I'm rambling, so I shut up. I count the street signs passing by. When I get to fifty, I will tell him about Richard.

"Hey, do you mind if I leave you with Lori and call an Uber for your ride home?" he asks.

I swing my head and look at him for a moment. His forehead has that wrinkle he gets when he is stressed. He keeps peeking at his phone whenever we stop at an intersection. I can see it buzzing with messages. He must be having a hell of a day with this transition. I can't tell him. This is not the right time.

"You can leave me with Lori, honey, of course.

And—I'm so sorry I'm ruining your birthday."

"Don't be ridiculous. I'm the one ruining it by going out to dinner with the boss. We'll celebrate tomorrow, okay? My family is coming for the turkey anyway."

We pull up at a tall glass building. Before we get out of the car, I turn to him, hold his face in both hands, and tell him, "Aidan, be careful."

"Of what?"

"Your meeting with the new president. Just be careful what you say. You don't know him." My voice shakes. I hope he doesn't notice.

"Oh, so you did remember him from Westview? What's he like?"

The lying rips through me like lightning, but I can't stop. "No, never knew him at Westview. I just think you need to watch him for a while. You are a very kind and trusting person. I love you for that, but you should be careful with this guy."

"Sweetheart, don't worry so much. It's not my first president to deal with. I just want you to feel better. And then you can meet him yourself and help me out."

"How can I not worry? It's our jobs on the line. Sophie is about to go to college."

"I've got this. Go see Lori, and then go home and rest. I'll try to get home as soon as I can and will tell you all the details. I love you." He takes hold of my hands and kisses them. "Let's go. I do need to get back to a meeting."

He holds my elbow all the way to the elevator. We slip past the receptionist and into Lori's private office. With a quick kiss, he takes off, and I start crying. I'm a little relieved that he is gone. I'm still so embarrassed about what happened. And frightened, so very frightened.

Lori walks in a few minutes later and washes her hands. She is no longer wearing her lab coat, and her dark brown hair is out of the ponytail she always wears when she sees patients. She must've been ready to go home.

"Sorry," I say. "I didn't mean to keep you at work longer."

"I'm sure you didn't mean to get a concussion at the mall, either," she says. "What happened?"

"I don't have a concussion. I passed out because I skipped breakfast. My head is fine. Why does your office smell so nasty?" I make a gagging motion, then grab a tissue and wipe my eyes.

"It's just disinfectant. You're nauseated because you've hit your head."

"I barely hit my head. It hurts, but only because I had a headache since this morning."

"Any previous fainting episodes?" She shines a small light in my eyes.

"Stop it. No."

"Any other headaches lately? Any weakness on one side of your body? Follow my finger."

I follow her finger obediently. "No, I haven't had a stroke or previous headaches. But I'd love some medication for the headache I have *now*."

She makes me stand up, and I try very hard not to sway and to walk straight and do her neurological tests, but they are all so exhausting. I collapse into a chair, too tired to climb back up onto an exam table.

"Lori, stop with all this. I fainted because I was on the phone and heard some bad news I didn't expect. I'm not sick."

"I still have to examine you. Just in case you hit your head harder than you are telling me. You'll need to take it easy for a while. I'll run some blood work on you as well."

Fifteen minutes later, after the nurse leaves with a vial of my blood and I feel even weaker, she finally sits down after she hands me a plastic cup of water and a package of graham crackers. "So what's the bad news?"

"John gave up control of D&P."

"What? Dana hasn't said anything."

"It just happened a few hours ago. He hasn't had a chance to tell your wife, since she is out at her research conference."

"She told me the Eli Lilly deal was in the works, but I didn't realize it would be so soon."

"It's not even Eli Lilly. It's this company I've never heard of—Avias Global."

"Never heard of them either. Wonder if Dana has."

"She must have. She knows everyone in pharma. John, apparently, is very happy. He'll be on the board, but we have a new guy in charge. I have no idea what happened to Eli Lilly. I mean—there was a good offer on the table."

"This Avias deal must have been substantial."

"Likely." I look away. "Aidan has to have dinner with the new president tonight instead of going to his surprise party."

"And Aidan skipping his birthday party was enough to make you faint? Is it because of the deposit the Blue Room required for the day before Thanksgiving?"

"That's a bad joke." I try to smile, then give up. "I

used to know the new president. Back in college."

"Ex-boyfriend?"

"No."

"Can you talk about it?"

"Can I tell you another day?"

"Yes. Are you in any danger?" Her eyes are zeroed in on my face. She is trained to spot lies.

"No, definitely not." I shake my head with as much conviction at possible.

She is quiet for a moment. "I hope you talk to Aidan about this. Let me get you something for your headache."

As she turns around and begins to search in her drawers, I allow the panic to wash over me. Am I in danger? Has Richard assaulted others? Did anyone tell him that I tried to get him kicked off the football team and expelled from Westview after he assaulted me? Will he come after me when he sees me?

Lori's eyes narrow in concern as she hands me the Tylenol packet and a cup of water. "You can talk to me about it when ready. Are you sure you'll be all right?"

"Yes, I'm just shaken up. This whole day has been shit. And Aidan's party—I've tried so hard to make today special for him, and now that's not happening. I took a freaking day off, and I had all these reports to finish. I might lose my job. And my head hurts." I sniffle and drink the pills.

"Emma, go home, get in bed, and relax. Binge on some mindless television." She wraps her arm around my shoulder. "I want to see you back here in a week. We'll discuss your blood work then."

****

My hands shake as I try to open the lock to the

front door, but it swings open and nearly hits me in the face.

Sophie frowns as she scans my head and the rest of me. “You look awful.”

“I should’ve never left the house today.”

She follows me to the bedroom as I take off my stained coat and boots, throw them on the floor, and collapse on my bed. Cookie jumps up and lies next to me. I stroke her furry neck, with barely enough strength left now to lift my fingers.

“Dr. Lori said I was to make you something to eat.”

“When did Lori call you? Never mind. Can you please get me some toast and a few slices of cheese?”

“She said lots of water and just plain toast for a few hours.” Sophie’s lips stretch into a smile. She knows I hate being told what to do.

I glare at her, and she runs away to the kitchen. I hear her giggling.

I’m sobbing inside. I’m so shaken by all that’s happened. I pet my dog to steady my nerves, but it doesn’t appear to help. My thoughts race. What do I do? How much danger am I in, exactly? Richard can’t possibly recognize me, can he? I look nothing like Katie Daniels, the freshman bio major at Westview. I use my middle name now. Even Aidan has forgotten I used to be called Katie. My hair is blonde now, and I’m at least thirty pounds thinner.

Katie was happy and carefree. Katie chose to go to a fraternity party and ruined her future. Katie was weak and couldn’t stand up for herself.

“Here you go.” Sophie walks in with a tray.

“Thank you, my love.” I give her a kiss and devour

my toast. She has cut it into a heart shape. Sometimes when it seems as if the world crumbles around me, Sophie can do a tiny thing like this and make me feel so amazingly loved.

"I'm sorry about Dad's party," she says.

I sigh. "We still need to make the cheesecake. He can eat it when he gets home."

"How are you going to make it if you have to stay in bed?" she asks.

I point at her and then in the direction of the kitchen. "If you're old enough to go to college—you're old enough to bake on your own."

"I knew I was going to get trapped somehow," she huffs, but walks off to the kitchen.

I grab my phone and start searching. I'm not sure what I hope to find, exactly. Maybe that this Richard is not the one from my past. But as my fingers finish typing in his name, and his face appears in Google, I can't deny it any longer. It's him. The football player who beat me, then raped me, twenty-one years ago at a college fraternity party. He is here. In the safe life I've managed to build for myself, away from those memories.

How could this have happened to me? What is he even doing at a pharmaceutical company? He was being recruited for the NFL, the last I heard. But I heard that from Shannon, my roommate, who also told me he was a nice guy right before he drugged and assaulted me. I take a deep breath and look him up. Never made it to the NFL. Seems he married someone named Jennifer, whose dad is the chairman of the board of directors of Avias Global. He lives in Connecticut with his wife and two sons who look a whole lot like him. I cringe.

Richard worked his way through the company and now has been promoted to the top. Not bad for a child of war refugees from Croatia. Or was that also a lie from Shannon, to get me to talk to him that night? There's nothing I find to help me understand why he assaulted me. Nothing helps me assess whether I'm still in danger from him now, today, or Monday when I return to work.

As I continue to search, a text from Aidan dings.

—Hope you are feeling better. Sorry I have to go out tonight. You'll meet the new president at the Gala. Don't worry, you'll have great opportunities with Avias. Richard says your marketing department was one of the reasons Avias wanted D&P. Love you—

So—Richard and I will meet.

No matter how hard I worked to get away from my past for all these years, it has found me. I've thought so many times of what I'd do if Richard was ever in front of me again. But now I'm lost for ideas. I've thought of a million ways to hurt him, to punish him for what he did to me. Yet all I want to do is find a new way to escape, to forget any of this ever happened to me.

Chapter 3

I slam the door of the bathroom stall behind me, press my back against it, and sink to the floor. It's unusually quiet, except for the sound of my pounding heart and the scraping of my heels on the tile as I collapse next to the toilet.

Aidan had just handed me a glass of wine when I heard Richard's voice. "There you are!" he said. And everything in me exploded. Then I bolted. I didn't plan to respond this way at all.

Two women laugh as they enter the stalls. I can't stay in this cramped space forever. I'll have to come out and go back to the Holiday Gala. I remind myself I'm part of the senior leadership team. I don't fall apart no matter what. My sales teams are here, and I must pull it together. I can always pull myself together. I close my eyes and breathe slowly—not an easy thing to do next to the toilet, on the cold tile, and in this skintight dress.

Minutes later, I'm a bit steadier. I stand up, holding onto the germ-infested porcelain bowl. The temptation to vomit is strong, but I hold it in. I won't allow myself to be ill. I leave the stall and check my face in the mirror while washing my hands. The sound of the water spouting from the faucet is rather calming.

My face is pale, but my eyes look determined. I add some more lipstick and pinch my cheeks. Better. I'm ready to go back. Maybe Richard is gone now.

Maybe I can handle seeing him next time. It's been a very long time, an eternity—I can't possibly still be traumatized by this. I'm not the person I was. I'm not a weak, pathetic Katie who was forced to run back home.

I stumble out of the bathroom, making sure to take little steps and search for my husband. If I can just hold onto his arm, I'll be better.

"I was wondering where you've been. I have your wine." Aidan takes me firmly by my shoulder. "I've been telling Richard all about your latest brand strategy for the new stimulant."

I'm gripped by terror, icicles spreading through me and freezing my entire body as I stare into the face of Richard Stolar. His hair is still dirty blond and cropped short. He is wearing a designer black suit, crisp white shirt, and an ugly purple tie.

"Yes, Aidan's been telling me about your latest product campaign. And I've been very impressed with the portfolios I've seen. Your department runs very efficiently." Richard stretches his hand toward me. "It's a pleasure. We need to talk new sales strategy ideas. We are about to bring a breakthrough drug on the market, and I'll need your skills."

Aidan is pushing me toward Richard, and I will my face to contort into a smile and my hand to shake his. I'm terrified of feeling the touch of his skin on mine. My mouth is dry as a desert. I try to focus my eyes on something besides his face, but then all I can see is his ugly purple tie.

Does he recognize me?

"It's a real pleasure to meet you, Richard," I say. He wanted "*my skills*"? A strong desire to lunge at his throat rises in me, and I take a step back. I look at

Aidan. "Will you please excuse me? I promised to help Dana with something. But I'll be back in a few minutes."

Richard waves in dismissal. "Don't let us keep you. But I hope to talk to you again later."

I walk away as slowly as I can without seeming to run, picking up a glass of wine on the way. There are conversations and laughter behind me. I sip my Merlot and hide in the hallway. My senses slowly return to normal as the wine works through my system.

Please don't let me have another flashback.

Did he recognize me?

What am I going to do? For the rest of this party and for the rest of my life?

There are at least two more hours of the party left. What if he recognizes me if he sees me again? If I stay that long, I can't control what I do. I search for Dana and see her standing in a large group. The Research & Development scientists always huddle together at these parties. I make signs to her, but she doesn't notice. One of my best salespeople from North Carolina waves at me, but I don't feel like talking about her sales numbers right now. There are groups of people everywhere, enjoying themselves, talking, laughing, drinking. This is a yearly celebration for our company. A day to dress up, show off, celebrate your achievements. Everyone is drunk, excited, and happy.

I am in agony. I need to get the hell out of here.

As a last resort, I text Sophie,

—Need rescue from party. HELP NOW. Text you are sick to Dad—

—GOT IT—

Grateful for my faraway helper, I hug my phone as

I walk back into the ballroom and stand by the bar. Aidan is at my side a few minutes later. "Hey, I just got a message from Sophie. She couldn't get hold of you."

"What? Let me see." I look at my phone flashing with a message from Sophie. "She is throwing up and has a fever." I look my most distressed. "Let me text her some instructions. Maybe it's nothing," I say, rubbing my forehead. Guilt forms in my stomach and crawls up my chest painfully. I hate lying to my husband. But I can't think of any other way to get out of here.

"What? You have to go home."

"Well, I can't leave in the middle of the gala," I say. "Richard wants to speak to me about something, too." My eyelid begins to twitch, and I wonder how long I can last.

"Our daughter is more important. We'll meet with Richard tomorrow. He's in town all day before he goes home to Connecticut."

There is a nasty taste in my throat. I cough. "I better go, then."

"I'll get a ride with someone. You take the car," he says.

Aidan walks me to the valet stand, and I give him a hurried kiss, averting my eyes. I jump into his Audi and drive away fast. The ride home from D.C. is less than an hour. I bet I can make it in thirty minutes. I'm anxious to put as much distance between me and Richard as possible. The city lets me escape quickly tonight, but then I approach the Roosevelt Bridge, and I'm trapped in the sea of cars, in the darkness, rain pelting at my windshield and my heart pounding in anger, grief, and fear.

How could this have happened to me? I thought I'd never have to see the fucking bastard again after I dropped out of school. After Westview refused to press charges against him. After they blamed me for Richard assaulting me.

There is loud honking and cursing. I shake my head and slam on the gas, then almost hit the car in front of me. Everything seems out of control, out of focus. I haven't felt this way in at least twenty years, not since Aidan came into my life. And especially not since I became a mother. "Get a grip," I whisper. I wipe my tears and focus on making it home.

To Sophie.

The tires screech as I pull into our circular driveway a little while later and come to a quick stop. The lights are on in every room of our house. I'm so glad Sophie is there. I'm badly in need of her company. She greets me at the door in her pajamas, hair in a ponytail.

"Mom, you look like shit."

"I feel like shit." I collapse on the couch. "I need a drink."

"Should you be saying this to me?"

"I don't have the strength to be a proper mom tonight, sorry."

Sophie sighs. "Hold on." She returns a few minutes later with a glass of wine.

"How do you know how to open wine?" I stare for a moment. "Oh, never mind."

"So what happened?" She sits cross-legged on the love seat with a can of ginger ale in one hand and her phone in the other.

"I honestly wouldn't even know where to begin." I

take a sip of my wine. "Why are you home? Didn't you have a date?"

"Never mind."

"Tell me. Please. I need a distraction."

"It was Nathan. He said he had an extra concert ticket, and then he gave it to this other girl."

"I'm so sorry. So who is this other girl?"

"Pretty. Blonde. Skinny. The popular type."

"Baby, you've never been the type to be jealous."

"I'm not. I just hate her."

"How much did you like him?"

"I didn't. I just wanted to see the band."

We laugh. I hug her and feel a bit better.

"So what was up with you needing a rescue?"

My heart skips a beat. "Nothing. I just didn't so much care to be at that party. Too many people."

"You like these snobby galas, and you've never had me make up a lie to Dad before."

I look down. "I shouldn't have done that. I don't want you lying to Dad. It's just that there wasn't any good way to get his attention and explain I needed to go home. Don't worry, I promise I'll tell him the truth when he gets in."

"So what happened?"

"You know how D&P has just been bought by Avias? Well, the president of Avias—I am not a fan."

She whistles. "Why not?"

"He is an asshole."

"All right, then." She raises her eyebrows. "Does Dad like him?"

"Yes."

"And why exactly are you calling him names?"

"I'd rather not say right now. I'll tell you later, I

promise. I'm just too tired."

"Does Dad know that you don't like him?"

"He doesn't."

"Are you going to tell him?"

"Maybe." I take a large sip of my wine. "Probably not. Not sure."

"Has he done something to you? Or other people?"

"Me. Likely other people as well."

"So why don't you get back at him for whatever he's done?"

"He is our boss, not a playground bully." I sigh.

"Boss or not, you can't let him get away with it."

"When you are an adult, your choices are much more limited. I can't just get back at my boss."

"In my experience, adults make whatever choices they wish. Wouldn't you just love to plan a revenge on him? If I were an adult in power, like you, that's what I would do, whether he was my boss or not." Sophie gets up and gives me a kiss. "Goodnight. I have people to chat with, okay?"

"Sure, go. Love you."

I finish my wine and settle myself on the couch with my dog, waiting for Aidan. As I close my eyes, trying not to think, the world slowly drifts into oblivion.

****

I startle as Cookie jumps off the couch. My heart pounds, but the dog's bark quickly changes to whining and scratching at the front door.

Aidan is back, I reassure myself. The steps in the hallway are familiar heavy steps. My breath slowly settles down.

"Sorry I had to leave early, honey," I stand up as I greet him.

"No problem. Is Sophie all right? Do I need to go see her?"

"No, she's gone to sleep. Hopefully, just a twenty-four-hour bug. She's gotten through the worst of it now." The guilt of lying punches me hard in the stomach. "How was the rest of the party?"

"Fine." He gives me a kiss and begins to remove his jacket, then his tie. "Great, actually. I really like Richard. I know you met him just for a minute, but what did you think? He sure seems fond of you."

I look away, so he can't see my face. "What do you like about him?"

He sits down on the couch next to me. "Emma, I think he is brilliant. He'll take this company in good new directions. We've been in a rut forever, with the failing sales. He's already bringing a new drug. He'll ensure we survive the market."

"I don't think the company is ready for new drug applications." I frown. "Not with all the new FDA requirements."

"Just a few weeks ago, I was sure I'd lose my job, but now he guarantees I'll have a promotion within a year."

"Can we possibly trust this guy? You've known him for a few weeks. John pulled this company out of nowhere. We know nothing about them."

"I've done some looking up. Avias has an above-average reputation. Their board is solid. Their stocks have done well. And besides, Richard and I think on the same wavelength. We have a lot in common. I'm looking forward to developing a friendship with him."

Something inside me breaks. "Be right back," I say in a strangled voice as I dash to the bathroom and lock the door. My husband wants to be friends with my rapist. I can't stop a flashback from coming on and sending me into the world of terror. Richard's face is in front of me in my mind, as if we are back in that gray stairway so many years ago.

The metal door slams behind me and Richard throws me against the wall. I scream, and the sound of my terror echoes through the floors below. He slaps me then—hard. My ears ring, my eyes are flooded with tears, but I fight, my arms flailing. I can't think; something is making my brain terribly fuzzy. I feel a hand holding both my wrists as he drags me down the stairs. Someone will come and help me, any moment. I remember I have a boyfriend—Jeff. He will come—I know it. I kick Richard as hard as I can. I taste blood. This can't be happening. I'm a good person—this kind of thing doesn't happen to good people. I feel him pushing inside me. I concentrate on breathing. I must survive this. I pretend to faint, and stay silent. I stay still and silent. I figure he'll stop if I don't respond.

But he doesn't stop.

"Did you catch the bug too, sweetheart?" I hear Aidan's worried voice as I begin to vomit my fear.

"I did… Let me be…" I mumble, as I crouch near the toilet.

"Okay. I think I'll go check on Sophie real quick."

I lean my back against the cold wall as Aidan's footsteps disappear down the hall. I want it to go away. I want it all to go away. The pain. The memories. The nightmares. The agony of his fists on my ribs. The feeling of my skin being ripped apart by him. The sight of blood on my thighs. I want a time machine. I want to say to my roommate Shannon that I'm busy, that I have a headache, that I changed my mind about going to that frat party with her. And then none of it ever happens. But that's not possible. That's never possible, no matter how much I wish for it every single day.

And then what Sophie said flashes in my mind. Getting back at Richard. Revenge. I've thought so many times over the years about what it would feel like to get justice. Is there such a thing as justice for me after all? All those years ago, I thought there was. I did my rape kit and then went to the police to file a report. And I answered all their questions. And there were so many questions…

"Maybe you gave this boy the wrong message?"

"And how much did you have to drink before you had sex with him?"

"What color were his eyes? If you can't remember any details; how do you know it was really this young man?"

"Do you have any witnesses who can support your statement?"

And the same questions were repeated everywhere I went—the police, the Victim Services office, the dean's office. Until the day they forced me to leave Westview.

Suddenly, my dreams of revenge return, and I wish for Richard to feel pain. The same pain I felt when I was told by everyone it was my fault I was assaulted and left in the stairway alone, without any help, while the fraternity party continued all night. What would've happened if I hadn't managed to crawl down ten flights of stairs and get to a pay phone? What if my friend Eric hadn't come to my help and taken me to the hospital? Richard took away my worth, my safety, the part of me that knew who I was and knew I deserved love. I was no longer an intelligent, strong woman. I became only a victim trying to figure out how to put her life back together.

I get up and pace around the bathroom. My thoughts are on a loop, my blood races through my body, my fingers curl up into a fist, and I imagine pounding the wall over and over until I can't feel anything anymore.

Chapter 4

"Are you absolutely sure you're feeling better?" Aidan's eyes are full of concern, but his body is tense.

He is dressed and ready to leave for work. He's been pacing around impatiently, running out of reasons to delay his departure. His coffee mug is empty, and his phone won't stop ringing. He hasn't heard a word I've said to him in the last thirty minutes.

I need him to stay and climb back into bed, wrap his arms around me, and hold me in a bear hug. And tell me it will all be all right. And that I'll be safe—that he will protect me from Richard. But I can't come up with the right words to beg him to stay. I simply nod, stretch my lips into a smile, and watch him walk out as I'm left alone with my thoughts in an empty house.

The problem is Aidan doesn't know I need protection from Richard. I've never told my husband what happened at Westview, because I was so desperate to put that chapter of my life behind me. I met Aidan a year after I dropped out of college. I told him I left because I missed home. I didn't expect for him to fall in love with me. I never thought anyone would fall in love with me, a stupid girl who let herself get assaulted.

And after a while, how do you bring it up with your husband that you've been a rape victim? That you won't take stairs because every time you are in a stairwell you can feel your body being pounded. That you look over your shoulder anywhere you go. That, years later, you still wake from nightmares at least once a week. The best way I've come up with to explain any of it has been to tell him I suffer from occasional panic attacks. My mother and sister do, so it just made sense to use that explanation. And it wasn't quite a lie. I do have panic attacks on the stairs.

The house is too quiet now. Sophie is already at school. I took a sick day. I would've liked for her to stay with me in bed all day to watch Netflix and drink hot chocolate. I need some time with my girl. But there was no question of her staying at home faking sickness, as Aidan watched her down a large smoothie this morning. I wanted to at least make her lunch, but the sight of food made me too queasy. Maybe I did catch a bug.

I'd like to sleep for the rest of the day and pretend none of yesterday happened, but I'm unable to settle down my body or my thoughts. Justice. I'm consumed with the hope of justice. But my thoughts can't wrap around how it could be possible.

I need to talk to someone who knows. I shower, throw my gym outfit on, and get in the car. I know where my friend Eric will be at his usual early lunchtime. My hometown is only half an hour away, but I get stuck in two traffic jams, and as I crawl on the highways and bridges, my thoughts begin to untangle, and I realize the ridiculousness of wanting justice. It's too late. It's just not possible. It didn't work before, and it would never work now.

And what about Aidan? And Sophie? I need to put all this behind me. I come up with a new plan. We'll move. I'll convince Aidan that we need to move and look for jobs elsewhere. I mean—there's no way I can work for Richard. I can't even look at him without falling apart. My husband and I must find new jobs. Sophie is almost done with school, and she's leaving in a few months. We can go to work for Eli Lilly and live far away from here.

The Russo Italian Deli in Frederick still has the same beat-up storefront as when I worked here twenty years ago. It's home. There is a long line at the counter, as always. Hipsters, standing next to construction workers, standing next to doctors in scrubs, standing next to hungry teens. Eric's wife, Jenny, runs the Deli now. She makes the best sandwiches in town, possibly the whole of Maryland. It's loud, with orders being called in, the slicer going, the register dinging, people laughing.

I walk toward the back, where Eric and his patrol buddies usually hang out at a rickety table. Eric is alone today. I watch him for a minute. He looks tired as he scans the paper in front of him, a large coffee in his hands. I can see gray hair starting to show all through his dark brown hair. Latinos gray early, he always says. But I know that at least some of it is due to his long work hours and to Jenny's recent bouts of OCD. He's had some health problems he won't tell me about either. I try not to bother him with my non-problems usually, but today I have no choice.

"Eric. He's here," I say, plopping down on the chair opposite him.

"Hello to you too. Who is here?"

"Him." I can't bring myself to say the name. It's choking me as it slithers up my throat until it finally expels itself. "Richard Stolar."

"What the fuck is he doing here?" He slams the newspaper down, shaking the table violently.

"Our company was bought out. And he is the new president. Last night Aidan introduced me to him at a gala."

"You're shitting me. Wasn't he just a football player?"

"Well, apparently now he is a president of a pharma company."

"Did he recognize you?"

"I don't think so. At least he didn't give any clue that he did."

"Well, you don't look anything like you did when you were a college girl. Plus, asshole rapists never remember the faces of their victims."

"I don't even have the same name anymore. You're the only one who still insists on calling me Katie."

"You'll always be Katie Daniels to me. Are you all right? How are you holding up?"

"I'm terrible." I start shaking.

He covers my hands with his. "How are you able to work with him every day? Right in your office?"

"He only came into town last night. And I didn't go in to work today." I point at my casual outfit.

"You'll have to go in eventually. Did you tell Aidan?"

"I haven't figured out how. He…likes the guy. What am I going to say? 'Oh, by the way, I've never mentioned this in the twenty years we've been together, but I was assaulted, and my rapist is our new boss, and I want him dead'?"

"All right." Eric reclines in his chair. "You can't keep something like this a secret anymore, though. You must tell him."

"I keep thinking that, but then I also think—maybe he never needs to know."

"Katie, this is going to get out somehow, and it'll hurt you again."

"I won't let this get out. *You* won't let this get out. I've managed this far. I can keep this going." I hope Eric understands. Of all people, I need him to understand.

"Yeah, by telling him you have a mental disorder. And having me keep this a secret for you."

"So what? It's worked."

"But now this guy is in your fucking office, you'll be forced to confront him. What are you thinking of doing to him?"

"Why are you so certain I'll do something to him?"

"You've only mentioned it to me a thousand times."

"That was years ago. I'm a different person now. How am I going to fight him? I can't kill him," I say. "You'll be the first to come and arrest me."

"I don't think you are going to kill him, dummy. But you'll think of something. You're a genius. I know you'll want to get back at him for what he did to you. Legally. And that's why you have to talk to Aidan. He needs to help you."

"I already tried to get him punished back then. Remember what happened? That worked our really well, didn't it? Particularly the part when I was blamed for the rape and then had to leave Westview in shame."

"You had no power then, but now you do."

"True. I have connections. I have access to the company's records, and there is so much junk you find on people on Google these days." I look at him closely. "And you have access to all kinds of information."

"Hey, don't get me involved. I'll lose my job. I'm barely hanging on as it is." He gets up. "You want some egg salad? Jenny just made a fresh batch."

I follow him to the kitchen. "I'll take some, sure." I watch him make us two sandwiches on pumpernickel bagels, my favorite. He still remembers.

"Aren't you trying to get that promotion to detective?" I ask.

"I tried, but it's not easy for a brown-skin person to get promoted around here. What does that have to do with this?"

"I'm just saying—you are pretty good at detective work and finding dirt on people. Maybe this would help."

"How would this help? You mean, if I found out he's been raping other women?" He hands me a plate. "I can do some searching for you. Nothing illegal, though."

"Don't worry. You can't help me, anyway. He's from Connecticut. I don't want you involved. Justice is a nice idea in movies, but practically, in my life, I don't want any of it. All I want is a quiet safe life. Just like I've had for all these years."

"But it's not going to stay exactly like it was. How can it? It's already changed. Don't you understand? You can't pretend it hasn't. He's going to be right in front of your face all the time."

"Maybe I can handle it. If not, I have a plan."

I take a bite of my sandwich and allow myself to enjoy it for a moment. Eric watches me eat.

"So what will you do?" he asks.

I put my sandwich down. “On the drive here, I thought maybe I could ask Aidan to find another job. Start over. Maybe we’ll get out of pharmaceuticals. We have MBAs, so we can work anywhere. We’ll get back to the life we had before this company. When all we cared about was our family.”

“And he’ll be willing to do that for you? What story would you spin to convince him you both must give up your jobs and suddenly move?”

“He loves me. He’ll believe any story. But I don’t need to come up with the story. With Richard and his company taking things over, there’s too much uncertainty. Everyone’s feeling it. There are rumors flying around about who will be fired. Aidan’s been very nervous. He hates instability. You know how he is about money.”

“And what about Sophie?” he asks.

“Good question.”

“You are a good mom.”

“Thanks.”

He finally begins to eat, and I finish my food. The deli is getting quieter now, the lunch hour almost over. I look for Jenny, but she must be still finishing up. Always busy. Always cleaning. Not easy to keep up in the kitchen when you have OCD.

“Your mother should’ve never let you go to that school.” Eric sighs.

“I chose to go there.” I shrug.

“You just didn’t want to stay home.”

“I couldn’t handle it after the whole thing with Dad.”

“I know.”

“Mom and Patty were driving me out of my mind.

Didn't you ever want to leave? I mean, this town can really get to you, you know? And it's so hard for Jenny to run this place. Maybe somewhere else you could make detective and she wouldn't have to work?"

He wipes his forehead. "She'd never want to leave, though. She loves the place. It keeps her busy. And the kids have been happy. Thank you for helping them with school. If they make it big, maybe we can retire one day."

"You'll never retire. You love being in the force."

"I will. I'm sick of it. We picked up another wife beater just this morning. He was trying to shoot her and his kids. I always think of your dad." He places his hand on mine and squeezes lightly.

"Oh, Eric. Don't." I shake my head. "That was one incident. It's not going to happen to you."

"Never mind me. You know, there is one more thing you can do about the Richard situation."

"What?"

He takes the last sip of his soda and cracks his knuckles before looking up at me. "You could forgive him and move on."

I stare at him silently for a minute. "Are you seriously suggesting that to me?"

"Just think about it."

"After you saw me beaten within an inch of my life by this guy, and after you drove me to the hospital and watched me get a rape kit, and after you helped me put my life back together when Westview kicked me out while basically calling me a whore, you tell me that I should forgive him?"

He lifts his hands up. "Forget I suggested it."

"I know it's a man thing to say, but I never

expected that this would come out of your mouth."

"Just forget it, all right?"

"I don't think I can."

He grabs my hands and holds them. "I am so sorry. Stay a while. We'll talk some more. Jenny will be free soon, and she could really use to talk to a friend today."

Chapter 5

I'm stronger after talking with Eric and Jenny. They've been there for me always. When my dad was killed when I was sixteen. When I dropped out of Westview and came home without a degree and needed a job. I don't see them often enough. But I made sure their kids—Dominic, Lucas, and Julia—each got a scholarship to go to Sophie's school. Jenny doesn't mind the commute. The kids are smart; they belonged in a good school. The twin boys received early admission into Virginia Tech.

On the drive back, as I'm stuck in traffic, I imagine what it would be like to confront Richard. He didn't even remember me… He drugged me, beat me nearly unconscious, yet he couldn't recognize me when I stood right in front of him yesterday. How would it feel to watch his face as I tell him who I am? Who I was.

I tap on the steering wheel with my fingers. Could I tell Aidan about my past? I may have to if he doesn't listen to me about moving away. Will he tell me I need to forgive Richard and move on, just like Eric did, or will he go after Richard? Aidan is a very kind guy, but my mind goes through several images of Richard's face and perfect hair covered in blood as Aidan beats the crap out of him. I feel slightly better after imagining the asshole's bloody face. I laugh and see a woman in the car in the next lane staring at me. *Honestly, lady, you are the least of my problems right now.*

The ocean of cars finally moves forward, and so do my thoughts. My only option is to convince Aidan to start fresh. And it's a good thing Richard doesn't recognize me. This way, when I continue to bump into him at work on the rare occasions, he still won't know who I am. I don't need him to know. I want to take my family and get the hell out of D.C. Before my anxiety takes over my brain completely. Before I take any other choice. My hands hurt, and I look at them. I've been gripping the steering wheel so tightly my knuckles have turned white.

When I get home, I make Aidan's favorite lasagna recipe for dinner. The house fills with the smells of basil, tomatoes, and garlic. I inhale with pleasure as I set the table. My phone buzzes with a message from Lori. *Need to talk to you urgently.* I ignore it. There's too much on my mind. She was away for Thanksgiving and probably wants to tell me all about her time with her family. I can hear about it tomorrow.

We'll have dinner, a few glasses of wine, and I'll convince Aidan the company is obviously in turmoil and the safest thing for us to do is look for jobs elsewhere. I'm certain he'll listen. He always wants to make me happy. I pour myself a glass of wine and turn on Sinatra. Aidan can't resist Sinatra.

The door dings as Aidan walks in. "It's cold out there," he says and then sniffs the air. "Lasagna!" he exclaims, as he drops his bag and rushes into the kitchen.

I open the oven door in a hurry. "Hold on, let me check on it."

"What's the occasion?"

"I'm feeling better and thought we could use some comfort food with all the stress we have at work. Sophie is out with a friend, so it's just the two of us relaxing tonight."

"I love you. What stress?" he asks as he plants a kiss on my lips.

I regroup and try again. "D&P is in such disarray right now. It's just not fair that you worked so hard for this promotion, for so long, and now you have a new boss and might lose your job. I'm sure I'll lose mine. My numbers are terrible."

"Disarray? Things are going very well. Couldn't be better, actually, as far as I'm concerned." He washes his hands and sits down, fork ready.

I slice the lasagna, but my hand is shaking. "What do you mean? You must be worried about your job."

"Sweetheart, my job is perfectly secure. Yours as well. Why would you think we were in trouble? I told you—Richard and I get along well." He takes a bite and starts chewing. "This is amazing," he says a moment later.

"But you can't possibly trust him!" I burst out.

He looks at me in surprise. "Why not? He is a great guy. Former star athlete. Do you know his parents were refugees from the war in Bosnia? They came here and worked as janitors at a private Catholic school so he could get an education and be in a safe place."

I feel sweat dripping down my sides. I don't give a damn about Richard's parents. No, I do give a damn. Do his parents know he spent his time in college raping girls? If only Aidan knew what his precious Richard did while he was a star athlete… It almost slips off my tongue, and then I stop myself. I don't know why I stop.

Eric thinks I must tell him. I know I must tell him. Why can't I tell him?

Aidan pours himself a glass of wine and continues, unaware of my tumbled thoughts. "He has fantastic ideas about the company. We've had a few meetings, and I believe Avias will lead us in the right direction. He guaranteed me the next promotion."

"How can he guarantee you that?" I sit down and fidget with my napkin. "He just came here. He knows the company is doing terribly."

"Of course he knows. He's seen the financials. Avias was only interested in the company because they believed in its future profits. You know it can be done. Remember all the times you and I discussed D&P being run into the ground? All those drugs we began to develop but never got approvals for? Well, now Richard and the board will listen to everyone's ideas, including yours. This buyout is not only good for me, it's good for your career as well. So just relax."

I flinch, but he doesn't notice. He is swishing wine in his mouth happily.

"It's beyond just fixing the finances," he continues. "They have several breakthrough drugs in development, almost ready to propose to the FDA, and once they're approved, the company's future is assured."

"We're going to push new drugs to the market now, as we are struggling to make any money?"

"Absolutely. It's the only way we'll recoup our losses quickly. We'll need your help on this, of course. That's why Richard wants to talk to you. He needs a new brand strategy from you ASAP, for one of the drugs."

Blood flows to my face. "But this is a ridiculous

idea. The whole thing you're telling me sounds ridiculous."

"I don't understand, Emma. You should be excited about all of this. You finally have a chance to showcase all your ideas. Why are you upset?"

"Because…" I stop myself before I tell him that the reason I think this is all ridiculous is because he's made friends with my rapist. I get up and start cleaning up in the kitchen. I don't want to look at him. He is betting our future on decisions that will be made by the one man I hate more than anyone else in the world. How does he not feel it? Can anyone not feel Richard's evil when they are near him?

"If it all goes well, sweetheart, the company will make more money than ever. You'll hear all about it tomorrow when you're back."

I sit back down and place my shaking hands in my lap. Richard becoming wealthier. My husband and I will be helping him grow richer.

"Aidan, he could be lying about all of it. You don't know him at all. You hear stories like this all the time—a hostile company takeover and all the people are fired within two months. I'm sure Avias just wants us to do all the work and then we'll be let go."

"Sweetheart…" He sets his fork down. "It's not a hostile company takeover. John wanted to merge with them. He is very happy with Avias. And so am I. I've had Avias checked out. They have a great reputation. Just trust me, okay?"

"I do trust you. I just wish we could have a quieter life. Where we didn't always work so hard."

"I don't think I work so hard. And you had a day off today. This is exciting work, not hard."

"Well, I thought today about what it was like when Sophie was little and you'd come home early because you were afraid to miss her first steps." I know this memory makes him emotional.

"That's before we had to worry about her college tuition. There's also our retirement."

"We don't always have to worry about money. Wouldn't it be nice if we had a more peaceful life and spent more time together?" I place my hand on his thigh, rubbing lightly.

Aidan rubs his forehead. "I miss you too. I couldn't even spend my birthday with my family this year." He sighs.

"I don't mean just the last few months. I'm talking about these last few years. I hardly ever see you since you got the last promotion. I even miss the time before D&P."

He reclines in his chair. "Before D&P? That was a very long time ago."

"We were so carefree back then."

"Also so very poor. Remember that studio apartment we had, with a blow-up mattress as our only furniture?"

I smile. "Yes, and that was all we needed."

"You forget how hard we had it. You had that minimum-wage deli job, and I was just barely making ends meet as an entry-level broker."

"And we were so happy back then. And so in love."

"We are still in love now. My love for you hasn't changed. But we've worked so hard to get to where we are now. We can't just let this go. This is a dream opportunity for me. I want to make CFO. We have to make sure we provide for Sophie. My job is to take care of my family. I can't forget about it, ever."

I pour him more wine and try again. "But what if there is a great opportunity waiting for you in another company, where you could be hired as the CFO without having to prove yourself to a new boss?" I hold my breath. This is a good argument, I think.

"I know what I'm doing. And don't worry about it. I'll keep us secure. I'm certain I'll be the CFO by the end of next year." Aidan starts eating again and checks his phone, dismissing me.

I know this is a low blow, but I'm desperate. "But Aidan, all the discussions we ever had about how to improve this company never involved Big Pharma taking it over. You were the one who always said that these giants were unethical and you'd never work for one. What happened to that? What has changed?"

He lifts his gaze from his phone. "I think you've been really stressed out lately and you could use a vacation. Is your anxiety acting up again? Maybe Lori can prescribe you more sleep pills before you start having nightmares again. Or maybe you want to take a week off? I'm sure it'll be fine with Richard."

"No, it's all right, it's not anxiety," I say.

I get up and walk out of the dining room. But it's not all right. My mind is screaming as I pace back and forth in my bedroom. Aidan thinks my panic disorder is flaring up. But I need him to listen to me. I don't want him thinking I'm having mental health problems now. And he is not listening at all. I can't decide if I'm furious, scared, or heartbroken.

Eric was right. I'll not be able to run away. Aidan isn't willing to run away with me. And I don't have the guts to tell him about Richard.

It seems I'm trapped in this nightmare. I'm pinned against Richard once more. Alone.

Who will win this time, if I'm the one who starts the fight? Who will get hurt in the end? How far am I willing to go to get justice?

Chapter 6

I park the car in its usual spot in the D&P garage, by the security guard station. I turn off the engine and recline, closing my eyes for a moment. I have an extra half-hour. Should be enough time to sneak into the conference room through the back hallway. Today is the quarterly company meeting, and I'm on the schedule for a presentation.

In front of Richard.

I should know today if he recognizes me. I doubt he will—I look nothing like Katie Daniels. But I'm prepared if he does. I practice my glare in the makeup mirror. *Come and get me, Richard.* A part of me understands, though, that he won't. He never even looked at me as he pushed me into the stairway that day. He simply never cared to see my face. He had no idea whose life he was ruining, and I bet he's never given it another thought.

"Stop it!" I tell myself firmly in the mirror. "He didn't ruin your life. You are not a rape victim anymore. You are successful. You are respected. You are loved by your husband and you are a great mother. He can't do anything to you now."

Can he?

I grab my laptop bag and get out of the car. Sitting in the garage isn't helping. Might as well face the enemy.

The conference room is dark and empty at this hour. I push the lights on and search for a good seat, taking my time. The mahogany tables have been pushed together in a square, for the leadership team to face each other. There are chairs all around the tables and a second row for the less important people. The presentation podium is off to the side, with a large screen all set up on the wall. It's staring at me, menacing.

Where will Richard want to sit? I should probably sit as far from him as possible. Will he be in the corner by the front? Or will he want to face the projector screen? Will he stand next to the podium? Oh, God, I think I feel a strong wave of nausea again. Anxiety. I run to the bathroom and throw up, but nausea passes quickly this time.

I return to the conference room, pick a seat smack in the middle on the right, and my nerves settle a little as I log into the company's new computer system. I stare, speechless, at the "Welcome to Avias Global" screen for a few minutes, then review the quarterly numbers for my presentation.

My talk is not that long. I will explain our strategy for the last quarter and discuss results on the simplification of the ad campaigns. The last three slides will go through our final numbers. I have nothing interesting to report, but no one should be surprised. D&P's company profits have been flat for some time. Am I supposed to call us Avias now?

The phone buzzes with another call from Lori. I send it to voicemail. She may be calling with my lab work results. I have no time for bad medical news. I just hope I can make it through this meeting without looking away from Richard.

"What are you doing here so early?" Aidan's head pops in the door.

"I wanted to prepare." I give him a hug. It's brief. I'm still upset about him not wanting to leave. I have to keep reminding myself that it's my fault he doesn't know who Richard really is.

"You got any good news for us?"

"You know I don't. We haven't seen any uptick in sales for the last six months."

He pulls out a chair and sits down next to me. "I hoped things wouldn't look all bleak for Richard. At least some positives for him to hear at his first QBR."

I fidget with my pen, and he steadies my hand. "Don't worry. He is a super-nice guy. You'll get along great."

"Well, you know I get fidgety doing these quarterly presentations."

"You'll be fine. I have a quick phone call to make, and then I'll be back." He pats my shoulder and leaves.

Fifteen minutes later, the room is filled with people. There is breakfast on a side buffet table, and I pretend to be hungry. With food in front of me, I can keep my mouth full and avoid talking for a while. I desperately want Aidan to sit next to me, but he stands in the front, near the podium.

Dana is at a table across from me. She mouths, "Call Lori." I nod and roll my eyes.

The door swings open, and everyone turns their heads.

Aidan's face brightens. "There is the man of the hour!"

I don't want to look at Richard, but I can't help it. I

stare straight at his body, as he strides in, his admin struggling to catch up. He stands next to Aidan by the podium. Aidan is about to say something, but Richard dismisses him with a small motion of his head.

"I'll give the floor to you, then, Richard," Aidan says quickly and sits down.

Richard's voice booms through the room for some time. I can't understand what he says. The room sways. I stuff a bagel in my mouth and drink my coffee. I know I can get through this. I've managed to get through all the years since what he did to me. I won't allow him to rattle me. The food helps, and slowly, instead of the roaring in my ears, I begin to hear the words he says about the company's future and the new line of antipsychotics he wants us all to work on. I make a note on my phone to talk to Aidan about this: *Ridiculous plan of action: too many side effects—will be buried in lawsuits/go bankrupt. I'm not dealing with this.*

It is well into the meeting that Aidan nods to me, signaling it's just about time for my presentation, when the room erupts in piercing sounds of a fire alarm and blinding flashing of emergency lights. I can't help it—my head is immediately in my lap, with my hands covering my ears. Dana's arms are suddenly around me, pulling me out of the chair, as I grab on to the armrests, not letting go.

My brain is scrambled with panic.

"Aidan, she needs you," Dana calls.

Then I feel Aidan's arms, moving me out of the chair and leading my body somewhere. I finally open my eyes when there's a cold breeze on my neck.

"No!" I back up quickly. I look for Dana, but she's off to the side now, talking into her cell and lining up people to exit. How could she abandon me?

"We have to evacuate the building. I'm sorry, Emma," Aidan says, annoyance evident in his voice.

"I won't take the stairs. I can't do it, Aidan. You know I can't." I back up farther and tuck myself into a corner of the hallway.

He blocks me with his body. "You are causing a scene," he whispers into my ear. "Everyone has to evacuate. Shut your eyes and lean on me. I'll guide you out."

"You are a big boss here; can't you get an elevator pass for me? Please ask security—tell them it's an emergency," I plead, my heart pounding, threatening to burst out of my chest. And then I can't breathe, blood thrumming in my ears, when I hear Richard's voice.

"Mrs. Shephard, do you need some help? We have to clear the building with some efficiency."

Aidan moves sideways, and I see now that there's a group of people standing by the door, snickering, staring at me. My husband is breathing heavily and tugging on his tie. He hates this, I'm sure.

I make a mistake and look at Richard's face. His lips are stretched into a grin. Our eyes meet, and then he gives a small, almost imperceptible, nod to me. But it's not a friendly nod of encouragement. His eyes narrow at me, and my blood freezes, my heart instantly icy with fear.

My body instinctively moves forward and fits into Aidan's for protection. It helps, and I find the strength I need. "Come on, Aidan." I turn my head to the rest of the onlookers and explain, "Sorry, everyone. I stubbed my toe and couldn't move for a moment."

I pull Aidan out the exit door and descend the

fucking stairs, pretend-limping and biting my lip until I swallow blood over and over.

Aidan is silent. I can sense his annoyance in the way he no longer says anything to me as we proceed.

But I'm not annoyed, or any longer terrified of the stairs.

I'm furious.

Furious at Richard, who is stepping down heavily behind me, probably gloating in his knowledge that each step makes me remember the punches he landed on me that day. Furious that this is the first time I've been able to take the stairs in years. Furious that, even though I manage to descend the stairs, my ribs and my face ache terribly, as if they are still receiving Richard's blows on the tenth-floor stairway at Westview.

I feel the heat of his breath on my neck, I smell his sweat, and I want to fight back just as violently as he hurt me that night. By the time we get out of the building, I'm ready to strike.

My fingers ache from being clenched into fists, and I know the anger has given me power. The power I haven't felt since before Richard. Since I failed my dad by not getting justice. Since I failed all the victims who likely came after me.

"What's the matter with you?" Aidan resumes talking, looking at me with narrowed eyes. "You don't seem right. You look pissed off."

"I hate these fire alarm drills," I say through my clenched teeth. It's the best I can come up with.

The phone in my pocket buzzes and rescues me. "I need to take this," I say to him. I pretend to take the call but I don't answer. It's Lori again. I can't talk to anyone right now.

Aidan gives me a sideways look but walks off to talk to Richard. I watch them laughing a minute later, standing near the delivery bay, Richard casually leaning on the railing.

I pace along the sidewalk, counting my steps. Each step creates energy vibrating through me and generates more anger. I pick up some fresh snow in my right hand and squeeze the icy crystals until they begin to melt from the heat of my hand. But it doesn't help to cool me off. I imagine throwing the snowball at Richard's face and watching Aidan gasp in horror.

"Emma, the building is clear," Aidan yells in my direction.

"All right, I'm ready to present," I say, my body still vibrating in anger.

I'm on fire. Let Richard watch how he has absolutely no impact on me.

"Actually," Aidan says, coming closer. "We won't have time for your presentation. Richard said we needed to move on to discuss the financials for the next quarter. You don't mind, do you? We really have to get through the QBR by noon."

"So I prepared the Power Point for nothing?" My fingers curl into a fist.

"You said you didn't have any major news. Can you go ahead and email the senior team your slides? We must get everyone's attention on Richard's budget proposal."

So that's how it's going to work now. Richard will always get whatever he wants. He's always gotten whatever he wanted. And now he's going after my husband and my company, all the while laughing at me as still his victim.

"I guess no one wants to hear from me now that Richard is around. No problem. Of course." I'm boiling from my toes to the top of my head, and I'm frightened of what I might say or do next.

"You're not mad, are you? I need your attention on the budget, sweetheart."

"I'm fine." I kick the muddy ground with my right toe. "I have nothing better to do than spend hours putting together presentations no one cares to look at. I'll keep that in mind next time I'm bored. I'll just work on another hour-long pointless Power Point."

"Come on, don't do this sarcasm crap. It's Richard's first meeting. Don't give me a hard time."

I take a few steps away from my husband, alarmed at the fire inside me. I don't know if I can control it. "You want me not to give you a hard time? Fine, I'll go work at home, and you can hold whatever stupid budget meeting you want to hold."

"Whatever. Go home. Probably wouldn't hurt to call Lori about those anxiety pills." Aidan turns and storms off to Richard.

I run to the parking garage, find my husband's car, and kick the tires a few times as I wait for my assistant, Janet, to bring my bag down. I pull out of the parking area, my tires screeching.

I don't know where to go. I don't want to go home. I ought to drive far away—keep at it for miles, for days, until this out-of-control feeling disappears. Until Aidan misses me.

So Richard recognized me. Is that why he canceled my presentation? Could he see the fear in my eyes? Did he enjoy it? Did he enjoy watching me leave today as my husband stayed at work thinking his new boss is so great?

"Fucking bastard!" I scream, pushing on the gas.

My anger refuses to be contained now. I'm a volcano ready to erupt. He doesn't deserve this. Richard doesn't deserve his life. He shouldn't be here running my company, and laughing with my husband, playing games with me, while I can't even manage to go down the fucking stairs without having a flashback. I had to drop out of college. He made me into an angry, empty, lonely person who was afraid of anyone who came around her. But Richard never had to put his life on hold. Instead, he became a wealthy, powerful man with no obstacles in his path.

And as I look at the ocean of cars in front of me, I know I will right the wrong Richard has done to me. I can't let Richard win. He tried to destroy me before, but I managed to rebuild my life. No one knows how hard I've worked to stop feeling like a victim, and I won't allow him to make me a victim again. And I refuse to lose Aidan to him.

Richard deserves my anger, and he deserves to be punished.

Chapter 7

I park the car half way down the driveway, run into the house, and pull the heavy ladder of the attic with all my strength. My shoulder makes a loud pop and, for a second, I worry I might've dislocated it, but then the sharp pain is gone, and I climb the tiny steps to the freezing attic. I'm glad I still have my coat on. I stare at the uneven floor, pull off my heels, and throw them down. The sound of them hitting the wood below reverberates through the empty house. The pull rope for the light bulb still works, and I search through the neatly lined up cardboard boxes among the yellow insulation and discarded household junk.

The large box labeled with green marker "Dad's stuff" is way in the back. I climb carefully through to the back, wipe the dust off the top of the box, and peel off the tape holding it closed. I know what it contains: my dad's things I managed to hide as my mother was throwing them away just a month after we lost him. She couldn't cope with the fact that he was murdered. She wouldn't accept his death within a few months of being promoted to detective after never getting so much as a scratch in all his time as a patrol officer. Mother wanted to erase all the traces of Dad so she wouldn't fall apart every time she saw his shirts or socks lying around.

I dig through to find what I'm looking for. The first item at the top is a small photo album with pictures of my dad and me fishing, eating ice cream, and dad pushing me on my first bike. Then Dad's wallet that I gave him a week before he was killed. His watch. The glasses he always lost and I had to help him find. A tie he wore to church. A picture of him in his cop uniform. Another of him at his desk when he became a detective.

And then there is a green case. The lock is stuck a bit. It hasn't been open in years, after all. Dad's 1911 Remington. I hope it still works. Dad will be happy if I finally get some use out of my inheritance. I can finally get justice. It would've hurt Dad to know that my attacker never got punished. He never would have allowed me to leave Westview without making sure everyone there got punished for what they did to me. Nothing was more important to him than people getting what they deserved.

"Sorry, Daddy," I whisper. "I failed you."

Mom never officially allowed him to teach me how to shoot a gun, although I begged all the time. Dad loved his gun. He had his department-issued weapon, of course. But this was his prized possession. He showed me how to use it just once. He took me out in the woods, loaded a few bullets, and let me hold on to his arm as he fired it. I fell back from the impact, but I wasn't frightened, and he let me keep the empty casing from the 45-caliber bullet. The last time my father used it was sometime in the nineties. I remember him telling me that he had never shot anyone on the job. I wish he would've. Because he wasn't killed in a crossfire. He was killed by a man who'd been beating his wife for years and didn't like my dad interfering. Maybe if Dad had had his weapon out, it would have stopped the guy. And then Dad would have been around to help when I faced Richard and Westview.

I stroke the black metal and the ridged handle. I search the box for bullets, but there are none. Must get some. I also need to learn how to use it. I can't make a mistake. I wish I could ask Eric to teach me. But you can't ask a cop to help you kill someone. I think for a minute, look up the address of the nearest gun range, and then I'm in the car. My soundtrack skips to rap, and I let it. My blood is pumping to the rhythm. I can't wait to find out what it feels like to shoot. I assume shooting a person is different from shooting at a target, but I must start somewhere.

The range is quiet, with only one other person checking in at the front desk, with a small handbag. I watch a required safety video and then place my gun case on the desk for inspection. "I need some 45-calibers, please, a person target, and I'll pay for an hour," I tell the man at the front desk.

"Nice piece," he comments after inspecting the Remington.

He hands me the bullets, goggles, and earplugs, and I enter through a heavy door into the shooting area. All this wait had begun to make my anger dissipate, and I don't like that. I want to stay furious at Richard. And at Aidan, for sticking with Richard. How could he do that to me?

There are two men loading their guns next to me in their lanes, and I watch them carefully. Looks easy. I take Dad's gun carefully out of the case. It's heavier than I remember. The men fire, and the sound is so much louder than I ever expected that I drop the gun, and it falls with a loud crack on the floor.

There is a shout, "Cease fire!" and a man in the

gun range uniform runs to me. “Move away from your weapon!”

I step back, shaking, as he inspects the gun.

“It’s not loaded,” he says, turning back to me.

“I know,” I say, my voice breaking. “I just took it out of the case and dropped it accidentally.”

“You have to respect your weapon.” He shakes a finger at me. “If you can’t hold onto it unloaded, you can’t be here.”

“I can hold onto it.”

The three men can see right through me, I’m certain. I won’t let them see my fear. “Can I get my gun back now?” I say, my voice loud and firm now.

The man sets the gun down on the shelf in my bay, the barrel away from me. “Here you go. Mind your gun.”

I glare at him and return to my task. I close my eyes and bring back the memory of Daddy loading the gun. I remember. I know how to do it. One at a time, I slide the fat bullets in, push them in carefully. Then slide the magazine, lock in place. Ready?

No, not ready.

The fire on both sides of me continues, and I startle as my hands shake. My fingers struggle to hold on to the heavy pistol with both hands, staring at the target in front of me. It’s shaped as a man. I try to imagine it looking like Richard and think which shot would be best: head or chest. There is fire on my right, and a bullet casing flies to my side. I jump. Shit!

The head. I will go for the head because I want him to die quickly and I don’t want anyone to save him. If I miss the heart, they could save him at the hospital. Will I see the bullet go into his body?

I count, "Three, two, one," and squeeze the trigger.

The gun feels like it exploded in my hands. Sharp pain shoots up my wrists, and my arms jerk toward my head. I stumble but manage to keep on standing straight. The smoke and heat of the shot hang in the air around me, and I stand gasping.

I put the gun down carefully on the shelf in front of me and look at the target. I hit the top of the head. The brain. And, suddenly, I gulp for air. That's how Daddy died. The guy shot him in the head. He was dead almost instantly. The guy knew how to kill someone right. It wasn't his first murder. But the first one he was caught for.

Oh, God, what am I doing?

I put my face in my hands and feel a sob coming through my chest and then resolving in a shower of tears. What the fuck am I doing? Am I actually thinking of murdering someone? It would make me the same kind of horrible person as that guy who killed my father. The guy who is rotting away in prison right now. Is that what I want? To rot away in prison and abandon Sophie? And Aidan?

I'm not a murderer. My father's kind face appears in front of me in my mind, and then the image of his dead body in the coffin, when he was no longer recognizable because the mortuary did its job of draining his blood. I'd like to drain Richard of his blood, but I'm *not* a murderer. I've never hurt anyone in my entire life. I've only hated. First, the man who murdered my father. Then—Richard. Hated and dreamt of revenge. And now that it's in front of me—I can't do it. I can't kill him.

"Ma'am, is everything all right?" I hear behind me.

"It's fine. I'm leaving," I cry out.

I take out the bullets, pack up the gun, and drive away as fast as I can.

I pace in the living room when I reach home. The gun is still in my car. Cookie paces with me with her ears pressed back on her head. She knows something is up. I kneel and pet her to help her settle down.

I walk to the bathroom and wash my face. My hands smell like the metal of the gun. The scent is vile. Suddenly, I'm at the toilet, and my anger has turned into violent vomiting. When I finish throwing up, I scrub my hands with lavender soap over and over until the metal smell is obliterated.

I fall face first on my bed, spent physically and mentally. My anger isn't spent, even though my head spins. I need a new plan. I'm clearly not going to hurt Richard physically. What else can I do to him? How far can I go to show him that he can't just show up here and damage my life again? He has to leave me alone. And my husband. And my company. I need to take something away that he cares about. Is there anything that he does care about?

I sit up, despite the dizziness. I know what matters to Richard the most. He was never smart enough or rich enough to get to where he is now, not by himself. But somehow he did. He made it to Westview, he made the right connections, he was protected by everyone there despite what he did to me, and he married his rich wife, whose daddy put him where he is now. Money and power. That's what I need to focus on. Jeopardizing his position and making sure Avias loses money. All those plans he has for bringing in the new drugs and making profits off his D&P position—I will sabotage them. All of them. Then let's see how his wife and his father-in-law feel about him.

I'll show him I am no longer that weak Katie Daniels he tried to destroy.

Chapter 8

The doorbell rings and startles me. I consider pretending I'm not in, but Cookie runs to the door and gives us away. A few minutes later I'm glad I changed my mind. After I stumble to the door, I see Lori, with a large paper bag of groceries.

"If you don't call me back for days, I have no choice but to come check on you." She hands me the bag as she walks in, the drops of rain coming in behind her. "And I didn't enjoy taking a detour in this weather. Dana and the kids are going to have to come here too, after the gymnastics. I got takeout. Here."

"Thanks." I hug her. "I haven't even thought of dinner yet." I'm so happy she is here. I'm teary-eyed in gratitude. I'll figure out what to do with Richard later. It's been yet another shitty day, and a hug from a friend feels like the ultimate kindness to me right now.

"Is your anxiety acting up again?" she asks as she hangs her wet coat.

"No, I'm fine. I really am."

"Dana said there was a fire drill at work today, and you had a panic attack and then left for the day. I don't think you are fine at all. I wish you would answer my phone calls."

"I'm so sorry I didn't call you back. I did freak out a bit during the fire drill. But I'm better now. There's just been a lot going on, and then the president cancelled my presentation after the drill."

"It's all right. We can talk about all that." Lori washes her hands in the kitchen sink. "Those packages need to be heated up. I got the food about half an hour ago."

I take out the packages of Chinese food gratefully. I'm so exhausted these days, with Richard having descended on us, I haven't even thought of restocking the fridge. Hot food is just what I need at the moment. I sneak a water chestnut before placing the first container in the microwave.

"Aren't you the least bit interested why I've been trying to reach you?" Lori asks.

"Oh." I pause, finger on the start button. "I hope it's not bad news. Is it bad news? Is that why you brought me all this food?" I'm suddenly going through the list of my symptoms lately: dizziness, fatigue, confused mind, nausea.

"Well, I do need to tell you something about your blood work." Lori opens a cabinet, takes out a glass, and pours herself some water.

I groan. "This is not a good time to give me bad news, Lori. It's been a shitty day. A shitty few weeks, really. Ever since Avias sent the new president here, it's just all been a mess." I wonder for a second whether I should just come out and tell Lori all about Richard, but then I realize she'd tell Dana, and I don't want Dana to know who her new boss is. Not yet. Or maybe not ever.

"Well, you can tell me all about this new president later. But first I get to talk. It's not bad news." She smiles. "The opposite, actually. You are about nine weeks pregnant."

"I'm what?" I whisper, dropping a container of lomein. I gag, looking at the mess, and put a kitchen towel to my mouth, covering my nose.

"Yep," she replies, as she picks up the noodles off the tile with another towel and throws away the mess. "That's probably why you fainted that day when you came to see me. Early pregnancy. I called in prenatal vitamins a week ago, but I haven't been able to reach you. You need to get in with your OB for an ultrasound. So congratulations!"

"Stop it! I'm entirely too old to be pregnant. I'm forty. I have a daughter graduating high school soon." I start pacing. "Aidan and I don't even have time to have sex."

"Well, you had sex at least once." She laughs and hugs me.

"But could the test be wrong? I mean, we've tried so many times before. After Sophie. How could this be happening now?"

We did try, for so long. Aidan always dreamed of having many kids. But we've had years of failed pregnancy tests. Years of miscarriages. We went through multiple tries of IVF, back when I wasn't too old to have children.

"You can't predict what human bodies will do. For some reason, your ovaries decided they wanted to be active again. I don't know what else to tell you." She clears her throat. "You are going to keep it, right?"

"Of course I'm going to keep it, but I can't even wrap my head around the idea. I really never thought I'd have a chance again."

"Congratulations—I'm so happy for you guys. Perfect timing, with Sophie leaving for college soon. You'll have a little person to occupy your time."

"Don't bring up Sophie leaving," I snap.

"Okay. Heat up that food. You need to start eating more. You were too thin when I saw you. Oh, and you can't take any more of that anxiolytic I prescribed you. If you keep on struggling with panic attacks, we'll find you a psychologist."

A few minutes later, I excuse myself to the bathroom and sit on the edge of the bathtub for a while. I'm not hungry, anyway. I touch my stomach, but my hand feels nothing. All those years I counted days to my ovulation, and we tried repeatedly to conceive… All those days praying and hoping I wouldn't get my period… All those dozens of pregnancy tests that came up negative… And here I am, at forty, pregnant.

I cry, then laugh, then stand in front of the mirror, lifting my shirt. My stomach is so flat—the result of years of gym and rigorous jogging. I bend backward slightly, trying to imagine myself looking pregnant again. What did it feel like? I tap my fingers on my stomach. I remember kicking. It felt incredible. Carrying Sophie was the only time I was truly able to forget about being a victim. The only time I didn't have nightmares. I only had dreams about her—Sophie.

"I'm not sure I'm ready to tell Aidan yet," I say to Lori when I return to the kitchen.

She is setting the table for dinner but spins around at my announcement. Her hand is frozen in the air, holding a fork.

"What? How can you keep this from him, after all you've been through with the other pregnancies?"

"That's the thing." I wipe a tear. "I don't want to put him through it again. We've had so many times I got him all excited and then had a miscarriage. He's been heartbroken enough about it."

"But listen." She puts down the fork. "You've never come this far before, besides Sophie. You usually miscarry right away, and you are nine weeks already."

"Still time for something to go wrong. Let me have an ultrasound first. Then I'll tell him, if everything is fine." There are so many fears growing in my head.

Lori throws her arms up in the air. "Okay, it's your baby, your husband. Just know that secrets don't help a marriage. You do what you wish. But do get those vitamins tomorrow, please."

"I will."

I go to the garage a little later, get the gun out of the trunk, and hide it in a box labeled "Old Paperwork—discard this year." I let myself hold it for a moment before putting it away on a top storage shelf. I'm floating on hope that there is a life inside of me. I can't allow Richard to ruin this chance for me. He's already ruined so much.

****

Aidan and Sophie have gone to bed, but I can't sleep at all. Aidan forgot to close the curtains, and I watch his face in the moonlight as he sleeps. He looks very peaceful as he stretches his arm, reaching for me. He always knows when I come to bed, no matter how late. I wish we didn't fight earlier at work. It's not always easy to work together. It gets the best of us sometimes, when we get so hotheaded. I reach for his hand, place it on my chest, and stroke it gently. Then I pull it lower, to the spot where our child is growing. I hope Aidan's love can help him grow stronger. I feel guilty for not telling him about the baby, but I don't want to disappoint him again.

The day I met Aidan, nearly twenty years ago, we collided in the elevator. I was working for Jenny's father at the deli, and he sent me to deliver a cheesecake to a small brokerage firm. I was late and had two more deliveries to make. I ran red-faced into the building and was waiting a long time for the elevator. When it finally arrived, I rushed inside as a man was rushing out of it.

"Whoa!" I yelled out, trying to hold onto the cake.

"It's all right, I got you," he said, smiling.

Aidan held onto me, then helped me carry the cheesecake upstairs to his office, where I learned that it was for his birthday. He asked me out for coffee and we talked for hours. And he has held on to me ever since. Through my bad moods, through miscarriages, through IVF, through holidays with our families, and through my nightmares.

What do I do now that I'm pregnant? What would happen if my husband ever found out about Richard? I don't want Aidan to hurt or worry about anything that's ever happened to me or is happening to me. I need to protect Aidan. If he is happy, then I'm happy; it's that simple. That's how it's always been. Aidan feels his job has always been to protect me. If he knows I'm in danger, he'll lose his mind. His dad left his mother and sister when they were young, so he always feels this need to be a super-protective person to all the women in his family. I can't put yet another responsibility on Aidan. If I can figure out how to get Richard to leave us alone, to get out of our lives, it could all return to normal and Aidan would never need to know, would he?

I so wish Aidan would stop liking Richard. Does he not feel how much it hurts me? Of course, I can see why Aidan finds Richard so fascinating. Psychopaths are very skilled at charming people, right before they hurt them. I fell into his trap once.

I shudder as I recall meeting Richard that evening at the frat party. My roommate Shannon introduced us, had a drink with us, and left. He was tall. Handsome. Popular. Slight hint of an Eastern European accent. Charming as he brought me drinks and made jokes. I felt mesmerized. Until everything began to sway, and I lost track of where I was anymore… Until I found myself in the middle of any woman's worst nightmare.

I hope there is enough time for me to get back at Richard and to get him to leave us alone. I return Aidan's hand to him and stroke my stomach, right below the navel. Suddenly, I'm certain. It's a boy. I can feel him growing inside me. He needs another thirty-one weeks. Maybe a bit less. So I have that long.

I don't have much time at all.

Chapter 9

The best plan—the only plan—still must be to sabotage Richard's success with his new job at D&P. If Richard makes no money with D&P, then maybe his father-in-law will send someone else to manage it. And if Aidan sees the company struggling, he may have to accept my plan to move out of Great Falls. Goodbye Richard, for sure, then. I will just need to make sure that my husband never finds out about my involvement in any of this.

"So what exactly do you want to know?" Dana asks as she enters my office.

"I know you are upset about the Avias deal. I need to understand why." Besides Aidan, Dana is the only one at D&P I can trust.

"I wanted to work for Eli Lilly, not Avias."

"So did everyone. But what exactly is wrong with Avias?"

"Why don't you ask Aidan?" She sits down.

"I want your opinion. You are the head scientist. If anyone knows anything, it'd be you. I just feel like Richard is sleazy."

"Well, as a company, Avias has a terrible reputation. Especially with women and minorities. What did Aidan tell you?"

My shoulders drop. "Only that they are doing well in the stock market." Did Aidan lie?

"His Richard is worth fifty million. Yeah, they are doing great. I hear he also owns a lot of D&P stock now."

I twitch at "his Richard" but try to restrain myself. "Great—rich and sleazy," I say.

"The rumor is—Avias is known for acquiring smaller companies with existing drugs, laying off employees, practically stopping all research, and then hiking up prices on the drugs."

"Yeah, that would get you to fifty mils."

Dana raises her finger in emphasis. "He'll make a lot more now that they get our stimulants and antidepressants. Also, Richard said something about Parozex, the new antipsychotic they've developed. We're supposed to file the New Drug Application and then your department will need to market it. He is really counting on it to be a big deal."

"So Avias does research new drugs?"

She smirks. "In India and China only."

"Overseas? We never did that."

"It's cheaper. It saves thousands. No, maybe millions. Fewer regulations. You can do whatever you want there. No ethics committees to go around. Do you know how much it costs us for that NDA?"

"Yes, half a mil."

"And the extra in lobbying. Now you see how Avias gets that money?"

"By saving on the cost of trials."

She nods. "Overseas trials cost one-tenth of ours. Also, Avias can get anyone to sign a consent form to be in a study in India."

"But isn't their government having an issue with this?" I ask.

"No, they're happy to have drug companies in India. It's a lot of money. And the people enrolled in the study will agree to anything. They get compensation and free health care. Also, sometimes they are forced to do it by their doctors, who are well paid by the company."

"Are people in India and China suitable subjects for US drug studies? Does FDA find this acceptable?"

"They are not. You should test drugs on people of all ethnicities. Drugs can metabolize differently. But FDA lets it slide."

This is better than I expected. I'm sure she'll agree to go against Richard with me. Having Dana on my side would be incredible. And given what she just said, I won't need to tell her why I'm against him.

"We must do something about this, Dana," I say.

"What am I going to do?" She shrugs.

I lean forward on the desk. "Can you stall any NDA Richard wants filed? Especially for that antipsychotic he is so excited about? That would give me a chance to talk to Aidan and look into this some more. And it gives *you* a chance to make sure the research is solid. We can't allow our reputation to be ruined with any poorly done applications."

Dana shakes her head. "I'll get fired, Emma. My job is already on the line. R&D are the first to be let go by Avias."

I didn't think of Dana losing her job. Another casualty. How many people am I willing to sacrifice for this? I can't turn back now. I get up and walk around the desk. I grab hold of the armrests of her chair and look straight into her dark brown eyes. "Dana, you are likely to get fired anyway, given what you are telling me, so why not do something good on your way out?"

She pushes my arms aside, gets up, and walks to the window.

"Good for who? You?" she asks, leaning on the windowsill, her arms crossed. "And why are you suddenly so interested in making things difficult for Avias? Don't you want them to succeed? Your job should be safe."

"I don't trust Richard. I don't trust how he's sucking up to Aidan so much. Something is wrong, but I can't quite put my finger on it. John sold the company too fast." Keeping secrets is becoming second nature to me now. I'm disgusted with myself.

Dana is quiet for a while as she plays with the plants on my windowsill. My heart is in my throat as I wait for her to decide. She is my friend, but what I'm asking her to do concerns her professional integrity.

"I can maybe try to hold up the data. FDA will not review any NDA unless all the data is included. But it's not just my department who is sending it out. And I can't quit. I don't have another job lined up. For sure I'll be looking for one in January." She rubs her forehead.

"Can I tell Aidan about this?" I ask.

"What does Aidan care? He's a money guy. And Richard is his new best buddy. Don't you see them always hanging out together? I bet Aidan is thrilled we're finally turning a profit. This place has turned to shit. And I don't think your husband gives a damn." Dana shakes her head and walks out.

"You are wrong," I whisper behind her.

****

I don't like being up when Aidan's gone to bed. No

matter how many lights I turn on, there are always strange noises in the house. There is the odd scraping noise that Aidan assures me is just the branches of the old trees touching the roof and the wall of my study when the wind is strong. And the floor creaks underneath my feet as I close the drapes to keep the dark out.

My eyes are sore, and I stretch and yawn. I've been researching Richard and Avias. My old chair doesn't have nearly enough padding for this job. I should get a new one. The lighting in the office could use some updating too; it's too dark in here at night. I can hardly see anything besides my screen. My dog lies on top of papers by the desk, keeping me company. I wish my mind would settle down.

I go to the kitchen to grab a snack. I insert two slices of bread into the toaster, then pause with my finger on the slider as I hear steps behind me. I spin around and see—nothing. I need to calm down.

After the toast is done, I listen for noise upstairs, then tiptoe to Sophie's room. A sliver of light shows underneath her door, and I open it gently, risking her wrath. She is not asleep. She is lying on her pillows, typing away, smiling. Her laptop is on her lap, as usual.

"You were supposed to be sleeping. Don't you have a calculus exam or something tomorrow?"

"Then why are you here bothering me?" she retorts.

I sigh. "I need your help." I sit down on the bed next to her and pretend I don't notice her hurriedly closing her laptop. "Don't bother hiding your stuff. You are not in trouble. You see—you're really good at hacking into sites and you always hide it from us, but we know you do it anyway."

"I have no idea what you're talking about." She turns a bright tomato color.

"You know exactly what I'm talking about." I can't help it—I kiss the freckles on her nose even as she pulls away. "Anyway, can I ask for your help in doing some research on a few people?"

"Use my hacker skills with your permission?" She's grinning. "Yes, please. But then you have to allow me to go on whatever sites I want at other times."

"You absolutely can't expect me to say yes to something like this."

"Well, then you absolutely can't expect me to help you."

I take a deep breath. "You can't blackmail me. Can we just agree that you won't do anything illegal?"

"I'm hacking; it's already illegal. But fine, I'll stay out of trouble. I promise." She opens her laptop back up. "What do you need?"

I give her the three names to search for, then hesitate, trying to find the right words. "One more thing—I don't want Dad to know about this yet. It's just that he is so stressed with the transition at the company. And this has nothing to do with him."

"It's all right, Mom. I'm a big girl. I know you won't ask me to do anything that's bad."

"But I'm asking you to lie to your dad."

"Not really. You are asking me not to tell him that I'm looking up information for you. He doesn't ever ask me what I do besides my grades and who I'm going out with. It's fine."

It stings, this lying. The guilt gnaws at me. But I push it aside.

"Mom, this will take a while," Sophie says. "Go do something. I need to find his social media, work profile, digital footprints, criminal records. You think this will be fast? I don't need you hovering over me." She waves me away.

I go to the kitchen and make two bowls of ice cream to pass the time. I add whipped cream on top. I'm not raging anymore. I'm hopeful. I'm fueled by the desire for revenge. What does my daughter think of me, I wonder? What will she think when she stops searching and realizes what I'm asking her to do?

When she comes downstairs, I gesture for her to whisper so we don't wake up Aidan. We scroll through pictures of Richard at his country club. She shows me his bank account, his stocks, his wife's social media. We make a list of his user names and passwords.

As she flips to yet another picture of him at yet another social event, I exclaim, "Hold on!" I grab the laptop from Sophie and click the image to magnify. I must be mistaken. This surely can't be… Barely distinguishable, a face of the person taking the picture, reflected in the mirror behind him. It's Shannon, my college roommate. I gasp, then cover my mouth.

"What is it?" Sophie asks.

"You see that shadow right there in the right corner?"

"Where? Oh. That's a face."

"It's a woman I knew a long time ago."

"Huh. He knows her?"

"He does."

"What's her name? Let's confirm."

Sophie's fingertips fly on the keyboard. I hold my breath. I'm not sure what I wish for more: for her to find Shannon or to *not* find her.

"There she is. Shannon Tomak, but she is married to Jeffrey Rawley now, so Shannon Rawley. They have a son, Benjamin."

The ice cream bowl falls out of my hands and crashes into a million pieces on the kitchen floor. I stare in horror at the melting puddle in front of me, while Sophie rushes to clean the mess.

"What's going on?" Aidan's sleepy voice comes out of the bedroom.

"It's all right, Dad. I broke a bowl, but I'm cleaning it up." Sophie rescues me.

I sit down on the bar stool.

"Who are these people, Mom? You're white as a sheet."

"I'm sorry. It's just such a surprise to find that they all…know each other. I knew them a long time ago."

"In college?"

"Yes. These people really screwed me."

"What exactly did they do?" Sophie asks, her eyes wide with curiosity.

"I made a mistake and got into trouble and felt I had to leave college. And—they were involved."

"Is that why you had to work at the deli? And didn't go back to college until I was older?"

"Yes. This Shannon—she was my roommate in college, and she wanted my boyfriend, Jeff Rawley. She invited me to a party, where I drank too much and did something stupid, and he broke up with me. That's how she ended up with him."

"I suppose you don't want me to know what it was that you did?"

"No, I don't want you to know."

"So she not only stole Jeff, she married him and they have a kid. I get it now."

"Exactly."

"And how is this Shannon person involved with Richard now? Wait." She grabs my arm. "You don't think they're having an affair, do you?"

"Why would they, if she got the other guy?" I say.

"Her face in the mirror, Mom. She looked too happy. And this Richard—he was smiling at her in a creepy way too. I bet you they *are* having an affair. Let me look them up some more."

As she types again, she asks, "You don't still…have feelings for this Jeff Rawley, do you, Mom?"

"God, no, Sophie. I love your dad very much."

"All right. Give me a flash drive. I'll load up all the info for you."

Some time later, Sophie still can't find any more information about Richard and Shannon having an affair. False thread. But the flash drive is full of information on Richard, Shannon, and Jeff. Enough for me to lose sleep over for the next few nights, I'm guessing. "What are you planning to do to them?" Sophie asks, handing the flash drive to me.

"Why do you think I'm going to do something to them?"

She rolls her eyes. "Honestly. You are having me look up information on this guy. Then you panic when you see these other names. You haven't quite been yourself lately. You must have some sort of a reason. Are you planning revenge?"

"Absolutely not."

"Sure, you're not. I'll keep looking tomorrow for

evidence of the affair. I'm just too tired tonight."

"No need. It's fine. Even if they are having an affair, they have enough money to hide it well."

"You'd be surprised. I can look for recent trips they both took, recent restaurant charges, stuff like that."

"Fine, you can look." I kiss her and begin to walk toward the bedroom.

"Hey, Mom," she says. "The Rawleys' son? Benjamin?"

"Yeah?" I turn around.

"He's been picked up twice for drinking, but he didn't get the points on his driver's license. They pay their lawyer well to make sure he gets the DA to drop the charges."

"And?"

"I just thought it's something you might use for your revenge. Because Shannon belongs to a lot of clubs. She's, like, a socialite. They're having a New Year's Eve party, and it's, like, the party to be at, in their social circle. Everyone's trying to get an invite."

"Figures," I mumble to myself. "Thanks, baby. Goodnight."

I climb into bed with my laptop and plug in the flash drive. There is Jeff: LinkedIn, Facebook, a donation to a hospital, a marriage certificate, and several images. The images are unmistakably him. An older, graying hair him, but still him. I click on the image of Jeff playing golf with a couple of guys. He is smiling and fit. He looks happy. My heart skips a beat. Wait a minute—he works for the FDA? He did get his M.D., but how did he end up working for the FDA? He always wanted to be a pediatrician.

I click through a few more images, and then I see

her. Shannon. She is in a low-cut silver gown, standing next to Jeff at a party of some sort. He is wearing a tux, and his arm is around her. The picture is not very old. She looks like she's had some work done. I look through multiple pictures of Shannon. She looks the same in all of them.

I need to know more about them. Benjamin is a tall teen boy who looks just like Shannon. I wonder if Sophie would find him handsome. Why am I thinking like this? They live in Chevy Chase. That's too close. Way too close to my life. I drive past their neighborhood several times a week. I could've bumped into them so many times, I realize, shuddering.

Shannon became a trophy wife, as she always wanted. They were a perfect match for each other, I guess. When I was assigned to be Shannon's roommate at the freshman dorms, I thought I was so lucky to have found a friend right away. A friend who knew the ins and outs of private school life that I'd never been exposed to as a small-town girl who grew up in a policeman's family. She seemed kind and helpful and introduced me to her friends, who all threw lavish parties. She gave me fashion advice and helped me learn how to use a blow dryer. Until it was too late, I didn't realize that girls like me were the ideal victims for girls like Shannon. Easy to influence and easy to manipulate. I must have been a constant source of entertainment for her and her friends.

It was clear she wanted Jeff from the day I started dating him. Their families knew each other, and she made it obvious they belonged together much more than we did. "Katie, you just wouldn't fit in well with the whole scene. Women in Jeff's family are expected to stay at home and raise children. You are much better off finding a boy who will let you become a doctor, like you want." That's the bait she used to get me to come to the frat party that day. "So many great down-to-earth boys you will meet. And wait till you talk to Richard. You'll just love him."

All of them—Richard, Shannon, and Jeff—are rich and successful. Years after they ruined my life, they continue to prosper. They haven't suffered through years of failures, they haven't struggled with nightmares, they haven't doubted themselves over and over. They drive fancy cars, belong to private clubs, and attend exclusive events.

My father was wrong. Bad people don't get what they deserve. There is no such thing as justice unless you fight for it. "Sorry, Daddy, but I have to get back at them before I become a victim again," I whisper.

I close my laptop, wrap Aidan's arm around me, and put my head on his shoulder. And then I finally sleep.

Chapter 10

According to my assistant, Janet, Richard's been leaving for lunch at the same time every day. If I know anything about the men in suits, it's that they always lunch with someone else to write these lunches off as a business expense.

"Janet," I ask. "Can you discreetly find out where Richard is having lunch today? I want to try to surprise him with a bottle of wine."

"Sure thing, Emma. Do you want me or his admin to set it up?"

"No, I don't want Ally to know. It should be a surprise. And I'll set it up; you can go to lunch."

Janet pops her head in a few minutes later. "His admin says he has a reservation with your husband at Gaskell."

I thank her and laugh inside. Aidan has a dentist appointment during lunch today. Was Sophie right, and he is having an affair with Shannon?

I grit my teeth and plan to spy on Richard at lunchtime. I've sunk low, but I can't turn back now. I time my departure exactly five minutes after his calendar says he is out of the office, but I run straight into him at the elevator.

Fuck!

"We need that new marketing strategy from you," he says as he pushes the down button.

"Sure," I say, pretending I was passing by and attempt to rush past him.

"Whoa, whoa, slow down," he grabs hold of my shoulders.

The shock of his touch is pure pain. I see sparks in front of my eyes.

I…must…not…let…him…see…this. I fly off with the speed of lightning, resolved more than ever to seek justice. As soon as the elevator is gone, I take another, get in my car, and hurry over to Gaskell. It's only a ten-minute drive.

Richard should really choose his locations farther away from here, I think, as I wait for an hour, feeling idiotic. And terribly hungry. I can imagine him inside, eating a hundred-dollar steak, drinking fine wine, laughing at my expense. Anger bubbles inside me, churning my stomach even more.

Then I see them. Walking out of the restaurant, standing under the green-and-white canopy for a while, talking. Doesn't he have to get back to work? Shannon opens her umbrella as they come out from under the canopy, but I can still see them. I slide down in my seat but put my phone up to the window and snap pictures repeatedly. I beg the gods of photography to let me have just one decent shot of the two of them together. I hear several cars drive past me a few minutes later, so I peek and see the back of Richard's BMW.

I sit up and flip through my pictures. They are all awful, fuzzy, with images that no one would be able to tell who, only the bushes, the wet road, the canopy, the windows of the restaurant. And then I find one. They are half covered with the umbrella, but you can see enough of their faces to tell it's them. And Shannon is leaning in for a kiss, her lips puckered and eyes closed.

Bingo. I feel absolutely elated. It's a small victory against Richard and Shannon, having this photo. I'll contact Richard's wife right away. Or should I go straight for Richard's father-in-law? I can't decide, as I drive back to the office. Both, definitely both. I need to make enough trouble for Richard that he has to go back home to Connecticut and have to deal with this crap instead of being here, in front of my face, ordering me to create new campaigns and making nice with my husband.

As I walk back to my office, though, the feeling of elation and the adrenaline from earlier begins to dissipate, and I feel disgusted with myself. Do I have this little dignity? What would Aidan think of me following Richard and spying? I guess I'll never know because I'm not telling him. He doesn't need to be bothered with this. I can take care of myself for once. I don't always need him to protect me. This is a fight between me and Richard.

What would my father think of me? Following people, spying, lying, wanting to hurt Richard's wife. What about his kids?

This isn't the person you raised, Daddy, is it? I sit in my office, looking at my father's photograph on my desk. "But you weren't there to help me when no one would press charges against him," I whisper. "I tried to do it the right way. And they made me leave. They blamed *me*."

That pre-med counselor, Steven Moss. I remember him like it was now.

"Maybe you gave this boy a wrong message, Ms. Daniels." He reclines in his chair.

"I fought and screamed for him to get off me. I begged for him to let me go. What exactly was the 'wrong message' in that, Mr. Moss?"

"Listen." He narrows his eyes at me. "Richard Stolar is a top athlete and student at this school. He is about to graduate. But you're still here, and you don't want anything to jeopardize your status."

"How would this jeopardize my status?"

"You have an academic scholarship. If you continue to focus on this social issue you had, this will go into your pre-med file. You'll lose your scholarship, and you may not gain admission to a medical school."

"Are you saying I'll lose privileges because I was a rape victim? Even though I've done nothing wrong? Are you serious?"

"You are in the pre-med program. You're expected to behave as a future physician. And getting drunk at fraternity parties is not what your scholarship is for. Come to think of it, I'll have to make a note in your file about this." He begins to write.

"I came to you in confidence. You are supposed to help." My eyes are welling up with tears.

"I'm going to ask you to write an essay to include in your file. A reflection paper from the perspective of the boy you are blaming for what I hear is your inappropriate behavior and how this accusation can impact his life. And if you continue to struggle with drinking, I'll ask you to consider taking a year off to work on your mental health."

Yes, maybe what I'm doing is not exactly honorable. But what Richard did is so much worse, and what they did to me at Westview by forcing me to leave was so much worse also.

So I swallow my pride and create a fake Facebook account and send the picture to Richard's wife's Messenger. I look up how to hide IP addresses, open a fake email account and send the picture to his father-in-law's work email address from my tablet. I title the email *Proposal.*

There. That ought to teach Richard a lesson. I wait a while to see if either of them responds. It shouldn't take long for them to see the picture. I pace around my office, refreshing every so often on the open windows of my screen.

But they don't respond.

****

I leave work early and head out for my first ultrasound. Today has been full of secrets and anger. I need something good to happen. I deserve some good news. I'm desperate to share this with someone, but I guess Dr. Hernado will do. I remind myself that it will all be worth it when I see Aidan's happy face as he holds his newborn, healthy and strong, tears in his eyes.

It's dark and quiet in the ultrasound room. I can hear myself breathing. My eyes are glued to the monitor where I'm looking for a flicker to mirror the beat of my own heart.

"Am I too old to be pregnant?" I ask my doctor.

The monitor is bright, and then I see the little bean of a life inside me. I can't help it—I burst into tears.

She is quiet for a moment, searching. "Clearly you are not too old." She smiles and points to the screen.

There it is—a tiny flicker, a life. Hope. Love fills my chest with warmth, and a tear pours down my cheek.

"Is it okay? Is everything how it's supposed to

look?"

"So far, so good." Dr. Hernado looks closer at the screen, makes some measurements, and prints three pictures. "Here you go. Nine weeks." She hands me a towel to wipe off the gel. "Bring your husband next time. He'll be thrilled after all the losses you've had."

"I want to be certain before I tell him. I never thought it could happen again. We stopped using birth control years ago. There was really no point." I'm still crying.

"Well, God works in mysterious ways, you know." She washes her hands and writes me a prescription. "Prenatal vitamins. You need extra iron—you are anemic. See me in a month, unless there are problems. Don't run around too much."

I walk out of the office with the pictures of my baby safely tucked into my wallet. He is doing well. He is healthy. His heart is beating. Nine weeks. Most of my pregnancies never went past seven.

Pangs of guilt wash over me. Aidan should know about the baby. He should've seen the ultrasound of his son today and should've cried with me. But that's the thing—I can see him crying there with me. He's done it many times before. We've cried over so many babies. I don't want to see him suffering again. I want to tell him he is having a son after I'm certain there's absolutely no chance of anything going wrong. When he is guaranteed to have a healthy baby. When I can't disappoint him again.

My phone dings when I get in the car, and I smile. It's Lori.

—How was the ultrasound?—

—Everything is good!—

—Did you tell Aidan?—

—Not yet—

I see her typing for a while, but then no response comes back.

I type back.

—I will, after the amnio. I just don't want him to be hurt again—

I drive home, smiling the entire way. Everything will turn out all right.

Chapter 11

I'm so glued to my laptop screen I pay no attention to the heavy steps of a man entering my office. I turn my head too late—much too late—to catch Richard-the-Mother-Fucking-Rapist sitting opposite me, in *my* chair, filthy shoes on *my* desk.

"Richard! What are you doing?" I gasp, holding onto my chair. I look for Janet. Where is my admin? She is nowhere to be seen.

"That's what I'd like to ask you," he says, eyes boring into mine. "What *are* you doing, exactly?"

"What do you mean?" He must know about the picture. But how does he know it's me? I scan the hallway outside my door. There is no one there. We are completely alone.

"I ask for the New Drug Application and marketing strategy, and the next thing I know the application is stalled and the FDA has suddenly postponed approving our greatest moneymaker for the next few years. Why is that?"

A corner of his mouth twitches, and I find it unnerving.

"I really don't have anything to do with the NDAs. That's all R&D, I'm afraid," I tap my pen on the desk and stop myself. I point at his shoes. "Can you, please…"

But he doesn't move. "Aidan tells me we should

know each other."

Sweat begins to trickle down my back. "How so?"

"Turns out we were at Westview at about the same time."

"Really." I raise my brows in pretend surprise. "What a small world."

"I told him you would've said something to him if you recognized me." He finally removes his feet from my desk and leans forward.

Too close. I can smell him.

"So. Do you?"

"Do I what?" The sweat is pooling around my waist now. I shift in my seat.

"Recognize me?" Richard stares at me like a cobra paralyzing his victim.

I know I must resist or die. "I'm sorry. I don't. It was so long ago. I wasn't very long at Westview. I transferred out. I didn't like being so far away from home."

"You didn't graduate from Westview?"

"No, I graduated from the University of Maryland."

"When did you transfer?"

"1996." Why am I even answering his questions? I feel for my phone in my pocket. *Fake a phone call, Emma.*

"I graduated that year. And you don't remember me?" His tone is icy.

"I'm sorry. I don't. Am I supposed to?" I relax a bit; I might be winning this game.

"There are certain people you meet in college that you just don't forget. Certain encounters are very memorable." The corner of his mouth twitches again.

And I realize he is toying with me like a cat with a mouse. He doesn't believe for a second that I don't remember him. Fury balls up in my stomach and begins its slow rise to my head, the heat of it boiling through my body.

"Look…" He leans farther forward. "Let me be clear. We are a long way from Westview. I've been willing to put our past behind and let you work here. But you must do your fucking job. I won't waste my time with you or your husband. I can fill your jobs in a day. You are in or you are out. I won't stand for any nonsense." He nods, stands up, and walks out of the office, slamming the door behind him.

I lunge for him, but he is already gone. I hit the wall, my knuckles bruising instantly. He knows exactly who I am. He made it clear also he knows I recognized him.

And it doesn't bother him. He simply doesn't care.

Does he honestly believe I don't care? That I am afraid of him? He is not worried in the least to have me as an employee.

I do believe he just threatened to fire me and Aidan. Was this a test of some sort? To see if I would tell Aidan? How dare he act as if our past didn't matter at all? "We are a long way from Westview," he said. No, we are not, you bastard.

My heart pounds violently in my chest. Adrenaline rush. I need to hurry with my revenge. I hope he thinks I am okay with going on with the pretense that we have some sort of understanding, because I need to convince him of this as I continue with my plan.

I guess he doesn't know about the picture. Or does he? Is that why he is so angry? I check the fake

Facebook account Messenger, and I see that Jennifer has seen the picture. She didn't reply. There is no reply to the fake email account either.

I search through my purse for the flash drive Sophie gave me. I need to get rid of Richard fast. Before he figures out how to get the application back to the FDA. Before he fires Aidan and Dana. I search frantically through files, and I see nothing I can use. Does Jeff have any idea about Shannon and Richard? Maybe I tell him next. I cringe at the thought of seeing him and telling him. On the other hand, I can't stand the idea of doing another fake account email.

Out of ideas, I dial Eric's phone.

"Let's say I decided to get justice and go against Richard," I begin.

"Hello to you too."

I hear his radio going off. "Sorry. You busy?"

"I'm only a cop, I do nothing but eat doughnuts, right?"

"Sorry, call me back when you are off duty."

"No, it's fine. I need to take a smoke break. And Jim won't let me smoke in the car."

"You can't be serious about still smoking!"

"I have a wife to lecture me already, remember?"

"Fine. I need to talk to you about something."

"Give me a sec."

I hear the flicking of a lighter and the puff of a cigarette. I need to talk to Jenny about the smoking. I make a mental note to drop off samples for him of the latest drug we are promoting, guaranteed to stop cigarette cravings.

"I thought about what you said the other day," I say.

"About what?"

"About fighting back."

"And?"

"I got mad. Like out-of-control kind of mad. Felt like shooting him." I pause. "I didn't, of course. And I asked Aidan if he would be willing to look for another job and move. You were right."

"He wants to stay. Maybe Aidan will be like best friends with this guy?" Eric laughs.

"It's not funny."

"Sorry. I really do like Aidan. He is just so rational sometimes. So what's your plan now? You *are* calling to tell me something, right?"

"I've been trying to get rid of him. I'm sure he knows exactly who I am. And I think he is maybe having some fun watching me squirm because I have to work with him. I'm trying to do something. Like get him in trouble in some way and get him to hate being here, so he goes back and stays away."

"What exactly are you trying?" Eric's voice sounds serious.

"I found out he's having an affair. With that woman who set me up with him in the first place—my supposed friend, Shannon."

"Her? Really?"

"Yep. She married my old college boyfriend, Jeff. But she's having an affair with Richard."

"God, you have to love these people for keeping it in their own circle. So you told him you know of his affair?"

"No, I told his wife and father-in-law, who owns Avias."

"Don't you think they already know? Especially if

it's been going on for a long time?"

"I don't know. But nothing is happening. So now that I think about it—you may be right. They probably know."

"These company suits always have affairs. They think it's normal."

"Aidan doesn't think it's normal."

"Fine, not Aidan, but you know what I mean."

"Not all corporate guys are bad."

"Look, what you should be doing is looking into his tax records. Stocks. Recent purchases, bank transfers. Things like that. If he's worth a lot, he'll be hiding something. I'll run his legal history, but I'm sure we'll find nothing. He can afford good lawyers."

"Thanks for doing that. And thanks for the ideas. He's worth millions, I hear. I'm sure there's something I can find."

"There's always something if you look hard enough. I gotta go, all right? Call me when you find something."

"I will. You be safe out there."

"Love you, Katie girl."

"Love you back." I make a kissing noise and hang up.

I want to see Aidan. I miss him. But he and his business team are locked in another budget meeting for most of the day. I open the blinds and let the winter sun enter through my wall of windows. Hopefully, it will keep me awake for the afternoon. My office brightens instantly. I had forgotten about the first trimester fatigue. I smile, thinking of the baby.

My inbox is full of unread emails, many with attachments. I groan. Do I need to be cc'd on every conversation everyone has with Richard? Work is exhausting these days, when all I want to do is get rid of Richard and get back to my normal life. I look through a few of the emails, making sure that the NDA is still stalled and Richard is still angry about the missing application materials, but it doesn't look like Dana and I are involved.

I close the emails and search through the flash drive files again. I follow Eric's advice and follow the financial records. I didn't ask Sophie to look for tax records, but she did give me his bank and credit card information. Large deposits to the bank lately. Not abnormal, though, for someone who is wealthy. No stock information. Of course, a kid wouldn't think to look for stocks. Oh, but here is his brokerage account login and password.

Bingo. Ten thousand call options in D&P. Date of purchase November 1st. The company wasn't sold until the 22nd. Of course, he knew the stock would go up and he could sell it and make money. Good thing I pay attention to Aidan's ramblings about the stock market and insider trading. I know someone else who could benefit from D&P call options. Would he do it? Would he tell Shannon? Why wouldn't he? I make a note to ask Sophie to see if Shannon has a brokerage account tonight.

My phone dings with a text from Aidan.

—Do you mind if I go to happy hour with Richard? We have a few things to discuss—

Richard is getting me back. Bastard.

—Sure, honey— I text back, gritting my teeth.

If I get Richard for insider trading, what will he do to me and Aidan then, I wonder? Will I get rid of him before he does something else to me?

I get home in the evening to an empty house. It's Friday night. It used to be our night, when we would cuddle up in bed and watch a movie, and then Aidan's fingers would begin stroking my hips ever so gently and then… I stop my thoughts from going there.

My husband is out with my rapist. That's the reality of my life now.

When Sophie comes in, I don't hesitate. She helps me find Shannon Rawley's record of purchasing thousands of call options in November. And then I use my fake email account to send a letter about Richard's and Shannon's fraudulent activities to the U.S. Securities and Exchange Commission, and I pray this investigation won't take long.

Because I don't know how long I can keep all this up.

Chapter 12

The conference room is stifling hot. We've been sitting here listening to Richard for over an hour. He loves hearing himself talk. The trash cans are stuffed with empty coffee cups. The boxes of doughnuts and bagels gape empty. Everyone is checking watches and shifting in their seats. But Richard won't shut up.

I'm no longer terrified at being in the same room as Richard. I visualize him choking on doughnuts, then falling and suffocating slowly with me standing over him, watching, doing nothing. I feel the power of revenge surging through me. Richard keeps on talking. I try hard to focus on what he's saying.

"Our final item on the agenda is Parozex. Avias has developed what we like to call a third-generation antipsychotic. Avias received a breakthrough designation when we filed the IND earlier. The government has been encouraging the FDA to speed up the approval process, and we fully expected to receive approval on our new drug application shortly. However, the NDA was rejected by the CDER for being incomplete." Richard glares at me.

I stare back at him openly. I hope my eyes will burn a hole in his chest. Bring it on, asshole. And wait till you get a notice about your insider trading investigation.

"An Executive Order was signed a while ago

relaxing the regulations, so we have the best timing. I had someone at the FDA reopen the application. We just need to hurry up and get that application completed, people."

"But Richard, the drug didn't do very well in the trials. We need more time to collect the safety data. The NDA is not going to look very good," Dana says.

Good job, Dana.

Richard zeroes in his stare on Dana, and I swear it gets colder in the room instantly. "No one ever needs to see those 'first-in-man' results, Dr. Kapur. This drug will fly through the approval. It's the first one of its kind not to carry a risk of metabolic syndrome."

"What about the cardiovascular side effects?" Dana asks.

Side effects? My attention perks up. Is she serious? Is there a problem with the drug? I thought she was only stalling the application to help me.

"Should Emma talk to our contact at the FDA about the priority review?" Aidan interrupts.

Why is Aidan interrupting? I need to hear more about the side effects.

"Avias has its own contacts. Not to worry," Richard says.

"Were all the trials registered?" Dana raises her voice again.

"They were overseas trials. Avias has a CRO running trials in India and China. Aidan will tell you that it saves us millions and guarantees everyone in this room can finally have a bonus," Richard answers.

Dana knows that, you nitwit.

"We will take a hit with the penalty for not registering, Richard."

Dana is sweating. Something is not right. My curiosity suddenly replaces my anger. I wonder what's up. I can't wait to talk to Aidan and Dana after the meeting. I should've been paying more attention to all those emails about Parozex.

"Our people at the FDA will take care of that." Richard narrows his eyes. "Even if we do have to pay the penalty, Aidan can tell you it's pennies compared to what the drug will make. Last I checked, the penalty was still a few thousand a day, but Parozex is expected to bring in forty billion a year."

I hear whistling around the table.

"You guys like that, huh?" Richard appears pleased. "Let's put all of our resources on this now. The normal process through the FDA is ten months, but I'm told we can expect to be approved in less than sixty days. I want daily updates on this. We'll need to have more frequent meetings with the FDA, but that's nothing our team can't handle."

"Will we have trouble publishing the data if it's not registered?" someone asks.

"Absolutely not. Medical journals couldn't care less if it's registered or not. We'll sponsor a few CMEs for the editors, pay for a medical conference, and it will all be fine." He turns to me. "That's Emma's department. And she is more than capable of handling that."

The asshole has an answer for everything, doesn't he? I roll my eyes and see Aidan looking at me with disapproval. I stare back at him defiantly. He can take his new friend Richard and shove him…

After the meeting is over, I try hard to cool off as I look for Aidan in his office. I don't want to keep arguing with Aidan over Richard.

"What's up?" he asks. He is glued to his computer screen and not looking at me.

"Nothing," I reply. "Take me for some lunch? I'd like to know what that was all about."

"Sorry, I've got no time. What was all what about?"

"All that sweating Dana was doing in there. Did you notice it?"

"It's her job to sweat the ethics and my job to calm her down." He shrugs. "Don't worry about it. I'll take care of it."

"You don't pun well." I don't buy it. His forehead is tense. He is not happy. He knows something. "You can keep your secret for now, but I'll get it out of you later." I kiss him right in that wrinkle on his forehead.

"It's nothing. I do have to pull some new numbers for Richard tonight, and then I promised to have drinks with him later."

"Again?"

"It's not like it's every day."

"Feels like it," I whisper as I walk out.

When I get to my office, planning to call Dana, she is already waiting for me, her fingers tapping impatiently on the files stacked on the corner of my desk.

"The weasel found someone to approve the application," she begins.

"I'm not surprised." I stretch my neck. Sitting in that conference room gave me a terrible neck ache.

"I suspect Richard knows you and I were the reason the application was incomplete before."

My heart skips a beat. She's right, of course. "What

makes you think that?"

"Because he pulled me off working on it, now that they're scrambling to get it back to the FDA. Also, he is openly hostile to me."

"I'm sorry, Dana. I was worried I'd get you in trouble." I sit down and stretch my legs.

"Don't worry about it. I don't care that he knows, but I went through the new draft of the application they are sending out. I've got my people, you know. It exaggerates the benefits of the drug and underreports the side effects."

"So the drug doesn't work? It's not a breakthrough?" Figures. I don't expect Richard to be anything less than a liar and a criminal.

"As far as I can see, it's no better than any of the older antipsychotics. The studies are reporting an impressive-sounding percentage of negative symptoms reduction, but the older drugs were already doing that."

"You mentioned the side effects in the meeting."

"High risk of cardiovascular complications in several early studies. This drug should not be on the market. It's going to kill people."

I get up and close the door. "Keep your voice down. Will the FDA make the right decision and stop the approval?"

"Honestly, Emma, it's like it's your first day on the job. You know anyone can bury the data on side effects on the NDA. And Avias already paid people to break up the research data to make Parozex look like a miracle drug. One study split the results by gender and the older women improved significantly. Well, it's a schizophrenia drug, and the patients who most need it are younger men. The results for them were no better than an older generation antipsychotic."

I rub my forehead. She is right, of course. But how on earth do you fight the FDA? Luckily, I have the backup plan of my insider trading report on Richard. Hopefully, I don't need this drug to fail.

"Dana, there's not much we can do if Richard has paid off someone at the FDA to approve the application. We tried to stall it, we lost, and now it will get approved no matter what. What are you going to do—find someone else to pay to deny it?"

"That's actually not a bad idea." She taps her fingers again.

"I was kidding."

"No, no, listen." She begins to tap into her phone. "I'm going to send some emails. Maybe we could find someone honest at the FDA, someone we can send the side-effects data to, all the data that Avias probably will hide from the NDA with shitty statistics. And if that regulator recommends for the drug not to be approved"—she looks up—"maybe there is a chance?"

"Do you know someone in particular, or are you just blindly searching?"

"Blindly. There has to be an honest scientist at the FDA, though. We just need one."

"In the right division. A medical officer evaluating NDAs."

"I'll get all my friends on it." Her fingers are tapping fast.

"Here is another idea." I feel myself getting excited now. "What if you publish some of the side-effects data and create a negative buzz? I won't be able to get enough psychiatrists to prescribe it then."

"I've thought about it, but there isn't enough time.

Parozex is on priority review. It will be approved by February. I can't get an article in by February. And Avias already published several articles lauding its positive effects from the early trials. They've been ready with this forever."

"Did any of the published studies report side effects that we can point out?" I ask.

"Cleverly buried in the data. Positives outweigh the negatives. If we find that honest medical officer, I can prepare quite a portfolio with information, though."

"You'll definitely lose your job, then."

"I have another job lined up. I told them March. I don't want my name associated with this company when Parozex is here."

"Oh, Dana." I walk around the desk and hug her. "I don't want to lose you. You are my best friend. I can't be here alone."

"You won't be alone, silly. You have Aidan right here with you every day."

"Right." I feel tears sliding down my face. Aidan and his new best friend Richard and their loads of money they will make when this useless drug will hit the market and begin to kill people.

I wipe my eyes. "I'll help you do whatever you think is best about the drug, Dana. Just tell me what. Please don't leave yet. Don't give up on us."

"I'm not giving up. Especially not on you."

"I have another thought." I pull away from her. "I think we ought to find out who it is that's pushing this application through at the FDA. Maybe we can scare this person with exposure somehow."

As I say this, I suddenly have a very bad feeling that I know exactly who this FDA regulator is. Jeffrey

Rawley was a scum when I knew him in college, and I wouldn't be surprised if he's still a scum.

Chapter 13

The text from Aidan arrives as I'm about to call him to ask what to pick up for dinner.

—Having dinner at the country club with Richard. He needs some financial advice. Love you—

I drive straight home and sulk. About the fact that these texts are becoming too frequent. About the fact that Aidan doesn't want to spend time with me. About the fact that Richard is likely asking my husband to get him out of the trouble I got him into. Richard should've gotten a notice about being investigated for insider trading by now.

Sophie is out as well. Only Cookie seems to be happy to see me. I contemplate changing into my pajamas, but I see the Christmas tree and it makes me weepy.

—You got any meatball subs?— I text Eric.

—Jenny just made a fresh batch—

"Mom, you're home!" Sophie comes in, cheeks red from the cold.

"Hey." I hug her tight. "I thought you were out for the night."

"In this weather? No, thanks."

"Don't take your coat off. We're going for meatball subs," I pronounce.

"Are we driving all the way to Russo's? That's a bad idea, in the holiday traffic. It'll take hours."

"We'll be fine. I'm craving some good food. I'm starved."

"Well, only if you are driving." She shrugs.

Forty-five minutes later, we are trapped in bumper-to-bumper traffic on 15 North, still very far from the bridge over the Potomac to cross into Maryland. I hear fingers tapping on the leather.

"Fine," I say. "You were right."

"Good thing I've had a snack."

"I haven't." My stomach has been making itself known for about half an hour now, with spasms.

"I have a Snickers in my pocket."

"I'll take it." I dig into the candy bar with delight. I didn't realize just how hungry I was.

"You sure you don't want to turn around? Daddy will be mad we're driving so far this late."

"Daddy doesn't care. He's at the country club with his boss."

"Wouldn't that be your boss too?"

"Yep."

"The man you want revenge against?"

"What?" I spin around to look at her, and the car swerves into another lane.

"Watch out!" she yells.

I fix the car, my heart pounding. "Why do you think I'm getting revenge on our boss?"

"Do you really think I'm not going to know who I was looking up? If Dad wants a promotion so bad, what's he going to think of you setting this guy up to fail? Doesn't that mean Dad is going to lose his job?"

I take a deep breath and straighten up. "Look, there is a lot in play here that you don't quite know about. Everything will be just fine with Dad's job. I'm doing this to save his job. And mine."

"I don't believe you."

"Have I ever lied to you?"

"There is always the first time."

"Let's talk about something else."

"I do know something you might be interested in. You know this girl at my school, McKenzie—she's having a holiday party in a few weeks, and guess who's invited?"

"You?"

"And get this." She leans forward. "She lives in Chevy Chase. She's on my debate team. You've dropped me off at her house for practice before. So think—who else lives in Chevy Chase?"

A flash in my mind, but I don't get a chance to respond.

"The Rawleys. I can get McKenzie to invite their son, whatever his name is, to the party, and then when he drinks and leaves the party, we call the cops and they pick him up for another DUI. They'll probably find drugs on him as well."

"Why do you think I might be interested in this?"

"For your revenge."

I hear a ding of an incoming text on her phone and she is momentarily distracted as I think her words over. "Wouldn't their lawyers wipe out the records again?"

Sophie lifts her eyes from her phone. "Yeah, but he gets kept for a few hours or overnight, and while he's there, we can leak the story to the newspapers, and then it's not so easy to hide it. Some sort of society pages or something. And I can spread it on social media."

I take another few minutes to think, as I watch the car lights glare red in front of me. "Seems like an awfully low thing to do. To use a child in revenge against his parents. And—what if they don't even care about their son?"

"Their only kid? Of course, they care. Plus they've already hired lawyers several times to cover up his legal trouble. They must care."

I stare at her as the car comes to a stop at another intersection. "I'm worried about how easily this comes to you."

She shrugs. "I get bored at school. We hardly do any work anymore."

"It's a wild plan, but it might just work," I say, stepping on the gas again. It's the most ridiculous plan ever. I can't believe I'm taking ideas from a child, but what if this works? My heart enjoys a second of pleasure at the thought of Shannon suffering. "So why aren't you doing any schoolwork anymore?"

"Quit small talk. I know your mind is going through the plan of how to get this kid now. It's a great idea, isn't it?"

"It is," I admit. "Especially if I can convince Eric to patrol the area and respond to the call. That way, he can take Benjamin in and hold him for a couple of hours."

"Ben, that's what his name is. That's perfect, to ask Eric, Mom. Because a different cop might just let him off."

"Also a different cop might hold him too long or be too rough with him. I don't want anything to happen to him."

"He drinks and drives. Don't you think he should get caught? Why are you feeling so guilty about it?"

"Because he's just a kid making mistakes. A kid

just like you. What if someone was doing something to use you against us?"

"You have to not be so moral if you're going to succeed with your revenge plans, Mom. And all that's going to happen is he'll have a few pictures taken of him. Then his attorney will show up and get him off."

"I know." It's nothing compared to what his parents have done to me. "You think a few pictures is all we need?" I'm doubtful.

"Someone will see it, and enough people will talk about it for weeks. I guarantee you."

"So…" I take an exit off the highway and turn onto the small streets toward the deli. "How would I know when he's on his way from the party?"

"I'll call you when he's about to get into his car, give you his license plate, and you call Eric."

"That sounds really easy."

"Doesn't it?"

"Too easy." I look at her and hope she can see the suspicious look in my eyes in the dark. "You're not planning to do something you're not telling me about, are you? What kind of party is this?"

"I don't know, Mom. I don't hang out with McKenzie and her crowd. I'm only going for you." She points a finger at me. "You are going to owe me big for this."

"I gave birth to you." I turn her finger back at her.

"I already repaid you like a thousand times in chores. You can't keep using that. I want you to tell me why we are doing revenge missions."

I feel my forehead sweating despite the increasing cold in the car. "I told you. Shannon stole my boyfriend and married him."

"I don't buy it. And what do you have against your boss?"

"You are being silly."

"If you don't tell me, I'm not doing it. You can go to McKenzie's party yourself."

"Fine."

"Come on. Why can't I know the truth?"

"None of your business."

"Will you ever tell me? Or Dad?"

"I will. Just not yet." I grab her hand and kiss it. "I absolutely will tell you. But not now. I…can't quite figure out how to tell the story yet. I love you very much, and I'm afraid the truth will hurt you. All right? Please just be patient."

"Fine, whatever, keep your secrets," she grumbles.

I love this girl. And I hate lying to her. But I have no time for self-loathing. And I'm way past regrets. After all—I'm doing all this to protect my family from Richard. To get them away from his evil.

The smell of meatballs alone is worth the hassle of the trip to Frederick. My appetite is ridiculous. I catch Sophie staring in surprise at my triple helpings during dinner. Soon, she'll know why. After dinner, I ask Sophie to help Jenny and the boys clean up as I pull Eric aside.

"I need a favor," I say as I pace in the den.

"Anything," he replies. "But sit down, relax. You're making my head spin."

I sit obligingly in one of his favorite recliners. "Can you pick up a drunk driver for me next weekend?"

"Is this about Richard?" He lights up a cigarette.

"No. Shannon and Jeff. Will you please quit this disgusting habit?"

"My house, my habits. And I thought you were going after Richard?"

"I need you to stop smoking because I'm pregnant, Eric."

Eric puts out the cigarette, gets up from his own recliner, and envelopes me in a tight hug. "Congratulations! Is everything going okay?"

"It is. So far."

"Aidan must be thrilled."

I stay quiet a moment. Thinking how to phrase this exactly. "I haven't told him yet. It's too early. I want to make sure this baby…sticks around."

Eric nods, then opens a window, waving the lingering smoke outside. "Have you told him about Richard yet?"

I look down. "Not yet."

"How many secrets are you going to keep from your husband?"

"I don't need a lecture. And Aidan doesn't need any more stress or disappointments. We've lost so many babies, Eric. I can't let him go through that again."

"I get that. But how can you not tell him about Richard? He works with the man, for God's sake!"

"What does that have to do with anything?"

"He needs to know not to trust him."

"I've told him many times, but he doesn't believe me. I keep warning him, telling him Richard's company has a poor reputation. But Aidan thinks Richard has all these great ideas. And Richard keeps weaseling out of everything I try to do to make him go back to Connecticut and leave us alone."

"You are going to have to tell Aidan. He needs to be able to protect you. What if Richard tries to hurt you? You have to think of the baby now, too." He points at my stomach.

"I will tell him. I promise. I just need to try this one more thing. Listen to me. I found out Richard is having an affair with Shannon. She is the one who took me to that frat party and set me up with Richard so that she could…"

"I remember," Eric interrupts. "So what are you planning to do?"

"Get Shannon embarrassed and humiliated."

"Wow, Emma." He reclines in his chair. "Never thought I'd hear you say something like that."

I feel the heat crawling up my neck, spreading through my face. "Well, I never thought she'd marry Jeff, the man I was in love with, who gave me up as soon as I was assaulted. I never thought I'd have to stare at my rapist's face every day I walk into my office. And you, of all people, should know what it's like for me."

"Shhh. I do know. I was there after it happened, remember?"

"I know you were. So why are you questioning my choices?"

Eric was the one I called after Richard left me on the staircase, bleeding, bruised, with a split lip and torn clothes. He wrapped me gently in his sweatshirt, carried me to his car, laid me in the back seat, and drove me to the hospital. After five hours of rape kit testing and examination, he took care of me for the weekend until he had to return to the police academy. He drove me to the police station, but I asked him not to go in. I thought he had had enough. I lay in Eric's bed and cried for a week. I couldn't face my mother or my sister or my boyfriend until my bruises slowly faded and I could speak without crying.

"I'm sorry. I'm not angry with you. It's all of them. Thank you for being there for me," I whisper. "No one else was."

"You have to tell Aidan," Eric says. "He needs to be there for you now."

"He is there for me. In a different way."

"You still have to tell him. Don't take another step without him. It's not fair to him."

"I'll tell him when he stops going out with Richard every single night like they're brothers separated at birth. Will you help me or not?"

Eric walks over to the bar and pours himself a drink. He toasts me as he drinks every drop. "I know I'll regret this, but I can't say no to you. What do you need me to do?"

"I want you to pick up Shannon's kid for DUI and hold him in jail for the night."

"Is he going to be drunk?"

"Yes. He's had prior DUIs."

"You want Shannon and Jeff to freak out for a while? Then what?"

"I'll play it by ear. Sophie says we can spread it on social media and cause them some embarrassment. Shannon is a socialite."

"Don't involve Sophie in this, jeez."

"She just helped me get some information."

"She's a kid, Katie. This is none of her business. I can help you with anything you need."

"Don't worry. I know what I'm doing."

"All right. I'll arrest the kid. Just text me details or instructions."

"You are the best."

"Love you."

He hugs me, and I know he holds me longer than usual. I can tell he's worried. I want to tell him I'm all right, but I'm not sure of that myself. I pull away and walk out. I can't afford to be vulnerable right now. I must be strong. What I am about to do requires all I have.

Chapter 14

It's the day of McKenzie's party, and everything moves with agonizing slowness as my mind rehearses the details of the plan. It's a good plan. Easy plan. Eric and Sophie are helping me. I have the actions worked out down to a minute. Which makes me absolutely sure that something will go wrong. I just can't figure out what, no matter how much I go over every tiny step.

I tap my foot impatiently and swipe at my sweaty forehead as I write down the sequence of events again. I check off the steps on my notepad. Shannon will be furious. Her reputation will suffer. And it's the holidays. This should be a neat hit on her and Jeff.

I wish I didn't have to resort to this. I check my fake email account. Nothing but spam. Why didn't Jennifer care about Richard's affair? Doesn't she have enough to lose? Her social standing, her reputation? And why didn't Shannon or Richard get arrested for insider trading? I check their brokerage accounts. The call options are still there. I shouldn't have expected the government to move that fast. It's only been a few weeks. Darn it. I have no other choice but to keep going.

Except for calling it off, or postponing this. *Don't do it at all,* my mind suggests. *You know deep in your gut this will not go well tonight. Cancel.*

I sit for a while, watching the white glistening

snow outside my window. I'm tired of lying. I'm so sick and tired of lying to my friends. To my daughter. And most of all to my husband. I need to wrap this up quickly. For my son's sake.

For my marriage's sake.

For my sake.

"Ready for lunch?" I ask Aidan when he enters my office.

"Sorry, I can't. An emergency meeting of the leadership committee."

"It's not on my schedule." I frown.

"It's a finance meeting."

"I'm always included on budget meetings."

"This one doesn't include marketing. It's R&D budget."

"Is Dana invited, then?"

"I'm sure she is."

"Don't be sure. Richard doesn't like her."

"Nonsense. Richard likes everyone," he says, sitting down on the edge of my desk, fidgeting with my pens.

"Sure he does," I grumble. "He is just everyone's best buddy."

"Don't be grumpy. He's trying very hard to make everyone happy. And it's not easy around here. People are not necessarily very friendly to him."

"You are," I point out. "I've hardly seen you in the last two weeks. You're always out with him."

"Well, as I told you, I'm working on a promotion. And we are in the middle of a massive project. We need to pull this company out of the hole it's been in. We'll need your department's help very soon."

"Oh, I know. I'm already swamped with emails

from your Richard."

"I wish you'd be happy. We are finally productive."

"I just miss you." I touch his hand.

"I'm right here." He looks at his watch. "For another five minutes. Have a meeting with Richard. I told you, I like him. I haven't had a nice guy to hang out with in a while. You always go out with your friends. Why can't I have a friend, finally?"

"You can," I say. "Feel free to go out with him tonight," I add. "I have to take Sophie to a party, and I'll stop by Lori and Dana's."

"See, I need to have someone to spend time with when you girls are having a night out."

He starts to walk away. Without kissing me, as he usually does.

Come back and kiss me, Aidan. Hold me in your arms and I won't do what I plan to do tonight. I'll call off this ridiculous thing. I'll go home and watch Netflix with Sophie and go to sleep early and forget all about it.

Maybe if we got to spend some time together I would finally have the guts to tell him. But he doesn't come back. I'm eleven weeks pregnant, and he still doesn't know.

A few hours later, I'm off to go home. Alone. Until I can pick up Sophie and take her to McKenzie's party, where we'll proceed to ruin the Rawleys' lives as I planned. I know deep inside that what I'm doing is wrong, but I can't stop. I must do this. I need to do this. It's too late for me to turn back. Soon my son will grow and I will have to take care of him. I must hurry. I will finish this before my love for my son, my Sean, grows any greater.

****

I wake up with a start. It's dark, the icy rain is pelting my windshield, and the temperature in the car is freezing.

What time is it? I check my phone. It's full of messages from Sophie. Fuck! How could I have fallen asleep?

—He is not drinking—

—OK now he is—

—He has pills on him—

—He is a real jerk—

—Leaving the party in a few, black Jeep—

—Plate 600HCA—

—Where are you?????—

—Going with him, will you please text back!—

"No, No, NO!" I scream, the sound echoing in the car. Then I type furiously into the phone.

—Sorry, sorry, sorry, I'm here. Don't get in the car with him!—

—Too late—

I have to think. But I can't. I'm too panicked.

—Where are you?—

—Track my phone—

Okay, I know how to do that. I track her GPS location, and I'm so relieved. She isn't far at all. Just a few blocks off. I start the car and press the gas. The GPS is giving me a bit of peace of mind. But I know she's not out of danger. She is in the car with a teenage boy who probably drank too much and has drugs in his pocket and… I order my mind to stop. I can't do this right now.

I dial Eric as I search for the Jeep and give him the license plate.

"Got it."

"It's driving down Jefferson right now, toward Creek."

"Perfect. So you want me to just put a bit of a scare into the kid, right?"

"Eric, listen." He is going to be very angry, I know. "Sophie got into the car with him."

"She did what? Didn't I tell you not to involve Sophie in your plans? What are you thinking, Katie? This is so reckless, honestly. I got my lights on. I'm on it. But you and I will talk."

"I'm following right behind," I say, but he has already hung up.

I'm a shit mother. Worse than shit. And I know he'll yell at me, and I deserve it.

I see them now. A black Jeep. The kid drives well, not swerving or jerking. Nice and slow. I sigh and follow at a distance, just wanting Sophie to know I'm there. Eric's patrol car arrives a few minutes later, and I back off even farther, then stop. I figure Sophie will go to the station as well, so as not to raise suspicion.

I'm about to text her about it even though I feel terrible asking her to do that for me. I swear I would never ever ask her to do anything to help me with this revenge ever again, when I hear the roar of an engine. I raise my head to see what's happening, and my phone drops as I watch the Jeep speeding out of my sight into the darkness.

Eric puts on a siren and disappears into the darkness as well, and I sit in my car alone, absorbing the horror I've just put my daughter through. And then it occurs to me that Sophie is in the speeding car in the middle of the night with a drunk driver who is trying to get away from the police. And the roads are wet and slippery, covered in sleet.

I have just set up events possibly leading to my daughter's death.

I pick up my phone off the floor and try to text her, but my hands shake so violently that I keep misspelling. I finally manage.

—You will be OK don't be scared—

I don't know if she'll be okay.

I'm goddamn sure she won't be okay.

Now I see another patrol car racing past me. Good. Eric called for backup. I don't know what to do. I want to go chase after them as well, but what if I make things worse? I can't just sit here, either.

My heart is about to explode with fear. I want to call Aidan, but how can I possibly explain what I've done? I finally remember I've got my GPS app tracking her phone still. I'm afraid to look for fear the car is no longer moving. But I get over the terror and look. It's still moving, thank God. It's moving so fast the app is having trouble tracking it. I see the streets, though.

And then I know what to do. I look up Jeff's phone number and text it to Sophie. I add,

—Call this. His dad. Get him on speaker. Tell him what's going on. Eric is coming—

Chapter 15

I bite my nails as I watch the GPS tracking the drunk driver speeding away with my daughter. Then I check the time. It feels like agonizing hours have passed when it's been only about two minutes. The app finally shows the car has stopped, and my brain screams fearful thoughts. Did the car crash? Is the Jeep flipped over? Is Sophie lying there, covered in blood, limbs broken? I slam my foot on the gas pedal and race to the location, my car sliding through the slippery streets, my hands barely holding onto the steering wheel.

The street block is surrounded by white patrol cars. It's impossible to see anything for a moment, with all the flashing lights and the crowd of patrol officers in brown, but then I see a tall boy walking slowly in front of Eric, then turning and walking back. The Jeep looks fine.

Where is my daughter? I finally see her, sitting in one of the vehicles, watching the boy. I race to Sophie and wrap my entire body around her. My fingers are busy scanning for injuries, but I feel none.

"She says nothing hurts, ma'am," an officer says, tapping his brown hat.

"I'm okay. I really am. I had a seatbelt on." Sophie is laughing, but it doesn't sound like laughter. She is trembling.

"Good girl." I sob and rub her arms. She is in

shock. I can feel it.

"We are going to have to take her to the station to file a report on this," the officer says.

"That's fine." I wipe my tears. "What are you planning to do with the driver?"

"We are doing a Standardized Field Sobriety Test, and then we'll take him into custody."

I watch as the boy is handcuffed by Eric. I can't see his face as an officer tucks him into the back seat and the car drives away.

I brace for Eric's anger. I deserve everything he will say to me.

"She can go with you, Emma. You all right to drive?" Eric comes closer.

"I'm fine. I'm just happy she's safe now." I look up at him, apologizing with my eyes.

"She did a clever thing and called the punk's dad. Don't know what he said to him, but it made him stop," one of the officers says.

"It was Mom's idea." Sophie points at me as she stands up.

"Your mom has good ideas. Sometimes." Eric gives me a stern look.

I hug Sophie's shoulders and lead her to my car. My tall girl seems very frail right now, shrunk to half her size. She is no longer seventeen, she is barely ten, back to fourth grade when she was being bullied by two mean girls at school. I don't need Eric to lecture me. I am tearing myself up on my own. How could I have done this to my child? What kind of horrible mother am I? How could I even think of being a mother again? My uterus aches, and I rub my son gently. I have to do better. I must become a better mother.

"Are you okay?" I ask over and over on the way to the station.

"I just want to get this over with and go home, Mom," Sophie moans. "I'm perfectly fine. I'm just tired."

"Why did you get into his car?" I shouldn't be questioning her, but the adrenaline is still pulsing through me, and I need answers.

"You weren't answering my texts, and I was afraid he'd leave and all of this would've been for nothing."

"All of this? None of this was a big deal, baby. This wasn't worth your life!"

"I thought he'd stop when the cops showed up. But he just cursed and slammed on the gas. He said his dad would kill him if he got stopped by the cops again."

"How drunk was he?"

"I'm not sure. I only saw him drink one beer."

"Did you drink anything?"

"I pretended to him that I was drunk and needed a ride."

"Did you tell him where we lived?" I nearly stop the car when the thought occurs to me.

"No, of course not. I gave him Jenna's address. Who do you take me for?"

"The thought that this guy would know where you live…"

"He is quite nice, actually."

"I still can't believe I put you in so much danger. I'm so, so, so sorry."

"Don't worry. I'm fine."

"That's not what I'm worried about. I think you finally found out that I'm a horrible mother."

"You are a perfect mother. I couldn't wish for a

better mom. Who else could think this fast in a situation when her daughter is kidnapped?" She is laughing again, but it's not her laughter. It's hysterical, a shaking, jerky kind of laughter.

What have I done to my daughter? I try to smile at her, but the fear is deep inside my chest. It has settled permanently in me, next to the guilt. I never thought I'd hurt Sophie. I've worked so very hard to protect her. No matter what happened to me, I was always sure I'd keep her safe. But I put myself before her today. And I'll never let that happen again.

****

The police station is crowded and smells awful. Christmas decorations don't seem to belong, and there is no sign of doughnuts. But I don't know much about police stations. The last time I went to one was to file a report against Richard.

Eric comes and grabs my arm and ushers us into a small room. He pulls me back a little. "You realize what you just put Sophie through? You can't involve your kid in this. Period."

"I know," I whisper.

He points to a chair, and I sit, my head down.

A hot cup of coffee appears in front of me, with a pouch of powdered creamer. Sophie gets a water. She doesn't touch it.

I hug her. Tight.

"It's not your fault, Mom. He is the dipshit."

"Don't curse."

"Are you kidding me?"

Eric takes Sophie's statement in less than thirty minutes.

"What now?" I ask him.

"Well, we have citations for reckless driving, endangering the welfare of a minor, and fleeing police. We can hold him for a while. Then we'll see if the DA wants to do charges."

"What about intoxication?"

"His blood alcohol wasn't above the limit."

"And kidnapping of my daughter?"

"Well, that's the endangering the welfare of a minor."

"No, Mom. Don't do that," Sophie interrupts.

"What? He sped away and nearly killed you." I'm aghast.

"He just got scared. He made a mistake. He stopped like a minute later. And he wasn't even drunk, I told you."

"He only stopped because his father yelled at him."

"Not because of that alone. I also talked to him. Please don't write this down, Eric. He doesn't have a very good life. He was running because his parents are about to split up and he thought his dad would leave for sure if he got in trouble again."

"What are you talking about?" This is interesting. Shannon and Jeff are splitting up? Must be because of Richard.

"He said he heard his dad say that he wasn't his real son. That his mom…slept around. So his dad doesn't want to stick around for him, because he keeps getting in trouble."

"Ouch," Eric says, closing his notebook and raising his brows.

I didn't expect this. The kid is not Jeff's. Is it Richard's? Or someone else's?

"All right," I say. I owe this little to Sophie. "I

guess we don't need to pursue kidnapping or the minor welfare whatever."

I mouth, "Thank you," to Eric as we leave. He mouths back, "We need to talk."

I help Sophie put her jacket on. When the outside door lets in a gust of frozen air, I whip around because I feel her behind me. Shannon. My skin crawls uncomfortably.

"Mom, you dropped your gloves," Sophie says, and I bend to pick up my gloves, glad to have a moment to hide my face.

"Hold on. We can't leave yet," I whisper and pretend to struggle with my coat.

We watch as Shannon talks to the desk sergeant, to Eric, and then to another officer. I stop breathing for a moment as I see Eric point at Sophie and me, and Shannon turns slowly to face us.

This is it. It's time to have it out with Shannon. My breath returns. I'm ready. I square my shoulders as she glides toward me, her face contorting. Is it recognition on her face? Is it fear? Defensiveness?

She approaches much faster than I expect, and I step back, nearly knocking over Sophie.

"Mom!"

"Sorry."

Shannon grabs my shoulders and hugs me.

What the actual fuck?

"Thank you."

She is holding onto me still. My body is stiff as a statue. She reeks of perfume. I don't know how to shake her off. I'm counting in my head, hoping that I won't get to a hundred. She lets go at twenty.

"I can't thank you enough, really." She wipes her

heavily mascaraed eyes.

Is she seriously crying or just pretending?

"It's okay," Sophie says from behind me. "He really didn't drink that much. You shouldn't be mad at him. He stopped as soon as I asked him to. Please tell his dad."

"You can tell him yourself, dear. What's your name?"

"Sophie Shephard."

"Shannon Rawley." Shannon smiles at Sophie through the tears and then stretches her hand to me. "And you are?"

I stare at her eyes for a moment, but there is not even a flicker of recognition. Really, Shannon? Was I that disposable?

"Emma Shephard," I finally say, shaking her hand.

"Your daughter is very kind."

"She is. Also reckless."

"Aren't they all. I honestly don't know what to do with Benjamin. I have tried so hard with him. He's had the best education, counselors, church. But nothing is helping. Ever since his dad and I separated briefly last summer, he's been getting into trouble. It's his third time getting arrested in six months." She looks at me and then Sophie. "I'm sorry, I shouldn't be telling you all this."

"Maybe his dad should go easy on him," Sophie says.

"Maybe you could suggest that to him." Shannon wipes her eyes again and points to the door.

We follow her finger and watch as a tall man storms through the door. His brown coat is wet with melting snow, and his black hair is speckled with streaks of gray. But still, I recognize Jeffrey Rawley, the man I loved so deeply at eighteen. The man who shattered my heart into a million pieces. As I see him, my mouth emits a gasp of recognition, and I turn away, unable to control it quickly enough.

"This is the third time, Shannon! What the hell are you doing to fix this?" he yells, and Shannon begins to sob.

"Why are you yelling at me? You are the father who refuses to discipline your son," she says through the tears.

"He is *not* my son," Jeff whispers.

But it's loud enough for us to hear, and Sophie's eyes widen in shock.

Jeff spins around and notices us for the first time. His eyes lock on my face, and I see him flinch. He makes an arm movement to reach out to me, then pulls his arm back.

It's unmistakable. He recognized me.

Then he controls his face and arm and gently reaches for his wife. "I apologize, Shannon. I'm behaving inappropriately. Where is Ben?"

Shannon slows down in her crying and inhales some air. "He'll be out in a second. Here, this girl, Sophie, was in his car when he went speeding. And this is her mother, Mrs. Shephard."

"Sophie, yes. Glad you called me," Jeff says. "I am Ben's father, Jeff Rawley."

"I'm glad I called you too," Sophie says. "It was my mom's idea, actually. But Mr. Rawley, please don't be angry with Ben. He didn't drink much at the party. He only drove away because he was upset and afraid to get into trouble. He stopped as soon as I started talking to him, and as soon as you told him to. He is not a bad kid. I think…he just doesn't want to make you mad, not anymore."

"I'll take that under advisement." Jeff turns to me. "So calling me from the speeding car was your idea? Mrs. Shephard, is it?"

My voice shakes only a little as I respond. "Yes, *Emma* Shephard."

"It's a pleasure to meet you."

"They are not pressing charges, Jeff," Shannon interrupts.

"That's very kind of you." He is still looking at me, eyes scanning my hair, my face.

I stare back at him defiantly. "I'm just happy everyone is safe. I'm certain you'll take steps to make sure your son will not be in further trouble," I say after some time. Why do I sound so formal?

"We absolutely will. But I do feel we need to repay you for your kindness," Jeff says, equally formal.

"Oh, here he is," Shannon exclaims, walking away from us.

The jerk who nearly killed my daughter is led out. Shannon immediately starts hugging and talking to him, but he ignores her and keeps looking at Jeff. I watch as the boy seems to shrink in his oversized clothing, under his long bangs, as Jeff's ice-cold stare finds him. Suddenly, instead of throttling him as I planned, I feel pity for Ben. What is the deal with this family? What happened to the kind boy I dated in college, who spent hours being tender with me and reading poetry?

"You are off the hook again," Jeff says curtly. "Mrs. Shephard will not press charges."

"And no DUI—the alcohol level was not high

enough. So just citations for reckless driving, and we can take you home," Shannon adds, kissing the boy's forehead and clinging to him still.

"Thank you," Ben says to Sophie. Then, as he notices me, "I'm very sorry. I didn't mean to hurt her."

"She told me. It's all right," I say. I no longer feel angry. I feel sad for him. I want to give him a hug. I want to make up for Jeff's coldness and his mother's mistakes.

"I appreciate your consideration for Benjamin." Jeff comes close to me.

I instinctively take a step back. "No problem. Well, we are off. Goodnight." I grab Sophie's arm and walk toward the exit. I just want to get her away from them.

"Wait," Jeff calls after me. "We'd love it if you could join us for our annual New Year's Eve party. It's a bit of a thing around here. We'd like a chance to thank you."

I freeze, my back to them. They are having a party? Even though their marriage is falling apart? That's very Shannon. I hesitate. I should jump at this chance to find another weak spot in their lives. Yet I am not sure I want anything to do with these people any longer. This evening has been quite enough. This may be my best chance to find out if Jeff is the one pushing our drug application through the FDA, though. I grit my teeth.

"It would be a pleasure. My husband and I would love to attend," I say as I turn around.

We exchange phone numbers, and Sophie and I finally leave. I glance one more time at Ben and Jeff as we walk out. The kid is sitting on a chair, his head in his hands. Jeff looks back at me. He is pale, and his eyes are filled with some emotion I can't quite place.

Chapter 16

It takes me ages to select my dress for the Rawleys' New Year's Eve party, and Aidan almost gives up on going, but I bribe him with the promise of good food and Scotch. We arrive hours late, but the party is clearly still going. The valets are rushing back and forth from the side entrance, somehow managing to maneuver the cars on a narrow street.

I'm well familiar with what their house looks like, from Google Images, but it's much more impressive in real life. The three-story brick colonial seems to go on forever, recent additions making it even wider. It's all glitzy with holiday decorations, and each window is brightly lit. Well, Shannon always did have a talent for flair.

"These people don't mess around, do they?" Aidan remarks as we walk down the stone-paved entrance to the front door.

"No kidding."

He takes a step back and absorbs the sight. "This is at least three million."

"You think?"

"At least."

"Pretentious."

"How do you know these people, anyway?"

"Sophie knows their child, their son Benjamin. I was picking her up at a party the other day and struck up a conversation with the mom. She invited me." I think for a moment of how much to tell him. I'm worried Shannon or Jeff will mention the incident. Better tell him more. "And then Sophie told me Benjamin was picked up for drunk driving, and I spoke to Eric to make sure he was released to the parents."

"Was that a good idea? We don't want Sophie hanging around with a troubled teen."

"She is not hanging around with him. I'll make sure of that."

"All right. Can we keep this short?"

"Absolutely."

The front door underneath the tall white columns opens. Jeff, in sweater and slacks, appears in front of us. He stretches his hand to Aidan. "Jeffrey Rawley. Glad you could make it."

"Aidan Shephard. Thanks for having us."

"Hello," I say. "I'm Emma. In case you…"

"I remember," Jeff says. "Come on in, Mrs. Shephard. And thank you again for helping with my son. He's been in too much trouble lately."

"Well, teens are a handful, aren't they," Aidan chimes in.

"They are, they really are."

Jeff continues to smile and shows no signs of recognizing me as we walk in behind him. Why would he? I must have been mistaken the other day. He never truly loved me, did he? He switched very quickly to Shannon when she told him I slept with Richard. He never believed my story of Richard assaulting me. No matter how much I begged and cried and needed his help.

"Emma?" Aidan taps my shoulder.

"Oh, sorry, I was just admiring this sculpture." I point. The metal mess in the niche of the hallway is…something. I can't tell exactly what it is. Birds? On top of limbs?

"It's new." Shannon comes in, in a silver top that exposes her breasts entirely too much, a cocktail in her hand. "We brought it from France two years ago. From Paris."

"It's lovely," I say.

"Shannon bought us an apartment in Paris. She likes to go for the fashion shows." Jeff says, taking our coats.

"Do you like Paris?" I can't help but ask. The Jeff I knew hated anything French.

"No, it's not my speed. I'm more of a country person. Cities tire me."

"He'd rather sit in the woods than admire art," Shannon says and purses her lips.

"I find nature more beautiful than any canvas," Jeff says. "But let's not stand in the hallway. Let me show you to the bar. You need cocktails."

As he ushers us in, I scan my surroundings. Everything in the house has Shannon's decorating touches. I don't see Jeff in anything. It's all white and gold and glitz. I only knew Jeff when he lived in the dorms, but he took me to his parents' home for a weekend, and it was a warm, cozy home, with country accents. Jeff doesn't fit into this mansion. And neither does his son, apparently. Why are Jeff and Shannon even having this party if they plan to divorce? Or do they? Is this party in their reconciliation plan or just to keep up the pretenses?

Sometime later, I make small talk with a nice older

couple sitting on the couch and look for Aidan, but he is off somewhere already. Always the life of the party. I'd like a drink, but I feel awkward leaving the conversation. I can't ask Aidan, because I need a non-alcoholic one.

"I took the liberty of mixing something up for you."

I lift my head and see Jeff standing in front of me with a cocktail.

"What is it?" I ask, examining the drink.

"Rum and Coke."

My hand shakes, and I look up at his face. I always drank rum-and-Cokes when we were together. It was the only drink I knew when I was eighteen. Is this a coincidence, or did he recognize me after all? I scan his face, but it's blank. His eyes show nothing.

"Thank you. Very thoughtful of you," I say, making the best attempt at controlling my voice.

"No problem. Let me know when you need a refill." He walks away.

I take a sip to calm my nerves, then choke as I remember I can't drink alcohol.

"You all right, sweetheart?" Aidan is by my side.

"Yes, I'm fine. This drink is lousy, though. Can you get me some plain tonic to get the taste out?"

I walk to the backyard door and go outside. I take a gulp of the icy air. I came here hoping to find out if Jeff helps Richard with his drug approvals. I need this information so Dana and I can figure out how to prevent Parozex from reaching the market. My plan may not work if Jeff recognizes me. But does he? I need to test it somehow.

The door behind me opens and closes, and I turn,

startled.

"You don't need to hide from me," Jeff says. "I'm glad to see you after all these years."

"So you do recognize me," I whisper.

"How would I not?" He approaches and looks at my face. "You are just the same, Katie. You haven't changed a bit. Well, the hair. But your eyes are still the same."

"I *have* changed. You are wrong."

"You mean inside? We all have changed. Of course. But you are still my Katie."

"*Your* Katie? When was I your Katie? When you tossed me aside to marry Shannon?"

"I didn't toss you aside."

"What exactly would you call what you did?"

"I was angry, all right." He runs a hand through his hair. "I was furious that you gave me up for Richard. He was a football superstar. He had a new girl every night. You were not the kind of girl who would fall for a guy like him. I thought so much better of you." He looks at me quietly, then adds, "I loved you. And then you just picked up and left. Without ever speaking to me again."

"You loved me? Where were you when I told you I was raped and no one believed me and no one was there to help me?"

He pales. "There were witnesses who all said you went with him willingly. It was a frat party. Everyone has sex at frat parties, that's what they're for. All my friends told me not to believe you."

"You believed what you chose, Jeff. I had to leave campus because no one would listen to me, not even you." I feel the heat of anger spreading through my chest and neck. "If you loved me, you should've believed me and protected me. You should've stood by me. You shouldn't have married *her*."

He looks out to the naked trees decorated with bright holiday lights and takes a rather large sip of his cocktail. "It feels like so much of it was in a different lifetime now. I shouldn't have brought it up."

"You shouldn't have." I begin to walk past him. Forget getting information about whether he helps Avias. I can find out in some other way.

"I'm sorry," he calls out after me.

I slam the door and return to the party. I didn't expect Jeff to be even more of an asshole than I thought. I'm glad Sophie snapped that picture of his kid at the police station. As soon as I get home, we are spreading it on social media. To hell with him.

"Look who I ran into, sweetheart," Aidan calls out. I turn around and have no time to control my face as he pulls me closer to stand next to him and fucking Richard.

"Small world, isn't it?" I defiantly straighten up and stare back at him, but stand as far away as the room will allow.

My blood hasn't stopped boiling from my encounter with Jeff, and this doesn't help. What is he doing here? Oh, but of course. Jeff must have invited him. It seems I have my answer. Jeff *must* be the FDA contact who is passing the application I'm so desperately trying to stop.

Richard puts his arm forward, and I take a step back. Is he trying to touch me? He follows me, and I grab onto Aidan's suit sleeve in desperation. But Richard succeeds and takes hold of my shoulder, and I concentrate on not punching him in the face. He knows the effect he has on me, because his fingers tighten on my bare skin.

"Emma, I'd like to introduce you to my wife, Jennifer," he says, the corner of his mouth twitching.

I shake off his fingers. His wife is a tall blond in a cream gown. Slender but rather plain-looking.

"Delighted to meet you," she says, but she seems as delighted to meet me as I am to be touched by Richard.

She looks with boredom around the room. Interesting. So, not a socialite, then. What's her deal, I wonder? Mentally ill? Eating disorder? What kind of a person could stay married to someone like Richard? And not care when I send her the photo of him with Shannon.

I'm dying to walk away, but Aidan is still talking to Richard, who is watching me out of the corner of his eye.

"Should we go get some wine?" I ask Jennifer.

She nods. She'd rather walk than talk, also. I grab a glass of white and pretend to sip it while I pump her for information. No, she doesn't plan to move to Virginia. Ever. Her children are at a great prep school in Connecticut. They have Brayden, who is twelve, and Alyssa, who is ten. She doesn't like moving, and their house was just remodeled. This idea of buying a company in Maryland was a sudden whim Richard and her father came up with, and she wasn't properly warned. Richard has his own life, and she is happy to have hers. She laughs at that and winks at me. Oh, *that's* how it is.

I excuse myself. It appears Jennifer couldn't care

less if Richard has an affair. She is happy he's gone. Goddamn it. Why did she ever marry him, then? What about Richard was possibly appealing to this girl?

I can't find Richard anymore. He's vanished. And Jeff, my ex-boyfriend, who says he loved me, is in business with the man who raped me. Not only did he not believe me, but he works with the guy. Even if he didn't trust that Richard assaulted me, how could he work with someone he thought stole his girlfriend? What a spineless piece of garbage!

I'm so full of fury, I remove myself from the party and pace through the rooms, watching out for my enemies. My mind is crawling with murderous ideas, and I need to calm down. I find my way to the kitchen, dump my wine into the sink and fill the wine glass with water. There is a long hallway off the kitchen, and I press myself into an unlit corner. Seems like a safe spot to spend a few minutes. This is a terrible evening to be without alcohol.

Heavy steps are suddenly in the kitchen, and I hear whispers. I press my back harder into my corner and try not to breathe too loudly.

"What the hell are you doing here?" A woman's voice, slightly hysterical.

"Your husband invited me. We have business to discuss." A familiar male's voice.

"Can't you discuss it over the phone? At work?"

"I wanted to see you."

"You can't be here, you idiot. He'll figure us out." It's Shannon, I'm sure of it now.

"He'll never figure it out. I need to improve my relationship with him. I want him to approve a drug for me. He's been the main FDA contact for Avias for a while, but he mainly deals with my father-in-law. He wants me to take the lead on breakthrough drugs now for D&P."

"Well, that's good news. I just wish it wasn't my fucking husband."

"I love the fact that it's your husband."

"Richard, he already hates me. Don't give him another reason."

"I'm doing this for us, baby. We are going to be very wealthy once this drug hits the market. All those options I told you to buy? Once we sell, you can leave Jeff, and we can take off together somewhere."

I cover my mouth with my hands to prevent sounds from escaping. I was right the entire time. Richard and Shannon are just as evil as they were years ago. Making money off the shitty drug that's going to kill people. Using Jeff and Aidan. Using me. Using my company. I force myself to keep listening to their conversation.

"You'll never leave Avias. I don't believe it," Shannon says.

"I will for you. And I can't stand my job. I have no idea what I'm doing. All those nerds look down on me. The meetings are a torture."

Shannon giggles, and then I hear nothing, and then moaning. "Richard, we can't be doing this here. The caterer will come back any second."

"Then where? I'm horny."

"You're always horny."

"You love me for it."

"Jeff is leaving for a conference in two weeks. I'm free for four days. We can go away."

"I can't go away right now. Too much going on with the company. And isn't your son in trouble?"

"It's our son. And he is always in trouble. I'm tired of dealing with it. I need a break. Can you please try to get away?"

"I'll see what I can do."

They walk out of the kitchen as I remain frozen on the spot. I will need to find a way to talk to Jeff again. If only Dana and I could get him to stop helping Richard. I lean against the wall. How do I find the strength to talk to him again, though? I can't stand that weasel of a man. He abandoned me, and my guess is he takes bribes from Avias. How could he marry Shannon and treat his kid the way I saw at the police station?

Oh, wait, but it's not his kid. Does Jeff know whose kid it is? Would he change his mind about helping Richard if he knew whose kid he was raising? I just need to figure out how to tell him. I think it's time for quite a few secrets to come out.

Chapter 17

I count minutes at work until my ultrasound. I'm certain it's a boy. There is no need for more ultrasounds. My clothes could barely squeeze on top of my large hips and stomach this morning. I left the zipper open on my skirt and wore one of my largest sweaters.

I can't hide this anymore. It's time to tell Aidan. Tonight. I will tell Aidan tonight. And then we'll celebrate with Sophie. How should I tell them? I want it to be something fun. I'll have my OB appointment today, get a new ultrasound picture, and then present them with blue cupcakes. I imagine Aidan's face when he finds out. I do hope he'll be excited. He's always dreamt of a son.

I check on the private Facebook page for Shannon's Women's League as Sophie showed me. They are still discussing Ben's arrest. They've been going on for over a week. Sophie managed to snap a few pictures at the police station while I was talking to Jeff. I forgot all about it until the next morning when she uploaded them to my laptop. We posted them from a fake account right after her New Year's Eve party. Shannon will never live this down.

I still haven't figured out how to get to Jeff Rawley and tell him about who he's working with. Dana has been out of town, and we haven't had a chance to discuss this. I've been tracking Jeff's meetings online and reviewing FDA open records, but I haven't had the guts to contact him. As soon as Dana is back tomorrow, we'll come up with a plan. All will fall into place soon. I feel confident Jeff is the final piece in bringing Richard and Shannon down.

And then I can relax and enjoy my pregnancy. And my family.

****

Dr. Hernando is cheerful as always. "Your weight is great. And you're measuring fourteen weeks, as you are supposed to. Are you ready to listen to the heartbeat?"

"Yes." I close my eyes to take it all in. I'm rewarded with an incredible whooshing sound of my son's heart.

"Nice and strong," she says.

"Can I listen for a few more seconds?" I beg.

"Of course. And where is your husband? Still worried about telling him?"

"Telling him tonight. Everything is okay with this pregnancy, right?"

"You are in the second trimester. You've been healthy. I see no reason to worry at this point. Just have another ultrasound in a few weeks."

"Do I need it? I know it's a boy." I smile.

"You are considered advanced maternal age. You need it. Talk to Aidan about doing an amnio. Otherwise, you should be in the clear now." She removes the wand and hands me a towel. "You should relax and share this pregnancy with your husband."

"I will. I have it all planned."

"What are you going to do?"

"I'm going to get him a cupcake with a Dad decoration on it."

"Cute. All right, see you in four weeks."

I stop at a bakery on my way back to work and pick up two cupcakes. Chocolate in blue paper cups, with cream cheese frosting, and tiny blue pearls sprinkled on top. Aidan's cupcake says DAD on a tag, and Sophie's says SISTER. I think through whether to tell them both at the same time or one at a time. Best to tell them both after dinner. Just serve the cupcakes.

I can't stop grinning as I pull into my driveway. Then I see Aidan's car. That's a surprise—I thought he was going to happy hour with Richard, his new evening ritual. I need a few extra minutes to hide the cupcakes. I set them in the garage refrigerator to sneak them in later.

The house is full of light, and music is blasting as I walk in from the garage. I hear Cookie whining in the bedroom from behind the closed door.

"Aidan, where are you?" I yell through the noise, then walk into the kitchen to see several bottles of his Scotch on the counter. Is he celebrating something? Did he get the promotion?

"We'll be right in, honey." Aidan's head pops in from the back yard. "I'm just showing Richard where we can see the river from here."

"Richard?" I gasp. Richard is in my home? The only place that's been safe from him? "What's he doing here?" I ask.

"I thought it was time to invite him. He's been quite lonely without his wife."

"Pfft," I say out loud. Sure, he's lonely. He's seeing Shannon every night, probably.

Aidan stares at me, brows furrowed. "Don't worry. I got Rosanna's delivering dinner in a bit. You don't need to do anything. Have a drink." He points.

"I'm good. Why is Cookie locked up?"

"She wasn't behaving. She growled at Richard."

Good girl. Well done.

"I think I'm ready for another," Richard says, walking in and bringing a gust of icy air with him.

I shiver. And not just from the cold. Aidan bringing Richard here is a blow. Tonight, of all nights. I think of my little blue cupcakes sitting in the fridge, and all I want to do is crawl into bed and cry.

"Emma." He nods. "I hope my being here doesn't distress you."

"Distress me?" I straighten up.

"I don't mean to cause trouble, stopping by at the last minute like this."

"It's no trouble." I pour myself a water and drink it slowly.

"So where is your famous daughter? I hear—early admission to NYU?"

My hand shakes, and the water splashes on my blouse. Aidan hands me a towel and gives me a look of, "What's the matter with you?" I ignore it. How dare he ask about Sophie? She is none of his business.

"Where is Sophie?" Aidan asks.

"Probably stopped at a friend's house. She does that quite a bit these days. I'll be right back. I need to change." I smile at them and proceed to hide in the bedroom. I hug my poor dog. She licks my face over and over. She knows something is wrong.

I text Sophie.

—Stay at Amy's tonight. Dad has Richard at the

house. I'd rather you not be here—

—But I need my jeans for tomorrow—

—I can stop by in the morning and bring you a pair—

—Fine—

I change my blouse and return to the kitchen despite Cookie's whimpers. "Sorry, baby," I whisper, as I shut the door.

"Food's here," Aidan announces.

I busy myself with serving dinner. It's better I have something to do. I try not to listen to their conversation, but it's not easy. Richard's laughter irks me to the point of not being sure I can stop myself from smacking him with the salad tongs.

"Are you going to give us some salad?" Aidan asks, and I snap out of it.

"Quite a coincidence seeing you at the Rawley's the other night," Richard says as I finally sit down. "How do you know them?"

"We don't, actually," Aidan answers. "Emma was invited to their New Year's Eve party. What did you say, sweetheart? Sophie is friends with their kid, and the mom invited you? Wasn't there something about their boy being in trouble, and Eric helped him out?"

"Oh, yes, Shannon did mention being very grateful that you and Sophie didn't press charges against Benjamin." Richard butters a thick piece of bread and shoves it into his mouth.

"Press charges? What kind of charges?" Aidan turns to me.

"Oh, it was nothing, don't worry about it." Shit. *Shut up, Richard.*

"Yes, nobody got hurt. No need to worry, Aidan,"

Richard chimes in.

"Nobody got hurt? What is this all about? I thought we hardly knew them." Aidan frowns.

"It was all a big misunderstanding, I believe," Richard says, filling his plate with pasta and not looking at me. "Ben drove Sophie, and she thought he'd been drinking, so she called the police. But he wasn't drinking. However, when he saw the cops, he started driving away. Cops don't like that, you know."

Aidan looks at me. "You didn't tell me any of this. Sophie was in danger?"

"I was right behind her."

"What?"

Cover up, Emma. "She texted me she was in his car. I was nearby and followed them. Then I called Eric, and he stopped them. I handled it. Sophie was safe."

Aidan rubs his forehead. "I don't hear that at all. What else have you been up to that I don't know about?"

Richard laughs. "Wives always have secrets. Best let them have their lives. I'd prefer we didn't have secrets at work, though, Emma. I'd like for you to talk to me directly if you have concerns about Parozex."

"What's that all about?" Aidan's face gets even angrier, if that's possible.

"Emma and Dana Kapur are not happy with our new drug," Richard says. "Never mind we have such high hopes for Parozex bringing the company high profits next year."

I feel such a mixture of anger, annoyance, and fear I wonder if I'm shooting fire out of my eyeballs. I want this man out of my house—now. Right this second. I can go grab my father's gun and threaten him out of here. But I'm guessing Aidan wouldn't like that very much. Do I even care what he'll think? What if I set the dog on him? Tempting.

"What exactly is going on, Emma?" Aidan asks.

"Can't we discuss this at the office?"

"Right now is good."

"Dana has some concerns, and I believe she has stated them clearly. I don't feel we need to discuss this tonight. Let's just eat our dinner."

"I disagree," Richard says, taking a sip of his Scotch. "I think we do need to discuss this tonight, given that you and Dr. Kapur have tried to stall our NDA, have sent the wrong data to the FDA, and have now been harassing my statistics team about analyzing the data incorrectly." He leans back and does his cobra stare at me.

It won't work. I won't let it. I return the stare. I'm not his victim anymore.

"Fine, Richard, we can talk about it. Your team made the data look favorable to the drug even though the drug is no better than any drugs it's been compared to. Your team broke the data in little chunks to come up with statistically significant results. Your team is lying to the FDA. That's not how we do business at D&P." I set my fork down and stare defiantly at both Richard and Aidan.

"Now, just wait a minute," Aidan starts.

"Don't interrupt me, Aidan," I say, slamming my hand on the table. "Richard here is trying to get this shitty drug to fly through the FDA on incorrect data under false pretenses. He wants me to market it as a breakthrough therapy, and this drug doesn't even work. And it causes high blood pressure and stroke."

"Emma, this is something we discuss in meetings. It's not something we discuss behind people's backs, while they are working hard on the NDA," Aidan says in a stern voice.

"Exactly my point," Richard says. "When I came here, I was clear that I wanted everyone on board with Avias. We need to be a team. And now it looks like I have you two working against me. We'll never get this company out of its failing condition while you and your pal sabotage it."

I sit with my mouth open. Aidan stares at me with what I assume is disdain. How dare he? How dare they?

"Did you invite him here to attack me?" I turn to Aidan. "In my home? You teamed up against me?"

"Be reasonable." Aidan waves at me dismissively. "You are the one yelling at him."

I stand up. "Don't you dare. I'm going to take Cookie for a walk. You can ask him how much money he's paying Jeffrey Rawley to get his drug approved quickly through the FDA." I point at Richard.

"Emma, stop it!" Aidan raises his voice.

I walk away without looking at either of them, put on my coat, and put a leash on Cookie. She barks violently as we pass by Richard. I don't tell her to stop.

It started to snow as this farce of a dinner took place inside. We walk slowly in the fresh white cover, watching the snowflakes settle on the winter grass. Everything is hushed outside, as usual when it snows. I hear the tiniest sounds: my footsteps, my heart pounding in rage against my chest, my blood rushing in my veins as I think murderous thoughts toward Richard…and my husband.

Oh, Aidan, why are you on his side? I lift my face

to the sky and allow the snowflakes to cover my face, hoping they will soothe my anger and pain. No such luck. I keep walking.

I return home only when my toes are ready to fall off. The lights are off in the dining room. I suddenly feel very hungry. If Richard is still there, I'll get in the car and go get some fast food. If he's gone, Aidan and I need to have a talk. He owes me an apology. And I owe him the truth—about the baby and about Richard.

"Aidan," I call out, but there is no answer. Only my office light is on. I walk there slowly, listening for my husband's movements.

He is sitting at my desk, still, looking at my laptop screen. My hair stands up on my arms. He never comes into my office.

"What are you doing?" I ask, my voice shaking.

"Just trying to confirm something." He doesn't sound right.

"What?"

"The fact that you are sabotaging D&P. Richard told me all about it. I found this flash drive in your purse." He points at the silver flash drive now plugged into the laptop. "It looks like you've been spying on Richard and on the Rawleys. I find this despicable, Emma." He doesn't look at me, just continues to stare at the screen, his finger scrolling on the pad.

My heart plummets. "Aidan, hold on, I need to explain. It's not what you think." I inhale and prepare to tell him about the baby. Forget the cupcakes.

"That's enough lies." He stands up and slams my laptop closed before he looks at me with such disdain I wish I could die instantly. "Who are you? What kind of person am I married to now? And how did you not tell me about Sophie being in danger?"

"I'm sorry," I whisper. "Please, can we sit down? I really want to explain."

"I don't want to know any more. I've heard enough tonight. All your lies…" He gathers his coat and wallet.

"I need you to listen to me. You have to listen to me," I beg.

"Sophie is staying overnight at a friend's house. I'm going to a hotel." He walks past me.

"Please. I want to explain. I have an explanation for all of this, I promise." I grab at Aidan's coat sleeve.

"I'm sure you do, but I can't talk to you right now. I'm too angry. I have to leave."

He walks out without looking at me. The door slams behind him.

I watch him drive away, then pace back and forth in the darkness. The house aches with emptiness as the evening settles in. And so do I.

I lie down on the bed and hold the baby boy inside me with both hands. I try to feel any hint of a kick. But there is nothing. It's too early yet. I'm alone with my shame. With everything I've done that led to losing my husband. I've ruined the little happiness I did have in my life.

Aidan asked what kind of person I am. I'm a liar. I'm a bad wife. I'm a terrible mother. I'm a person with a dark soul. I'm no better than the people I hate. I deserve to lose Aidan's love.

I could've just ignored Richard and pretended his presence didn't affect me. I could've forgiven him and moved on. I didn't have to seek revenge. I would be happily enjoying my pregnancy with my husband next to me, stroking my belly, feeling the baby kick. Instead,

I'm alone, being punished for lying and hiding things from the one person who loves me the most.

I could've just told my husband the truth. Instead, I'm caught in this mess of lies.

I walk to the garage, get the Dad cupcake from the fridge, and smash it against the wall. The frosting sticks for a moment, then begins to slide slowly down, tiny blue pearls falling over the cement floor. Pathetic. Just as I am.

I try to sleep, but the bed is vastly empty without Aidan. I move a pillow and a blanket to the couch and keep the TV on to combat the loneliness. I sit on the edge of the couch and stare at the boards of the floor underneath my feet. The grooves in the wood seem to go on infinitely. Each line is so different from the next. I don't know why I can't take my eyes from these lines. I don't know why I'm sitting here until it's pitch dark. I can't figure out what I want. I can't figure out what to do. My thoughts feel like they're swimming inside my head, sort of like a school of silvery fish. And I can't catch any one of them long enough to look at it.

I stroke my stomach and whisper to my baby, "I'm sorry. I'm so sorry, Sean. I was wrong to lie to your father. I wanted to protect him. I truly believed I was making things better for our family. I desperately wanted to put the past behind us. And now I see I've made everything so much worse by lying. I'm terrified I've lost your father."

Chapter 18

I'm driving in a snowstorm and it's a struggle to hold onto the steering wheel of my car with frozen fingers. The windshield wipers are useless. Nothing but white in front of me. The tires skid. I know there's a bridge ahead, but there is little I can do to stop the car from sliding toward the guardrail, suddenly clear in front of me. I lose control of the wheel, and it's absolute terror as I plummet toward the raging river below. I'm falling, falling, falling...

I wake from the nightmare, and all I feel is pain. I curl my knees up to my chest and wait for the spasm to pass. What did I eat today? Stomach flu can't be good for the baby. But after a few minutes, I realize it's not the stomach flu. The pain alternates between cramping and searing. I know this pain; I've had it many times before.

I slide off the couch, get on all fours, and make my way to the garage. I lift myself, holding on to the door handle, and crawl into the car. After I sit down, the pain is better—much better. I just need to breathe through it. Maybe it's just stress. I recline my seat and breathe. Again and again, I breathe. But the cramping starts again.

Please God, don't let me lose the baby. It eases a bit. My fingers shake as I try to dial Dr. Hernado. I keep pressing the wrong numbers on the screen. I give up and start the car. I'll just drive to her office; it's nearby. I know deep in my heart I can't waste time on calling. I drive slowly to protect the struggling precious life inside me.

When I get to the hospital's valet stand, I manage to get out of the car, but my legs give out. Hands pick me up, but I refuse to move. I feel like I'm being ripped apart from the inside.

"I can't stand up," I cry. "I'm going to lose the baby if I do."

As the stretcher arrives, every muscle in my body concentrates on not moving as I'm lifted onto it. My eyes remain closed as I beg my son to live through whatever it is that's happening.

There are too many nurses and doctors asking me questions, and the one person I need at this moment is not here with me. If only I could feel Aidan's hand holding mine, it would all be better. I want my husband. But he left me and he is never coming back. He despises me.

"I'm fourteen weeks… Yes, I've carried a baby to term before… Yes, I have gone for my prenatal care… Just call Dr. Hernado."

Minutes later, the emergency doctor puts my feet in the stirrups and does the exam.

"Your cervix is at eight centimeters. Have you had a problem with cervical incompetence before?"

I don't like the tone of her voice. I'm frightened. I'm terribly dizzy and nauseated.

"I don't know what cervical incompetence is," I croak through my fear. "Where is Dr. Hernado? Wait! Did you say I was eight centimeters? What do you mean? I'm only fourteen weeks. Make it stop! Sew it together or something. Give me some drugs." My pulse begins to race.

She is so quiet now, I can hear my pulse. "I'm not sure there's anything that I can do at this point. You're almost fully dilated. You must feel the contractions."

"No, I don't feel anything contracting," I lie. "The pain has stopped. I'm fine. Check again," I beg.

She pulls out the ultrasound wand and I quickly lie back. The lights are bright, and the ultrasound gel is very cold. I shut my mind, ignore the pain that's tearing my body, and look and listen for the heartbeat. I need to see his heartbeat. If I see it, I know it will all be all right. But it's too quick, she does it too fast. I can't see anything.

"There's no heartbeat." She puts down the wand.

"Check again." I lift up and kick the stirrups as another contraction attacks.

"I'm sorry."

"Why won't you check again?"

"I'm afraid you are about to deliver your fetus."

"It's not a fetus. It's a child. It's my son. I need you to stop this labor," I beg. "Give me some drugs, stretch this." I see people's faces peeking into the windows of the room, but I don't care. "Why are you all just standing there? Make it stop! Where is my doctor? I want a real doctor!" I shout, my throat straining.

I want them all to know that I need this doctor to make my son stay inside me. I'm not losing another baby.

I kick the stirrups again and try to jump off the exam table. I slip and fall off the table, another sharp pain gripping me violently. I crawl on hands and knees, trying to get away from the doctor as she holds onto my back. I keep on making my way to the door, kicking at her and screaming.

Screaming for my son.

Screaming for Aidan.

And then I feel a gushing between my legs, and I can't hear myself screaming anymore as everything goes quiet and dark.

****

My arm is trapped. I pull and pull and finally have it back. It's stiff and achy. I open my eyes to see where my arm has been, and they fall on my husband, asleep in a recliner next to me. His hair is ruffled, and he looks unshaved. What's the matter with him?

Aidan? Aidan is back. A cramp squeezes my stomach…and I remember.

Oh, God, I remember. I throw my thin white blanket off, and I remember more when I see my now-flat stomach.

"No!" A gush of tears. The pain of grief. All so familiar.

My husband's arms are around my shoulders in seconds. He's holding me so tight I can hardly breathe. I have no desire to breathe anyway. He lies down on the narrow hospital bed and wraps his entire body around me.

"Make it go away, Aidan. Please."

"I'm trying. I will. It will. I promise," he whispers in my ear.

The door opens, and I feel Aidan's arm moving, gesturing to someone.

"I'm sorry. I'm so, so, so sorry," I sob. "I'll understand if you'll never forgive me."

"This happens. This just happens." His voice

breaks. He is crying now too. He pulls away and sits up.

"You were right to leave."

"I was wrong, terribly wrong. I'm sorry I wasn't here fast enough."

"You were so angry. You had the right to be. I've made so many mistakes."

"Don't worry about it now. It's all in the past," Aidan says, stroking my hair.

"I was angry too, but now… It's been so many lost babies." I hide my face in my hands. "It was a boy, I'm sure of it," I whisper. "I wanted to name him Sean."

"After your dad."

I can't stop crying. The pain of this grief is crippling. "I was going to tell you…yesterday, but then you left," I manage to say.

"It's okay. Just rest. The doctor said you are still bleeding a lot." He strokes my back.

"It's not okay. I should've taken better care of myself…and him." I have caused this to happen. My revenge plans have cost Aidan the only chance he had of having a son. God has punished me for seeking revenge.

"It's not your fault. The doctor said you had a condition with your cervix. It opened early, and the baby couldn't stay in."

"I should've known about it."

"I spoke with Lori, and she said nothing could have been done unless they caught it early."

"So they could've caught it then. But my OB said everything was great."

"Probably because everything *was* great."

Something occurs to me suddenly. "Where is he?"

"The baby?" There is a tear on Aidan's cheek.

"He's in the morgue downstairs. It's not really…a baby. It…wasn't formed yet. You can't…" He swallows and looks away. "You can't look at it or hold it."

I cry so hard my monitor beeps, and a nurse pops her head in. "Leave me alone, please," I beg her when she's done pushing buttons.

"They gave me this box, sweetheart." Aidan hands me a small box as I sit down.

The box has prayer cards in it and a poem about losing a child. Information about support groups. I close the lid and toss it on the floor. I'm a grieving mother and I have no body to hold. I have nothing to cry over.

"You know we've had trouble conceiving for years. We are just not meant to have any more children. It's all right," Aidan says. "We have one amazing daughter, and we have to take care of her and give our love to her and stop trying to have more."

"I wasn't trying. I just got pregnant."

"I know. It was a gift for you to become pregnant. But it wasn't meant to be."

"You were so angry last night. Richard. Sophie. So many things. I need to explain…" I'm too tired to even begin explaining.

"I'm sure you want to explain things to me." He looks serious. "I want you to. When you feel better, I will be ready for you to. But we have a lifetime together for explanations. I love you. And I would've loved this baby."

And Aidan puts his head in my lap and breaks down. I kiss his soft brown hair and my heart fills with love for him. Not just for coming to the hospital, but for grieving with me and forgiving me and giving our marriage another chance.

"It will be better. It will be all better," I whisper as we hold each other and grieve our loss.

As my husband falls asleep crying, with his head on the side of my hospital bed, I stroke his hair and weep.

Chapter 19

It's strange to see everything in your home unchanged as you return with a child missing from your body. Same couches, same kitchen, same dust bunnies, a dirty cup left from where you drank tea just yesterday morning. Everything stood still in this house as our lives changed so tragically.

I stand in the hallway, not yet ready to enter the house, still holding onto the hope of another child joining its emptiness. Cookie jumps off the blanket on the couch, still where I left it last night, and runs to greet me. Aidan waits, a few steps behind me. I think he understands.

"Mommy?" Sophie comes downstairs.

She tears up right away, and then she is in my arms, and our hearts sync in rhythm. I see Aidan petting the dog. I am home. It will be all right. Eventually.

Sophie pulls me in. "I made you some soup. Lori said you need soup."

"I'm not hungry, baby."

"It's okay. Maybe later."

"Let Mom sit down," Aidan says.

Sophie pulls up an armchair closer to me, and I fall into it. She sits near, lost for words. We hold hands.

"I'm sorry," I say.

"For what, Mom?"

"For not telling you. I just wanted to be sure this

time. I wanted to make sure the baby was okay."

"I know." She looks down.

"You don't have to hide your face. We can talk about it."

"I didn't know I'd be so sad. I'm sorry." She runs off.

I'm half alive. I stare into space. My world feels as dark as the rainy morning outside. I shut my eyes. The dog nudges me, and I bury my face in her soft fur as she pulls herself up on my knees. I don't like to see her upset. I wipe my tears, scratch her neck, and hope the day moves faster.

"Why don't you lie down?" Aidan asks, his voice gentle.

I try to move, but my legs are lead. I try again. And again.

He lifts me up, and I hang limply in his strong arms. His face is wet. I know mine is as well. He places me gently in bed, and the dog lies on my feet.

"Will you eat something, please?"

I shake my head. "Just leave me alone."

"Not a chance. I'm staying right here. I'll be your slave for the day."

"You should go to work."

"I can't go to work. I can't leave you."

"I'll be all right."

He takes my limp hand and kisses it. "I won't leave you again, I promise." He coughs. "I'm so sorry I walked out."

"It's all right," I whisper.

"No, it's not all right. I was an asshole. I…" He hesitates. "I went to Eric's."

I try to sit up but have no strength. "You didn't."

"I told you I'm an asshole. I thought that maybe you were having an affair with him. Don't worry. Nothing happened. We just talked. He told me everything." Tears begin to roll down his cheeks, and he grabs both my hands and kisses them repeatedly. "No more secrets, all right? I should've known. I would've protected you."

I pull him toward me and fold my aching body into him. I want all my pain healed by him. I cling to his shoulders. He lies down next to me, with my head cradled in the crook of his arm, and we cry together—for the child we lost and for the years of missing truth between us.

"Can we start over?" he asks.

I take a deep breath. "Yes, no more lies. The other day—what Richard said at dinner about Sophie being in Ben's car—I wasn't fully honest. You need to know you had a right to be angry. I put our daughter in danger. I asked her to help me catch Ben being drunk so I could use it against Shannon, and Sophie being Sophie—she went a step further and got into his car. She could've died. I was lucky Eric and his buddies were there to help."

Aidan pulls away from me a bit and looks at me, his eyes serious but not blaming. "I already know. I asked Eric about this too. He explained and told me you also figured out how to make the boy stop the car. No one was hurt. It was a very stupid, reckless thing to do. But it's another thing we'll have to put behind us. I talked to Sophie. She is fine. She's more worried about this boy than about how she feels after the incident."

"Classic Sophie."

"Yep.

"You are the love of my life, Aidan."

He kisses my lips. "For better, for worse."

"Just keep remembering this. Thank you for forgiving me. We need to talk more."

He swallows, and I can tell he has a question on his mind. "Why didn't you tell me? Oh, God, sweetheart, why didn't you tell me what happened to you? I would've killed the bastard as soon as I got a chance."

"That's why."

He sits up fully and shakes his head. "Shit. How have you been going to work every day with him there? I don't understand. All those times we've had meetings…"

It hurts me to see him suffer. The pain is intolerable. "It's been a nightmare."

"Did you talk to him? Has he said anything? I have a million questions running through my head. I can't think straight."

"You are wondering if Richard knows it's me? He does know. He remembers me. He's been enjoying the power he has over us."

Aidan looks up, his face contorted. "All this time I've been out with him for drinks and dinners…"

"He pulled you away from me on purpose to hurt me, to make me feel horrible that my husband is spending time with my rapist and doesn't even know it."

Aidan gets up. "I'm going to kill him."

"Sit down. You won't kill anyone. You are the kindest person I know."

"I must do something. I'm furious. I feel out of control." His hands ball into fists, and he punches a wall. "I can't go to work ever again. I won't be able to stop myself from hurting Richard."

"You can't touch him, Aidan. Calm down. I'm begging you."

"How am I supposed to react the next time I see him? He's hurt my wife, he's lied to me, he's threatened my marriage, and now we've lost a child. Can I please at least beat the crap out of him?"

"You'll get arrested and lose your job."

"Fine, let's go to the police. Find a lawyer. Get him for assault."

"The statute of limitations has passed. There is nothing I can do to punish him legally for the assault."

"How can you live without punishing him?"

"I tried to just make him go away. Leave us alone."

"Why did you try to stop the drug? It wasn't to punish him?"

"Parozex really is a dangerous drug. But I just wanted Richard to make no money on it, so that he would leave. I've done some other things to him too. I'm not proud of them."

"Other things at the company?"

"No, personal things to Richard. He's having an affair with Shannon Rawley, and I tried to expose him to his wife and her father, but they don't care."

Aidan whistles. "I thought something was strange about how much time he was spending here."

"Also…" I hesitate. "I found out Richard and Shannon have bought call options for D&P right before the deal with Avias, before the stock went up, and I reported that to the Securities office."

"That explains it." He sits back down on the bed.

"What?"

"He came to me last week asking some questions

about what someone could do with call options to prevent an investigation. We drank a lot, so I told him."

"What did you say?"

"I told him the trick was not to sell them. If he holds onto them, he's fine."

"Is that true?"

"It is." He sighs. "It's not insider trading if he never makes money. I'm sorry. It's like I was fighting against you. I didn't know." He grabs my hand and kisses it. "I was so blind."

"It was my fault. I thought it was best for me to fight him all on my own. I wanted to protect you from worry. From the pain of knowing what happened to me. Nothing can be done against Richard directly. I just want to get back to normal life. Can we please leave now?"

"I understand." He strokes my hair and kisses my cheek. "I'm so tremendously sorry. We should look for jobs elsewhere."

"Sounds good." I smile.

"Or…" He lifts his head. "We can keep going with your idea of stopping Parozex from being approved. We just need to be smarter about it now that he's aware of your previous efforts."

"But what would be the purpose? Let's just leave. I want us both to stop being so angry."

"I want to leave too. But I want to stop him from ruining our company before we go. And from making money off a bad drug."

"Aidan," I say. "I've already lost a child trying to go against Richard. I almost lost you. I can't suffer any more losses. I want to give up."

"Oh, sweetheart, you were never going to lose me.

And the miscarriage was never your fault."

"You must be so disappointed." My eyes well up with tears.

"I'm disappointed you thought I wouldn't understand or help you in some way. Just promise not to keep any more things from me. I'm here for you always. Just allow me to be."

"You have no idea how sorry I am that I kept it all from you."

"I won't lie. I was very hurt when I learned. But I was glad you were not having an affair." He gives me a kiss. "Why don't you rest a little while. I'll see if I can make you something you'll actually eat."

"I'm not hungry. Stop trying to feed me." I smile. "You should really go to work. You'll be terribly bored playing my nurse."

Aidan takes a deep breath, and I see he struggles with the idea. "Fine. I'll go in to work for a few hours and try to talk to Dana and answer some emails. I guess we don't need Richard to wonder why I'm gone for the day. I'll tell him Sophie had a school event."

"Perfect. I'll be fine."

I'm glad he has a distraction from the grief and I will finally have a chance to rest. I'm glad I finally can rest. The grief is still crushing, but I'm no longer alone.

Sleep grips me fast, but I'm back to the nightmare world.

****

I'm climbing a ladder and it falls. I scream. I climb another and it falls.

I wake gasping as someone's hands hold my shoulders.

"Emma, wake up!"

"I'm awake, I'm awake." I open my eyes and see Eric. "What are you doing here?" In truth, I'm so glad to see him.

"Your husband asked me to come visit you. He said you could really use me to lift your spirits, and he had to go to work." He hesitates. "I'm sorry I told him."

"Don't be. I'm glad it's all out. You helped me get Aidan back."

"Too late, though. Sorry about the baby."

"Nothing could be done about that. I've had many miscarriages before."

He hugs me. "I'm so sorry."

"Thank you for coming. You are always here for me when I fail."

"What do you mean—when you fail?"

"When I failed in college by going to that stupid frat party and then not being able to fight Richard. When I failed now."

"How exactly did you fail?"

"I did all those things to Richard, and I hurt Sophie, and I lost my baby, and I almost lost Aidan. I should've listened to you when you said I should just let it go or tell Aidan. I shouldn't have involved Sophie or tried to go against Richard."

"No, you shouldn't have. But you have never listened to anyone." He laughs. "You have always been stubborn, and that's why I love you. Stop talking nonsense. This isn't the universe punishing you. I don't believe in this kind of bullshit. Here." He unwraps a package. "Jenny sent you fresh-squeezed orange juice and some muffins."

I gulp the orange juice, with pleasure, from a small glass bottle. It's the best orange juice I've ever tasted.

The muffin is blueberry. I take a bite and cry again.

"I'm sorry about the crying. It's the hormones," I explain. "It lasts for a few weeks after a miscarriage."

"Cry all you want," he says, stretching his legs as he gets settled into a chair.

"How is Jenny? This muffin is incredible, by the way. Are you working with a new bakery?"

"No, she baked it herself."

I sit up to get another sip of orange juice. "I thought she was afraid she'd set the place on fire if she baked."

"No, that was only during the holidays. Her current obsession is the plates and bowls. They are never clean enough. She has to wash them by hand. She won't go to sleep until they are done just right. Sometimes I have to pick her up at two in the morning."

"I'm so sorry. I didn't realize she's getting worse."

"She always gets worse in the winter." He looks down.

"Do you think the twins leaving for college is stressing her out too?"

"Likely. I didn't think of that."

"Do you need more drug samples?"

"She's got a psychiatrist's appointment in a month. I'm sure he'll give her something. If not, I'll let you know. Thank you. My department insurance covers us well for the meds. We are doing well, so don't worry about us. You just get better."

"I will. It's not my first time." I shrug, but then I feel pain spasming my body, and tears choke up in my throat. "It's just that I was so sure this was a boy, you know. And I went so far this time."

He bends down and hugs me around the shoulders

as I cry some more into his sweater. It's wool, and the smell is comforting somehow. I push him away after a few minutes. "Go. I'll be fine. I need to talk to Sophie. And you need to go back to work and get that promotion."

Eric leaves, and silence descends on my room, except for the dog's quiet snores on the corner of my bed. I stare at the ceiling and pray to go to sleep and wake up in a different life.

But then Sophie tiptoes into my room, climbs under the blanket next to me, and I take back my wish.

Chapter 20

We have a little routine going in the mornings now. Aidan dresses in the dark and tiptoes out of the bedroom. Neither of us wants to talk about when I'll be coming back to work. "When I'm ready" is the answer. One day. The doctor said—a week off. It's been five days. Day seven is looming ahead.

I sit up and drink the coffee Aidan left on my nightstand as always. It's hot and creamy. He put hazelnut creamer into it this morning. I lick my lips. I think there may be extra sugar in it. I stretch my toes, then my legs. And then I suddenly feel—better. Stronger. I place the coffee down and stand up, testing my balance and strength. I stretch some more. I'm still okay.

I need to go for a run. Anything is better than sitting still in the house, alone with my thoughts. I put on my running gear, put a leash on Cookie, and we bolt outside. The air is cold and wet, and I inhale it deeply. There are all kinds of wonderful smells—of wet winter grass, old leaves, and dirt. It's still freezing outside, but the snow has turned to drizzle and gray fog. It's beautiful to me.

We start moving, slowly, carefully. My muscles are stiff, but they warm up as Cookie pulls me along. I begin at a slow pace, first walking fast, then jogging slowly. What a pleasure to be outside and moving, feeling my body getting stronger. I keep going and, as the fog clears a bit when the road turns at the end of the street, my mind does as well.

Later, the fog returns, and it feels a little unsettling, but I persist, pulling the dog along now. I can't let it stop me, just like I can't let Richard stop me. I turn around after a mile. I don't want to hurt myself, but I resolve to make myself run every day.

Back at the house, I get ready for a shower. My face is wet and cold, but I feel victorious. My cheeks in the bathroom mirror are pink and no longer ghostly pale. It felt great to get out of the house. I'm going to be okay, and I smile, no matter what enemies are waiting for me.

I won't allow Richard to win. I will come up with a plan. And Aidan is on my side now that he knows Richard as a monster. I'm not alone.

As I get out of the shower, Lori calls. "How are you?" Her voice is concerned, quiet.

"I'm great, actually. I've been out running." I hold the phone tight between my ear and my shoulder, as I dry myself off.

"Running? In this weather? It's barely thirties out."

"Oh, it was glorious. I feel great. It's not that bad once you get going."

"You are so strange." Lori's voice then suddenly turns cheerful. "Are you excited for your therapy appointment today?"

"My *what?*" I stop toweling my hair.

"Your psychotherapy appointment? Dr. Lustig?"

"What are you talking about?"

"Please tell me Aidan put it on your schedule. He asked me for a referral when you first came home. I told you about it, and you agreed, but I thought you might forget, with how bad you were feeling."

"I don't remember this at all, Lori. Shit."

"I'm sorry, but I was sure Aidan discussed it with you. He made it sound like he did."

"Well, he didn't, and I don't need to see a shrink. I'm doing perfectly fine. I'll cancel this."

"Wait, don't cancel it. Just go meet Dr. Lustig. You might like her. It's not so bad to see a psychologist. I see her sometimes. She is super helpful. It's not that easy to lose a child," Lori pleads.

"There is no way I'm seeing a shrink. Just forget it. I gotta go." I hang up with Lori and pace.

I despise shrinks. I won't go to one. The last time I went to a counselor, we spent time discussing how it was entirely my fault that I was attacked. And just like that, my memory brings me back to the dingy gray chair of the poorly lit basement room of the Victim Services office of Westview.

The counselor writes something on a sticky note and places it on the table in front of me. "Here is the address of a Planned Parenthood clinic. They can provide an abortion."

"I don't want...an abortion." I manage to find words through waves of panic. "I want him gone from the campus. Expelled. Charged with sexual assault."

She slides back in her chair, tapping her fingers on the desk. "I suggest that, instead of blaming this boy, we spend some time discussing what you could've done differently to avoid the situation. We both don't want something like this happening to you again, do we?"

"What I could've done differently? This asshole slipped something in my drink and then dragged me to

the stairwell and raped me. Look," I stand up and show her the yellow and green bruises all over my ribs.

"Are you sure that's how it happened? No one goes to a fraternity party if they don't expect to have sex. And how did you make a choice to go with him to the stairway?"

"He drugged me. Aren't you listening?" I lean forward, my face growing hot, tears streaming. "Are you going to help me press charges or not?"

"What I hear is that you had a lot to drink and had sex with a boy and now you regret it. How can you be sure you didn't give consent?"

My heart hammers with rage. I stand up. "You are blaming me for the rape? It was his fault. Not mine. He is a predator. He must be sent away from campus."

"Sit down," she says and starts writing on a form in front of her. "I can tell you are very distressed. I can arrange for a few days' break at a nearby hospital."

"A crazy-people hospital?" It dawns on me. "You want to lock me up and let the rapist go free."

"That's not the case at all. I just want to get you help."

"I think I'll be fine," I say, getting up and walking to the door. "I'll just watch my drinking next time. You're right."

The last thing I need is another therapist telling me I'm crazy. But two hours later I somehow find myself in the psychologist's office, in the basement of a duplex. As I hang up my coat, I begin to shiver. I don't feel so sure about being here. I drink two paper cups of water and fidget with my purse.

When the receptionist shows me into the therapy room, I sink into the cream leather couch and worry it's going to swallow me. I worry I won't be able to say a word. I worry this is all a huge mistake.

"Hello, dear, I'm Dr. Lustig," a tiny woman in her late sixties with waffle-colored hair enters the room and offers me her hand.

I stare at the hand for a moment. It's small and bony, and I fear I'll break the fingers if I touch it. I take it out of politeness and then look at her in surprise. The hand is warm and very strong. And, somehow, very comforting when it holds mine.

The doctor hands me a pillow, and I cling to it for dear life.

"What brings you to me? How can I help you?" Her eyes are kind. She has a notepad on her lap as she sits down in a large armchair across from me.

I stare at her for a while. "I'm not sure how to start. I'm here because I had a miscarriage. It's not my first. I've had many," I finally mumble. I was right. This was a huge mistake. My stomach somersaults. I try to think of a way to leave without seeming crazy. I can't stop looking at that notepad.

"Having a miscarriage is very traumatic." She nods with encouragement. "Have you been struggling with sadness or worry? Or maybe feeling angry?"

"I've been sad. And angry. And scared." I admit against my best judgment. "But not about the miscarriage."

"No? How long have you been feeling that way?"

I didn't expect this question. I bite my lip, then go for it. I mean, I don't ever have to see her again. "For twenty-one years."

"That's a very long time to hurt." Her voice is kind. "Did something happen all those years ago to cause these feelings to stay with you?" she asks.

I look away, at the picture on her wall, of a boat stranded in the middle of a lake. She nods, and then the words come out. I tell her what happened that day when Shannon invited me to go to the fraternity party with her. I tell her about my boyfriend, Jeff, and that I didn't want to go, but Shannon said she needed someone to be her safe driver back home, because she wanted to drink. I tell her about Shannon introducing me to Richard and Richard passing a drink my way and assuring me it was just a soda. And then my feeling nauseated and Richard telling me he'd take me to a phone to call Jeff. And his hands pushing me out the door of the dorm and then through the stairway door and down the stairs.

I whisper the rest of it.

She sits listening quietly, not writing, just nodding her head at me. When I'm finished, she leans closer, takes my hands in hers, and says, "I'm so sorry."

A shock runs through me. I try to pull my hands out. "It's fine."

She keeps holding on to my hands. "I'm so sorry this happened to you and you've had to live with this."

I try to pull my hands away again, but she is not letting go. I begin to cry; I can't help it. She finally lets go and hands me a box of tissues.

"I'm so sorry," she says yet again. "You didn't deserve this. Did you tell anyone when this happened?"

"When it first happened, I reported it," I say, after blowing my nose. "But the police—they did nothing. And the campus Victim Services and counselors and all the administrators—they said I was making it all up and he was their star athlete and I needed to leave. And then…I tried to hurt him recently and had a miscarriage. No matter what I do, I am the one who ends up getting hurt. He always wins."

She touches my hand again. "Have you ever talked to any other victims?"

"Other rape victims?"

"Unfortunately, there are many women at every college who experience assault. And many victims at all ages. I was just wondering if you've ever spoken to anyone else who's been a victim like you, in college or after."

"Like in a support group? No." I can't stop crying. I go through the entire fucking box of tissues. "I never thought to find anyone else at the time. I felt alone." So alone. I still feel alone.

"Is this the first time you've talked about this, dear?"

"No," I mumble. "My husband and my best friend know."

"Have you heard of the MeToo campaign? There are many women opening up to each other about their experiences on the internet. It's been very cathartic to so many to hear they are not alone."

"Of course I have. But it has little to do with ordinary people like me. It's Hollywood, the media, bigwigs being taken down by movie stars and celebrities."

"Not just movie stars and celebrities," she says. "MeToo has helped many women open up about being sexually assaulted. It's no longer a taboo topic. No longer something to keep as a secret. I assure you, there are many rape victims on college campuses. You were not alone. And it's not your fault. Do you hear me? This was not your fault."

I lift my tear-covered face, look at her, and I see her eyes are watery now too. This is all I can handle. I grab my purse and I run.

I run out of the office, out of the building, and to the safety of my car. I start it and drive as fast as I can home. Why the fuck does anyone go to therapy?

Chapter 21

I return home and bury myself in bed, where I cry for a few hours. Then I log into the therapist's website, email her an apology note, and schedule another appointment. I don't think I'll go again. But I don't want her to think of me as a quitter.

Later that night, after everyone has gone to bed, I still can't sleep. I sit in my bed, with Aidan sleeping next to me, laptop burning my thighs through the blanket, my eyes glued to the bright screen. I search for "college sexual assault" and "campus rape" and "Westview sexual assault." I'm lost for hours on the web, reading media articles about Title IX investigations and campus sexual assault culture. I'm so agitated that I feel the little hairs on my arms standing up.

My eyes are near bleeding when I give #MeToo a try. Minutes later I can't stop reading the stories. There are thousands sharing. Dr. Lustig was right, and I was wrong. It's not just movie stars. It's high school teachers, doctors, mothers, students, scientists, waiters, men, women—all sharing instance after instance of sexual assault and harassment.

"Sweetheart, go to sleep. Turn off your laptop. You need rest," my husband mumbles.

"Yes, honey," I answer and close the laptop to let him sleep.

I allow him to wrap his arm around me and try to settle down, but it's impossible now. What is with this #MeToo thing? Why would people say out loud, on social media, to the entire world, that they've been assaulted? Aren't they embarrassed? Don't they worry about the perpetrator coming after them?

How incredibly brave…

I get out of bed a while later. Sleep is pointless. I must know more.

I'm exhausted, but instead of the comfort of my bed, I now sit in the bathroom, on the toilet, and continue to read the stories on my tablet. I simply can't stop. I'm not alone. There are so many others. Maybe there are some people just like me, reading these stories right now, hunched over the screens.

Hours later, my hands shake as I type out the three short painful words on Twitter,

#MeToo. Westview.

I wait a while, but there is no response. I blow my nose and go to bed. So much for my courage.

I wake from the repeated buzzing and blinking of my phone. Traumatized people don't sleep well, and my eyes pop open. I hide the phone under the blanket and swipe my finger through the screen. Dozens of Twitter notifications. Hearts, retweets, and replies that I'm too tired to read. Then one of the replies makes me pop out from under the blanket.

Abigail Davis@AbbyDavis

Replying to @EmmaDShephard

We should talk. DM me.

Abigail Davis? *The* Abigail Davis? KIPT News Anchor? Crap. I attracted media attention. I knew I should've kept my mouth shut.

Curiosity wins, however, and I follow her back. A direct message from @AbbyDavis arrives minutes later.

—*I went to Westview. I was assaulted there. Let me know if you ever want to talk*—

I gasp, and Aidan sits up.

He is not fully awake as he reaches for me.

I squeeze his fingers. "It's okay, honey. Go back to sleep, I pulled a muscle. It's fine."

"Turn the light off, please," he says, wraps himself in the blanket, and goes back to sleep.

I run back to the bathroom and type a reply.

—*Yes, I do. Free now if you are*—

—*Class of '95*— Abigail replies.

—*Dropped out in '96*—

—*I was a sophomore when it happened*—

—*I was a freshman*—

It feels good, really good to talk to her like this.

—*Why did you drop out?*— she asks.

—*They made me, threatened me*—

—*Dean Scott?*—

I pause a minute, my heart thumping. She knows.

—*Yes, and the pre-med program pulled my scholarship*—

—*So sorry*—

—*Thank you. It was a football player*—

—*It was a guy I was dating*— she types back.

—*Frat party*—

Her reply takes a while to arrive.

—*Halloween Party at his dorm. He pulled me into the bathroom. I said I wasn't ready to have sex. He slammed my head against the wall. I passed out and when I came to I was on the floor and he was behind me, raping me*—

I can hardly stop my fingers from typing. I hesitate a moment but then go ahead and push the little arrow.

—He slipped something in my drink and I felt really sick. He pretended to help me but he dragged me to the stairwell instead and then he beat me and raped me. Later I found out my roommate set me up to have sex with him just so she could come after my boyfriend—

—Bitch!—

—It was my fault for trusting her— I type.

—It was my fault for trusting the asshole. And drinking too much—

—I made a mistake in going to the frat party. I had a boyfriend, should've stayed home—

There is a pause. Then the words appear on my screen.

—What I couldn't understand is why no one would help me. I heard music and laughing. I came out of the bathroom later all bloody. No one offered to help—

I know exactly how she felt. I'm dying to tell her.

—No one came to help me either. Called a friend to come get me. He drove three hours to pick me up—

—My friends said my first time was supposed to be this bad. They said the athletes always get this rough and I should be honored—

—It feels good to talk to you— I admit.

—We should get together. Talk about what we need to do. Can you do lunch?—

—When? Where?—

Meet Abigail Davis? Lori will not believe me.

—I'll come visit. How is tomorrow? Haven't been to DC in a while. Could use a change of scene—

—Tomorrow is fine—

—Perfect. I'll make a reservation at my favorite place in DC—

I sit back. I'm having lunch tomorrow with Abigail Davis. *The* Abigail Davis, with all the awards. And then my heart falls. She is a rape victim, like me. Celebrity status or not, she must suffer just like me. And she must feel just as alone, or she wouldn't be reaching out.

I scroll through our conversation. What does she mean by "Talk about what we need to do?" I've already done everything I could've done. More than that. I guess I'll find out tomorrow.

Chapter 22

I scan the restaurant for Abigail. We are in a quiet place with dark-paneled interior and vintage chandeliers. There are few people here, and none of them look like politicians or lobbyists. It's still early, and the hum of conversations is pleasant, not overwhelming.

I know what Abigail looks like from TV, but I'm still unprepared for the real person when I hurry to her table. I stretch out my hand, but she envelopes me in a hug, even though she is much more petite than me. She has long, jet-black hair and olive skin with a perfect complexion—the kind that tells you she never skips her facials. Her hair is silky and smells so good I can't stop myself from inhaling. She is wearing a sexy sweater and tight leather pants combination, and I'm certain I saw her earrings in *Vogue*.

"I'm so delighted you came." She lets go and claps her hands. "Sit. I was just about to order a giant meal. I'm starved. I've been working since four. What are you in a mood for?"

She continues to chatter as I sit down. I feel somewhat inadequate in my usual outfit of plain skirt, blouse, and sensible heels, and I can hardly speak, overwhelmed by her exuberance, but I can't help but smile at her as well. She radiates charm, and I begin to feel more at ease.

"I'll just order us a few appetizers to start. How does that sound?" She motions to the waiter and gives a rapid-fire order as I remove my coat and check my phone. Then she finally settles down, stretching her hands across the old wooden table to squeeze mine.

"Sorry, I know I'm a chatterbox, but I'm just so excited to see you."

"How was your trip down?"

"It was easy, thanks." She smiles. "So what do you do?"

"Marketing. I work in pharmaceuticals."

"Not bad." She nods. "Where did you get your degree? You said you dropped out of Westview."

"At the University of Maryland. I took a break for a few years. Then went back. When I was ready."

She motions to the waiter again and taps the wine glasses. "Two house whites, please. You don't mind the white, do you?"

"Not at all." She's a strong personality, but somehow I like her.

"So they forced you to leave Westview?"

"They did. Pulled my scholarship, and there was no way I could afford it. Not that I wanted to stay and stare at Richard's face every day," I say as I take the wine from the waiter.

"I assume you reported it." Abigail sits back, sipping her wine.

"Several times. Went to the ER, to the police, to the Victim Services, to the dean. Then they said they were pulling my pre-med scholarship and I should leave. They threatened to lock me up in the psychiatric hospital."

"You're kidding!"

"I wish I were. What happened when you reported?"

Abigail looks away. "I didn't."

"What?"

"I heard from my roommate that no one would listen. She was assaulted a year before me. She said the administrators only protected the athletes, and everyone would just call me a slut and a liar. The story was that, at most, Westview would do a $25 fine or make a rapist write an essay. So I didn't bother—never told anyone."

"They said *I* had to write an essay. From his perspective. Because I was hurting him with my accusations." The anger stirs up in my chest. It's an ugly feeling, but I'm used to it by now.

"Right. Maybe you should be grateful they didn't make *you* pay a fine." Abigail takes a large gulp of her wine. Her smile suddenly disappears and so does her bubbling personality. "Mine was a football player too. We'd met a few times before. I liked him a lot. It felt good when he kissed me. I never thought he would rape me."

"How did it happen?"

"You know, these predators—they search for women like us—the vulnerable ones. They know how to pick us out from the crowd," she says, looking to the side.

"But I wasn't vulnerable. I had a boyfriend. I studied medicine. I was fit mentally and physically. I didn't even want to go to the party where it happened, but my roommate insisted I should. He drugged me, he asked if I needed help to get to the bathroom, and then he pushed me into the stairwell. It wasn't my fault," I say firmly.

"Well, I'm certain it was my fault. I let him do it to me," Abigail says.

The waiter arrives with a tray full of food, but neither of us is hungry anymore, leaving our plates untouched.

"It wasn't your fault. It was none of our faults. It was only theirs." I take her hands this time and hold them. "How did you manage to survive on that campus?"

"I ate a lot of fast food, watched sappy movies, and gained thirty pounds…so no one would ever want to touch me again. The worst part was seeing him everywhere again. He never acknowledged me. Like I wasn't even a human being to him. I managed to graduate. It got easier with time," Abigail continues.

"Did you carry pepper spray on your keys?" I ask.

"A pocket knife."

"I had panic attacks every day for a year, even after I left. I still do, sometimes."

"I knew a girl who hung herself after. I didn't have the guts to do it. I took pills—Benadryl—more each time. But I woke up—each time." Abigail takes a sip of her wine. "And then it got better. I joined a prayer group and made some good friends. Then I met Ryan, my husband. He never tried to touch me. We just talked, and I began to trust again. And that's it. In a nutshell."

I look at her in wonder. That's so not it. She is internationally famous. Successful. A true survivor.

"So we are both survivors, aren't we," she says, confirming what I'm thinking.

"I thought I was. Until he came to be my boss."

She spits out her wine. "What?"

"Richard is now the president of my company. I

have to see him every day."

"How are you possibly able to deal with that?"

"Well, I tried to make him leave. I reported him for insider trading. I sent a picture of him having an affair to his wife. Petty things. Nothing worked," I say.

She laughs. "That's not enough. Petty revenge is not going to be enough."

"I know. Learned the hard way. This also made my husband pretty angry at me. He works with me, and I'd kept the assault a secret from him. I've told him now, though."

"Does he want to kill your rapist?"

"He does. But I convinced him we should look for other jobs and move on. I can't let my past ruin my life now. I have a great marriage. I also have a wonderful daughter. Her name is Sophie. She is about to start at NYU. Do you have kids?"

She shakes her head. "Didn't think I'd make a good mother."

"I just had a miscarriage," I admit. It's easy to tell Abigail everything. I can see why she is famous for her interviews.

"Have you ever thought of going bigger?" she asks.

"As in how?"

"As in getting justice not just from Richard but from everyone who was involved. The people who made you write the essay, the people who made you leave—all of them at Westview."

"Oh, God, the amount of effort that would take. And likely would get us nowhere." I wave dismissively at her.

"I always think it would be futile, but then, every once in a while, I walk into the bathroom, tired, and I still see his fucking face in the mirror and scream." A lone tear races down her perfectly powdered cheek, and she takes out her compact and fixes her makeup. "I still can't go to the bathroom at night without all the lights turned on first. Ryan hates it."

"I used to not be able to go down stairwells without having a panic attack," I whisper.

"I still don't enjoy sex. Almost never," she says, looking down.

"I have nightmares at least once a week. I wake up crying."

"So maybe we can never be over it. And maybe we should make them pay for it."

It's quiet for a while between us as we both share the pain of survival. Then I break the silence. "I really just want to move on, Abigail."

"Sure."

"Did you ever try getting justice?"

"I've consulted some very expensive attorneys. The statute of limitation on rape has expired. Even if we were earlier, District Attorneys don't want our cases. It takes years to prosecute. Women change their minds about telling the stories. Perps graduate and leave. Colleges cover up the lawsuits. Can't do it through any legal channels."

"What other way would you do it?"

"I don't know. I thought that, maybe, if we put our minds together, we could find a way." She shrugs.

"I think it's too late for us, Abigail."

"Abby, please. Listen, what if it's not too late? I've been doing some research on Title IX and the complaints many women are making against the universities now there's #MeToo. Maybe things are different now. Maybe if we join the others in their fight…"

"Don't be naive. All the universities care about is protecting their image. I think I'll send Sophie to college with a gun."

Abby hands me a gift bag as we hug goodbye later. I hold it a while. I give out plenty of gift bags, but I don't usually receive them myself. After I arrive at home, I riffle through the scented tissue paper and find a teal box. Inside is a teal leather-and-silver bracelet. The silver is engraved with two words, "Be Brave." I slip the bracelet on my right wrist.

Be brave? I don't know if I can, Abby.

Chapter 23

It's dark this winter morning as I walk into the therapist's waiting room. I'm dressed for work, determined to make it to the office today. As far as everyone is concerned, I've had the flu, but I can stay fake sick for only so long. I'm here mainly because I need Dr. Lustig to get me back to work. And fast. Aidan has been in agony facing Richard alone every day. And Dana is just plain mad at me.

The coffee is mercifully hot in my gloved hand, and I have no fear this time. I know how therapy works now. I'm not afraid of Dr. Lustig. But I won't let her hold my hands, and she is not getting me to cry, either. I'm here because I think going to therapy is good for me. I certainly don't want to be picking up guns and thinking of shooting people again. And I must go to work today. Enough of all this whining and moping around.

I look around in surprise. The reception area is in disarray. There are boxes everywhere: some empty, some half-filled with files. The receptionist stares at me with her brows raised. Her arms are full of files. I guess it's my smile. I don't look like I belong in a therapist's office, I'm sure.

"Is the doctor moving to a new office, or is this just going to storage?" I ask, after signing in.

She continues to stare, so I sit down and ignore her.

I won't let anything ruin my good mood today. But she sets the files down on her desk and walks over to me.

"Can I help you?"

Now I feel a slight irritation. "I have an appointment with Dr. Lustig." I look at my phone. "In ten minutes. I know I'm early. I'll just wait. I just have to get to work by nine-thirty today."

She gasps and covers her face with both hands. "Oh, my gosh, I'm so, so sorry. Has no one called you? What is your name?"

"Emma Shephard." Worry is creeping up slowly into my chest. "What's going on?"

She sits down next to me on the couch. "Again, I'm so sorry. I don't know how we missed your name. We made phone calls all day yesterday. Dr. Lustig passed away a few days ago."

"She what?" I feel my eyes open wide and refuse to blink.

She tries to hold my hand, but I pull it away. She whispers, "She had a heart attack. It was very sudden. I'm going to give you a name of a very good psychologist who is seeing her female patients. Just give me a second." She gets up and walks back to her desk.

"There's no need. Thanks." I get up, grab my coat, and walk out of the office slowly, in a daze, ignoring the receptionist saying something behind me.

Is this some kind of sick joke? The universe must be making fun of me. The one time in all these years I try to get help—my therapist dies. I sit down in my car but can't seem to get it started. Then I pick up the phone and call Eric. He answers right away.

"What's up, Katie girl?"

"My therapist died," I say in a voice that sounds strangled to me.

"Your who?"

"My therapist."

"Why are you going to a shrink? You are less crazy than me, and I don't go to one."

"I went to see one. Just one time. And now I went to see her again and she is fucking dead."

I hear roaring laughter on the other side. It lasts a while. "Quit it," I hiss.

"I'm sorry, but this is the funniest thing ever. You tell the shrink your problems, and it kills her."

"You are such a jerk," I say, but then my lips stretch into a smile, and I begin to laugh as well. At first it's just a few giggles, but then I nearly drop the phone I'm laughing so hard.

"Think about it." Eric finally calms down. "You are the most normal person I know, but you finally let the shrink near you and then she's dead."

We both erupt in a new fit of laughter.

"Thanks," I say finally when I'm able to stop. "I needed it. But we are awful people."

"No problem. Hey, the next time you want to pay someone a ton of money to listen to your problems…"

"Yeah, yeah, I'll pay you."

"And it will come with a meatball sub," he says.

"All right, I gotta go. Love you."

I hang up, and a thought occurs to me. I walk back to the therapist's office and ask for my records. I don't want my story boxed up and sent to storage. A few minutes later, I'm back in my car, with an envelope clutched in my hand.

I drive to the office. The building is still quiet

inside. It's too early for anyone to arrive. I lock my door, take off my coat, and stand still, staring at the envelope on my desk. I'm afraid to open it. What did I look like to a psychologist? How much of a hot mess am I?

I take the papers out of the envelope and read them slowly. And read them again. And then stuff them into the shredder. The words "chronic PTSD," "rape victim," "guilt," scribbled in blue ink, wave at me as the paper slowly slides in. I wait for it to finish, and then I take out all the little slithers of paper and tear them over and over.

I don't want "chronic PTSD." I don't want any of it. It's not fair. I refuse to be a rape victim. I refuse to be a person whose symptoms are scribbled on those papers. I stop only when I find myself sitting on the floor, in the middle of my beautifully decorated office, in a puddle of shreds, my fingers sore from the effort.

It's all been destroyed. Hasn't it?

I hear people arriving at their cubicles outside my office. Janet will see the light in my office and knock any minute now. I gather up all the shreds, frantically stuff them into the trashcan, and hide it behind the filing cabinet.

I'm not a victim. I won't allow myself to be one. I will fight back. Every one of the people who tried to make me into a victim deserves my wrath. They won't get away with what they've done to me. Abby was right. We need to get justice. I will call her today and tell her I changed my mind. And I will tell Aidan we are not moving. No way. I'm not letting Richard off the hook.

"Janet, can you get me a strong cup of coffee?" I

ask, poking my head out.

"Sure thing. Are you feeling all better? I was worried about you. You're never sick."

"Yes, I'm totally fine."

I drink two cups of coffee, leave a message for Abby, and pace around my office. Then I make a list. Richard, of course. Shannon. Jeff. Coach Turner. Julianna Barlow, the Victim Services counselor. Dean Scott. The pre-med advisor—Steven Moss. This is my new list. I wonder who is on Abby's.

I'm deep in research a few minutes later when Janet knocks on my door. "Sorry, but there's someone here to see you."

"Janet, I just returned. I'm not taking any meetings today."

She turns beet red and whispers, "Sorry, he said he was FDA. I know I can't turn these guys away." And then she lets a male figure behind her enter.

Oh, crap. Jeff. Some first day back I'm having.

I put on a brave face. "Jeff? What are you doing here?"

"I'm here in an official capacity. You must know I work for the FDA. You have an NDA for a breakthrough drug with a priority review, so we have to do frequent visits."

I raise my eyebrows as I sit down. "You're a regulator. It's a reviewer's job to come visit here."

"How do you know what I do? Oh, never mind." He sits across from me, folding his coat neatly on his lap. "You're right. I don't do these visits. I just wanted to talk to you."

I begin to fidget. "What about?"

"I saw what you did to Shannon. I suppose she

deserves it. But Ben—he doesn't."

"I'm not trying to hurt your son."

"But you are out here getting revenge on me and my family, am I correct? I was a prick to you the other night. I'm sorry. I continued to act as if the whole thing was your fault. The truth is—I still hurt sometimes from what happened."

"*You* still hurt? What about me? You should've protected me. I loved you. I believed you would be there for me. But you left me all alone."

"I made a mistake. I can see I was wrong now." His eyes glisten. "Your husband," he whispers. "Does he treat you well?"

"Aidan loves and adores me. He'll do anything for me. He protects me," I dig in.

He nods. "I believe it. He seems like a great guy. You are lucky. My wife is a spiteful bitch, and she's ruined our son."

"What about what *you've* done to your son? Why does your kid drink and drive?"

I watch him sit there in misery, and I feel pity. He is the one married to Shannon. He is the one who gets to live in a terrible marriage and accept a son who is not even his. If I tell him Ben is Richard's son, will he stop helping Richard?

But I don't have it in me. "Benjamin is only seventeen. He can still be saved from her," I suggest.

"Maybe. But maybe not. I don't know. He's another mistake I'm sorry for."

"How can you say your son is a mistake? No child is ever a mistake. He's caught up in your drama, and he's miserable. You have to fix it if you want any chance at a relationship with him."

"I don't know if I can. He only listens to his mother."

"He doesn't. I watched him, and he wants your approval, not hers. He loves you. You have a chance to make it better. Don't lose this chance." A familiar ache for Jeff fills me. That part of my heart that used to love him still does, I know it. I don't have the heart to hold his son against him in this battle with Richard. I'll find another way.

"I'll try to fix it. I don't know if it's still possible. But I sure will try. I'm here with another offer, though."

Interesting. I recline and fold my hands across my stomach. "What exactly do you want to offer me?"

He leans forward, his eyes pleading. "A bargain. I help you with revenge against Richard and you leave Ben alone."

"I'm not going to hurt Ben, Jeff," I protest.

"You might not want to hurt him," he begins. "But I know you want to destroy Shannon. And she deserves it. It's just that, once you start digging into her life—" he hesitates—"you are sure to find things that will eventually come back to hurt my son. And I want life to be easier for him for a while. So here is my offer—I help you destroy Richard, and you leave Shannon alone."

I can't seem to find the right words to answer. "That's quite an offer."

"I've been working with Avias for a while. I'm not…proud of it." He looks away. "I was seduced by money. And other things." He looks back at me. "I have a lot of files. I know enough to start a Senate investigation. I can bankrupt the company. It will mean your job and your husband's job will be gone as well.

But you can choose what you do with the information. I'll just hand it to you."

"Good lord." I lean toward him. I didn't expect this, for sure. He is admitting it flat out. I want to take his hand and comfort him, yet I also think he deserves a good punch to the gut. What was he thinking? Where were his ethics? He is not at all the man I loved in college. "What about your job?"

"Don't worry about my job." He stands up and begins to pace. "I'm clean. It's all covered. I did the best I could with the data they gave me. I'll look incompetent, but most of us are incompetent to some degree. I'll get dropped a pay grade, at the most. It's the government. No one ever gets fired."

"I don't know what to say."

He stretches his hand toward me. "It's a deal, then."

Against my better judgment, I shake his hand. "I guess it is."

He begins to walk to the door. "And Katie?"

My entire body shakes at hearing my real name from Jeff. "Yes?"

"I've made many mistakes in my life, but I think failing you will always be the worst one." And he walks out.

Chapter 24

When Abby returns my call the next day, I'm so excited to hear from her, I forget for a second I need to close my office door.

"I'm glad you called, because I've done some research," she says, her voice bright.

"On what?"

"What do you think? On the cover-ups the Westview administration has been doing of the sexual assault cases."

"What did you find?" I sit down.

"Records of four settlements in the last ten years. I bet there are more. All involve the football players. Two are gang rapes. In one of the cases, a witness testified that the football team has a tradition of hazing new players to drug and gang-rape freshmen."

"And this is still going on now?"

"The last case was settled last year. There is more. The football head coach was fired about ten years ago, but he sued the university for defamation, won, and was reinstated."

"How is that even possible? What's his name?" But I know before she tells me.

"Edward Turner. He is always the one named in the lawsuits. Not the rest of the administrators."

"Are they using him as the scapegoat?"

"Exactly what I think. And he probably didn't like

it the first time, but now they are paying him off."

"What about the perpetrators? If there are settlements, nothing happens to them, right? They just get away with it?"

"The cases I've found never went to court."

Figures. My heart falls. "So nothing is done to protect the victims? Still?"

"There is some hope. There is now one student who has filed a federal suit against the university. The suit states she was assaulted by a football player at a fraternity party and the university covered up her report of the assault. She named Dean Scott and Coach Turner in the suit. So Westview is under Title IX investigation by the Department of Education."

"So they've joined the club of schools being sued?"

"Right. They may be forced to start new reporting and investigation procedures of sexual assault cases. Still doesn't mean that either the coach or the dean or anyone else will be punished. But at least it's a step in the right direction."

"So what can we do? Can we maybe expose them in the media?" I hold my breath, hoping she'll say yes. She *is* the face of the media, after all. If she takes this on…

"They've been exposed already. It's always hushed up in a day. Someone pays to make it go away quickly." Abby is quiet for a bit. "We have to come up with something more convincing, I'm afraid. I think the angle has to be something that's not sexual assault. Something else they are doing wrong. We need to investigate and look for what else they are guilty of."

I can't tell if she wants to expose them or not. "So

if we find something else, you think you can do a report on them?"

"Not me. I'll have someone else do it. I have to think about it, all right?" She chokes up.

I understand. Of all people, I understand. She is not ready. Am I?

"I'll start researching, Abby."

"Sounds good. Gotta run. Talk to you later."

As she hangs up, I sit quietly for a while. And I try to remember what I can about the head coach. The large man with greasy hair and dimpled skin. I only went to one football game before I dropped out. But I did meet him. Dean Scott invited him to our meeting. Turner was the one who told me I'd had way too much to drink and seduced Richard and wished to frame him.

****

"Who is the boy?" the coach asks, not even looking at me.

"Richard Stolar."

"Our quarterback? You know, Donald, we're counting on him this year."

The dean coughs. "Well, Katie feels he may have been too rough with her."

"He raped me," I interrupt.

"It must have been a misunderstanding. My boys get rowdy, sure, but they'd never do anything like that." The coach smiles. It's a sly, disgusting smile that makes my stomach queasy.

"He is a predator. He knew what he was doing. He punched me, slapped me, bruised my ribs." I persist.

"Correct me if I'm wrong, dear, but some girls like this sort of thing, nowadays." The coach winks at the dean, and I nearly vomit. "And how much did you have

to drink before you had sex with him?"

"That's irrelevant!"

"Not at all. Whenever you students have sex, there is alcohol involved, and there's no way for us to tease out what happened. But let me tell you this. A few minutes of action with a girl shouldn't ruin a star athlete's life," coach says, narrowing his eyes at me.

"A few minutes of action? Are you for real?"

"Listen," the dean intervenes. "The Wolves have important games coming up. We can't be stressing Richard with any more of this nonsense. This is terribly unfair to this young man. And to you, for that matter—you're trying to get into medical school, aren't you? The last thing you want is for this to go on your record."

"I don't care what goes on my record. All I care about is that you get him out of here before he hurts someone else."

The coach leans over the desk and hisses at me, "This is a huge football town. If you start an investigation against the top player here, there'll be lots of talk. Your name will be thrown around a lot. And not in a good way, I guarantee it."

I lean forward. "Are you saying that people will say I'm lying just because he's a football player?"

"He's a star, and you are a nobody."

I look at their smug faces. They seem so proud of the swift way they are handling this.

"I'm not going to let you get away with this. Or him. I remember everything that happened. Let's see who people talk about when he's in prison."

After I walk out, I stand outside the door, in the hallway, for a few minutes longer. I want to rush back in and yell at them and grab them and shake them until they hear about my pain. But I know they won't hear me. But I can hear their voices.

"We must keep him on the roster. The Wolves need him to win this next game, Donald."

"Well, what am I supposed to do here, Ed? She did a rape kit and filed a police report."

"I'll call Dan and make sure the case gets closed."

"I think the best course is to get her off the campus as soon as possible. I'll get her scholarship pulled."

"Whatever you need to do."

And then I run.

****

Yes, I do remember Coach Turner. I suddenly remember everything. My fingers tremble as I text Eric.

—Can you check on something for me?—

—Sure, what?—

—Back when I was assaulted I filed a police report when they did the rape kit at the hospital. But I never heard back from the detective—

—So you want me to look up the record?—

—Yes—

—Sure thing—

—Thanks—

For the rest of the afternoon, I'm deep into research on Coach Turner and the cover-up of assaults by football players at Westview. Abby sent me an email with all the details of settlements she'd found. I'm reading through legal cases and archived news articles and posts by students on social media. It's almost all clear to me now.

I'm most unsettled by what seems to be a pattern of football players being signed on for the team with the promise that they could have access to any woman on campus and any number of drugs they wish. One recent settlement discusses Westview waited a year to investigate a freshman's complaint about a sexual assault. There are statements by the deans and the president of Westview that they are "skeptical" of any reports of sexual assault on campus. And my favorite one—an article quoting the president as saying "the girls deserved a lesson for doing so much drinking." The stories of gang rapes get more disturbing as I read on. Three football players, five players, eight players, countless players.

An article about a student hanging herself in her dorm eleven years ago. Her mother reported she was raped by a football player, but the Victim Services Office failed to take down her complaint, and the administration failed to investigate the assault. The girl lived in fear of her attacker for six months until she hanged herself, leaving only a text for her mother.

"I know what you went through," I whisper.

It's too much to bear. All of it. My head aches. I feel nauseated. I look at my watch and realize I've lost track of time. I grab my purse and walk to Dana's office.

"How does a coffee break sound?"

"Perfect," she replies. Her desk is covered in files. Her eyes show signs of late nights and lack of sleep. I'm not the only one drowning in research, I can tell.

The nearby coffee shop is surprisingly empty, even though it's midafternoon slump time. The familiar fresh-ground coffee smell is all around me and helps calm my mental exhaustion.

"How are you feeling?" Dana asks a minute later,

taking a bite of her cake.

"I'm better."

"You bounced back amazingly quick. I'd be in bed forever. Seriously, how are you?"

"I don't want to talk about the baby. If I start, I'll fall apart. It's not my first time grieving about this. I'm used to miscarriages. I just need to move on, Dana." I sit back in my chair and switch the subject. "So what have I missed with Parozex? I can tell you've been working hard on it."

She accepts the topic change. "Have you not talked to Aidan at all? He and I met two days ago. I guess you got him to be on our side?"

"Give him a break. He was always on our side. He just got caught up with wanting to make sure his job is secure."

"You can't give up your ethics just because you want to suck up to the new administration."

"You're still here, aren't you?"

"Ouch." She raises her brows.

"I'm sorry. Look, can we not fight? You look as tired as I am. The bottom line is Aidan and I are behind you."

"Well, I want to know what changed his mind."

I swallow. "It's Richard. I'd like to talk to you and Lori about him, maybe with a few bottles of wine on the table. He is someone from my past. And someone who is a terrible person. Aidan and I have no wish to support him."

"I see." She pauses. "So you want to know some way you can bring him down, is that right?"

"Basically."

"Will people's jobs be in jeopardy? How far are

you going with this?"

"Not any farther than you are. I want to stop him from hurting anyone. Just him. Possibly Avias. The thing is—evil people don't change; they continue to do evil things. I never stopped him before."

"And you think you can stop him now?"

"I'm sure I can."

"All right. And you obviously want me to help. I'll go along with this as long as I don't see that anyone is getting hurt."

"I'm asking you to help so we can be certain no one gets hurt. You are the most ethical person I know. You'll ensure no rules are broken." I don't know if I can keep this promise. But I sure as hell will try.

"Okay." She pushes half a cake toward me. "Well, here is what's been going on while you've been gone. FDA has approved Parozex for Priority Review. We'll have our final approval in about forty days or so. Then we are going into phase four and marketing. The CDER sent the preliminary letter about a week ago. They used to approve only about a third of these, but now it's more like fifty percent."

"The application went through at lightning speed."

"It did. Someone at the FDA helped Richard."

"I know who it was."

"How do you know?"

"He told me. It's a man I used to date in college. I recently…bumped into him again. I heard he was at the FDA, and when I saw him at a New Year's Eve party, together with Richard, I put two and two together. And—" I pause dramatically "—he says he is going to give us some information about Avias we might be interested in."

"Why is he willing to do that?"

How can I possibly explain this? "It's a very long story. Part of the same story I need to tell you about Richard later. Basically, he owes me for being a shit to me in college."

"This is fantastic. I mean…" She touches my hand. "Not the part where he was a shit to you in college."

"I still don't know how much help he's going to be to us, though. So we need to have a backup plan," I say.

"All right. Well, here is what's going on with the drug for now. The package of clinical evidence Avias submitted for review had sham evidence with overblown statistical results from phases two and three. The end summary stated that the preliminary clinical evidence for the drug demonstrated it improved negative symptoms of psychosis without causing as many significant side effects as the second-generation antipsychotics cause."

"So it got the 'breakthrough therapy' designation Richard wanted." I nod. "I assume the CDER didn't care about the cardiovascular side effects?"

Dana sighs. "The FDA figures they have time to register side effects and slap safety labels on it later, after the drug is on the market."

I feel ill. "I'll get blamed for this."

"No, R&D will get blamed for this. But no one will lose their jobs. If people die, we pull the drug and get slapped on the wrist."

"We'll lose our credibility."

"No, we won't. Every pharma functions like this."

"D&P didn't." I pause as I see my husband's car approaching. "Oh, good, Aidan is here. I texted him to join us. We really need all of us on the same page."

Aidan walks in and smiles at me. His suit jacket is off and he looks dashingly handsome in just his gray pants and a white shirt with a blue tie. I haven't looked at my husband in a few weeks, I realize.

"Something on my face?" he asks, wiping at his cheeks.

"Nothing. I was just noticing how handsome you are." I smile and give him a kiss.

"Get a room." Dana smirks.

"We will. Later," Aidan responds. But he looks at me with concern. I can tell he is still worried.

"It's a good day," I tell him. "Dana's been updating me on what's going on."

Aidan orders a coffee while Dana and I catch up some more, and then he joins us at a small table.

"So what are we talking about?" he asks.

"CDER approved Parozex for the Priority Review. Final approval in forty days," I say, to catch him up.

"Even with the side effects?"

"They were cleverly covered up in the application," Dana says.

"How bad were they?" He stirs the sugar into his coffee.

"People who take the drug are about two times more likely than those who take an atypical to experience a cardiovascular event."

"A heart attack?"

"Heart attack, stroke, you name it."

"Give me the absolute risk."

"For every one hundred people who took Parozex, there was one person who had a cardiovascular event. It was double the risk of atypical antipsychotics."

"Do you see why we tried to stop the drug before?"

I shake my head.

"I'm sorry for that. You know I am." Aidan touches my hand. "I didn't know what was going on. You can't hold it against me forever. What if we somehow let the FDA know?"

"Yes, Emma, what if you use that guy you know from the FDA?" Dana asks.

"Who?" Aidan turns to me.

"She is talking about Jeff Rawley." If I take Jeff's deal, I have to stop my revenge against Shannon. So I either get Richard or Shannon. I can't have both. "Maybe he can help. It's worth a shot." I finish the piece of cake.

"Excellent," Dana says. "I can prepare a document outlining the clinical results we've obtained so far, which I am concerned about, and you can share these with this guy."

"Do you think this will be enough to get the FDA to pull the drug?" Aidan asks, taking a sip of his coffee.

"I hope so," Dana answers. "We have forty days. A drug can still get approved even if it has side effects. On the off chance it is highly effective and might be helpful to someone. They just slap a black label on it later. Like they did with the antidepressants for kids."

"That's not going to be good enough for this," I say. "I need it off the market. I want Richard and Avias to suffer."

"You really owe me an explanation," Dana sulks.

"I know. In time. How about this weekend?" I give a peace offering. "Meanwhile, collect some good info on the drug's dangerousness. I will pretend I'm putting together a sales portfolio to speed it up through the approval and get it out to the market. I'll get in touch with Jeff and tell him we want to give him some information."

"I will continue to buddy up to Richard." Aidan sighs. "He can't think that anything has changed. Right now he believes he caught you in preventing the drug from getting approved and that I'm on his side. He thinks this is the end of the issue. He's been quite pleasant with me."

"Go on pretending, then," I say. "We have no choice."

Chapter 25

Aidan is cooking dinner for us the next evening when we hear a knock on the door. There is only one person who knocks like this, and I open the door in surprise to let Eric in. He is in his brown uniform, slightly wet from the snow. The visit is unusual, but he says nothing to me as he walks into the kitchen.

"You want a beer, man?" Aidan asks opening the fridge.

"No, I'm working tonight, but thanks." He takes off his trooper hat and places it on a chair.

"Then what are you doing in Virginia?" I ask.

"I'm not on for an hour."

His tone is serious, and I sit down at the breakfast table. I fidget with the napkins. Something is wrong. Eric sits down across from me and places his backpack on his lap.

"I looked up your police file." He pulls out a stack of papers from his backpack. "You wanna see?"

A shudder runs through me. "You read it?" I feel Aidan's fingers on my shoulder, gently pressing.

"I did. There was nothing I didn't know."

"I'd like to see," Aidan says.

"No, Aidan." I stretch out my hand. It's shaking. I know this will hurt Aidan. Maybe more than it will hurt me.

I lay the file on the table and look through the

printouts as the men remain silent in respect for my tragedy. I can imagine myself, so young still, talking to the smoking cop. I asked him to put out the cigarette, but he refused. I told him I had asthma. He said he wasn't there to make me comfortable. My throat itches when I think of the thick smoke in that room. He did write my words down, I see them plainly in front of me, barely legible. I skip most of the report. I don't want to live through it again.

Then I flip through the pages frantically.

"Eric, it doesn't say anywhere that they took any action!"

"No, it doesn't."

"Are there more records?" Aidan asks, peeking over my shoulder.

"This is it. The case against Richard was never opened. All they did was take her statement."

"What? But my words are all right here! And what about the rape kit? I went through that horror of the exam for nothing?" I keep on searching, hoping. My mind refuses to believe my eyes and my ears.

Eric is silent, but his hands find their way over to mine and he stops me from shuffling the papers. His hands are warm and steady on mine.

"Does Richard even know she filed a complaint?" Aidan asks.

"My guess is he doesn't."

"Where are the test kit results?" I ask, still refusing to believe.

"They didn't test it, Emma."

"But…but…I did it. I did everything right." I stare at them, not understanding. How was this possible?

"I know you did," Eric says, shifting in his seat.

"But you also know that nothing happened to Richard. Your kit was destroyed a long time ago, and the case was closed."

"Destroyed? The evidence against Richard was destroyed?" I feel intense pain in my head suddenly, and I hold my temples with both hands. "So the dean and the coach made the police department destroy evidence?"

"I don't know if it was personal" Eric says. "The rape kits in that town are incinerated every six months. Well before anyone has a chance to test them or finish investigation."

"This is against the law, surely?" Aidan asks.

Eric shakes his head. "Not necessarily. Don't you watch TV? There are like hundreds of thousands of untested kits around the country. Some precincts keep them in storage, but some can't afford that. I just watched a documentary on it the other day. Some famous TV star is fighting to get these kits tested."

"How can they burn evidence? I don't understand." Aidan asks again.

"There's a rule that rape kits can be destroyed after so long in storage. You can cover your tracks really well by saying the victim didn't wish to press charges or that the statute of limitations passed." Eric gets up and gets himself a glass of water.

"The point is—they burned it and closed my case, Aidan. And they forced me to leave. How did you learn about this?"

"From a buddy of mine who has a cousin working nearby. He says the detective who was on your case"—Eric points at the papers on the table—"Daniel Thomas, is married to Westview's football coach's sister. He was also involved in an organization which fundraises for the football team."

"So it was all about money."

"And the reputation of the school," Aidan adds.

"I'm going to get them, Aidan. They are going to pay."

"Thank you for looking all of this up, Eric. You are not going to get in trouble for this, are you?" Aidan asks.

"No, not at all. I'm trying to make detective. Looking into closed cases is normal activity for me these days. I'm not doing anything illegal."

Aidan and Eric share a cigar outside later, but I sit staring at the fireplace. So they were all in it together: the coach, the dean, the police, the counselor, the pre-med advisor. I suspected it but didn't have proof until now. Did the dean and the coach call me into his office just to threaten me that day? I can't rule it out, honestly.

I walk to my office and search for Dean Scott on my laptop. He wasn't the first on my list, but maybe I should bump him up. Bingo. Still at Westview. Distinguished scholar. Must be a hundred years old now, yet still tenured. He was so smooth that day. I can see his face as if it's happening right now.

"Listen," the dean says, "It's your word against his, and according to Richard's statement, you flirted with him all night and then asked him to go to the stairwell with you and have sex."

"Are you saying I'm making all this up?"

"I'm saying...there are different ways to interpret a situation. He is a very popular boy, and girls often find him attractive. I understand, occasionally, things might not go the way you want. It doesn't mean you make up a

story to get him in trouble."

"I'm telling you your popular boy is a predator. He nearly killed me as he raped me, and he will do it again. And next time, he might kill the girl!"

"Now, let's not get hysterical about this. You had sex with a boy, and things got a bit rough, and now you regret it. I sympathize, my dear. I absolutely do." He points to the door, trying to dismiss me.

How can I possibly get to Dean Scott? He's likely had an impeccable career at Westview. Highly respected by the administration and the faculty. Liar, cheat, and fraud. But Westview loves his devotion.

I text Dana and ask her to look him up. She has many connections in the science circles, and she has a way of digging up information that I've always envied. Her curiosity will win her over, and she'll come through, I know it.

Eric leaves to start his route, and Aidan is taking items out of the refrigerator after I close the door.

"You hungry?" he asks.

"Lost my appetite."

"Dad is making shrimp scampi," Sophie says, coming downstairs.

Aidan gives me a look. I need to try and stay happy for Sophie. She's been through enough. I give her a kiss and sniff the air. "Yum!"

Aidan has a bottle of white wine open on the counter, and I pour myself a full glass. I don't tell him his garlic is burning in the pan. I lead Sophie to the couch. We snuggle up under the fleece blanket and watch some sort of beach house shopping show for a while, listening to Aidan cursing in the kitchen. He doesn't usually cook, but I so appreciate the effort. My entire body aches with pain and disappointment.

I try not to think about that manila folder Eric left. I stroke Sophie's hair. It's silky soft and smells like angel food cake. It's her special scent. "You okay?" I check.

"Yeah, fine." She snuggles closer into my chest.

It's quiet for a while. Then she asks, "Are you going to try to get pregnant again?"

"No." It's a firm no. I'm done trying. "One beautiful girl is enough for me. This was…unexpected."

"Do I need to give you a talk on birds and bees, Mom?" She turns and winks at me, but then notices my look and lies back down. "I'm sorry."

"It's okay. We're all a bit on edge still. How was school today?"

"Fine. No one is paying attention to the exams anymore. Everyone is in their college sweatshirts, and the teachers have pretty much lost control."

I laugh. "I can imagine. We haven't gotten you a college shirt. I'm so sorry."

"Dad got me one."

"He did?" I look at Aidan. He is mashing something I can't see. "Dad's been on top of things, huh."

"He has. It's all fine, Mom."

"Okay. I can relax, then."

We eat dinner with pleasure. It tastes great despite the burnt garlic, and there is plenty of wine to go around. I watch Sophie and Aidan exchange jokes. I try to insert mine, but they are lame, as always. Our lives seem to be almost normal for an hour.

Almost.

Chapter 26

This tension with Richard at work is taking a toll on me. We both seem to avoid each other, yet I feel him moving around the building. I hear his voice. I smell his cologne in the hallways. In meetings, I sit off to the side and look at someone else, but I know he watches me at times, because that icy sensation returns, and I shiver.

I'm shocked he doesn't fire me and Aidan. It would be the simplest thing to do. How does he not know we are planning to sabotage the drug further? He must feel my hate. I watch as Aidan tries to laugh at Richard's jokes and tolerate his remarks in a meeting. When I see Richard place a hand on Aidan's shoulder, I nearly stop breathing as I watch my husband's body stiffen and his fingers curl into fists.

"Soon, Aidan," I whisper when we are alone. "Very soon. Just hold on a bit more."

I'm on my way to work when Abby calls. I'm fighting a sea of traffic in the snow, and cursing. Her call is a welcome distraction.

"Hey, Abby. These snowy roads are driving me bonkers."

"Here too. I hate winter. Listen, I have some interesting information. I've been doing more research about what's been going on at Westview," Abby says.

"You are awesome."

"I have many assistants who are not good for much

but research. So here is something—Westview got themselves a brand-new football stadium the year after you left, well—were forced to leave. Football stadiums cost a few hundred million dollars. Athletic facilities—even more."

"Westview was fundraising for a new football stadium the year I was raped?" I try to make sense of what she is telling me.

"Right, and they couldn't let you ruin their donor campaign. Didn't you say the football player was Richard Stolar?"

"Yes."

"Well, he was a quarterback with a TV contract, pulling in hundreds of thousands of dollars in revenue for the college."

"I didn't realize all that. Never went to football games. I was a nerd."

"Do you understand now? You threatened their cash cow, so they belittled and threatened you and forced you to leave campus so they could have their football stadium."

I can't say anything for a few minutes. I continue to drive, the red brake lights of cars in front of me changing, flickering. The full picture is in front of me now, but it's so disturbing that I want it to break apart like a puzzle. I wait, but it doesn't disappear.

"Are you still there?" Abby says louder.

"I was sacrificed for a football stadium," I whisper.

"Yes," she says. "Now you know."

"We're going to get them all."

"God, Emma, I want to hurt them. My rapist was a football player too. It was the same football coach, the same football program, creating these assholes. We need to expose that program and Westview."

"So what's our next step?"

"As I said, the sexual assault angle doesn't work well for the news. Everyone is tired of it by now with all the MeToo stories. And the public opinion swings all the time too; you never know if the network will approve the story or not. But the fundraising may be interesting. Let's just keep looking. I'm sure we'll find more."

"I found out something," I say. "I had a friend check on the police report I made originally. The investigation was closed and my rape kit was destroyed. I remember I overheard Dean Scott and the coach talking about making sure the charges never got filed."

"I'm taking notes. Keep going."

"No, that's all I know. But my friend is a cop, and he said the detective who handled my case was on the fundraising committee for the football stadium and was also a relative of the football coach."

"That's fabulous. And the kit destruction is a great angle. A very hot topic right now. All the reporters are on it. Did you see that documentary the other day with what's-her-name in it?"

"I didn't."

"I'll send you a link. Anyone else you want to go against? Besides the coach and Dean Scott?"

"There's still the pre-med advisor who took away my scholarship and the Victim Services counselor who said it was my fault I was raped and I should be in a psychiatric hospital."

"Go for it. Find them. We'll come up with something."

"I will."

"All right, I got all this down. I'll have my staff do some searching and find a good investigative reporter who'd love this story. Will check on all this, and I'll get going on Coach Turner and Dean Scott. Those are the two I'm after."

"Sounds good."

****

It's a quiet evening at home, and I'm snuggled into Aidan's arm as we sip our wine and watch the new episode of Abby's show. He and I are both too lazy to light the fireplace, so I stretch for the blanket and throw it over both of us.

"I've missed this," I whisper to him.

He pulls me in closer and kisses behind my ear. "She is compelling," he remarks.

"I told you."

"So how do you know her again?"

"Long story, tell you later. Let's finish watching."

The show ends, and I get up to get the wine bottle for refills. I remind myself—no more secrets. "I met Abby through Twitter."

"Huh?"

"I couldn't sleep one night, and I was on Twitter looking through hashtag MeToo. And then she messaged me. Because she was also a victim at Westview. She came down to have lunch with me, and we became friends." I refill his glass.

He gives me a kiss, but it's a bit short. He is still worried about us.

"I don't keep any more secrets from you, Aidan. I promise."

"Okay." He takes a sip of his wine. "So what else do I need to know about Abby?"

"We are working on releasing a story in the media about Westview's football coach and the administration."

"Why do you need to do this? We are already fighting Richard, you and I and Dana. This might interfere."

"It's not only about Richard, Aidan. It wasn't just Richard who was involved in what happened to me. These people made me feel like Richard was the good guy, a victim of my slander. They forced me to leave. They threatened me. They did the same to Abby. And there are still girls getting assaulted on that campus every week and getting no justice. Didn't you hear what Eric said about the rape kits being burned? Evidence being destroyed?"

"I understand why you are doing it. I'm just worried that this will spook Richard, and he'll take his money and run." He rubs his forehead.

I sit next to him and put my arm around him. "It'll be fine. Trust me. I'm letting Abby and her media friends handle that one. She won't mention my name or Richard's. We will concentrate on Richard and his company. But can we not talk about it tonight? I just want to relax."

"I wish I could fully relax. There's so much happening lately. My mind can't stop."

"Maybe I can distract you? It's almost Valentine's Day. We can pretend it's here early." I snuggle closer, pull his shirt out of his pants and slide my hand up his chest. His skin is warm, and he smells divine. I need him more than ever.

Then we hear footsteps. Sophie. Aidan jerks back and tucks his shirt in. She puts on the lights in the kitchen and begins to make hot chocolate, giving us sideways looks.

"Hey, Soph, who is that new boyfriend I saw you with the other day?" Aidan asks, and I snap my head in surprise.

"New boyfriend? How come I know nothing about this?"

"Because I don't have a new boyfriend, Mom." Sophie doesn't turn around, but her back looks stiff suddenly.

I give Aidan a look, and he shrugs and continues. "I saw you. Last Thursday as I was driving to a meeting. On the sidewalk by the library. You were holding hands with a tall skinny boy, brown hair, leather jacket. Looked very much like a boyfriend to me. Been meaning to ask you since."

She finally turns around, eyes defiant. "Dad, it wasn't a boyfriend, it was just a boy from school. We've been friends forever. You read too much into it."

"Do you want him to be your boyfriend?" Aidan asks.

"Maybe." She smiles. She stirs her hot chocolate and walks back upstairs.

Sophie not telling me about boyfriends. When has that started? I'm hurt, but I try not to let it show.

"He wasn't in her school's uniform," Aidan says to me. "She's hiding him from us."

"That's never happened before," I say.

"How do you know? Could've happened many times, for all we know," Aidan points out. "She's growing up."

"One thing for sure. She is not coming back down again, now that we know that secret."

"She'll be fine. Where were we?" Aidan asks, taking my glass of wine out of my hand and placing it on the side table.

My heart quickens its beat as he begins to kiss me, gently at first, and then his lips are forceful on mine, and I can hardly contain my desire for him. My hands are all over his body, ripping his shirt open.

"Wait." He pulls away. "Aren't we supposed to wait a bit longer? Doctor said six weeks, didn't she?"

I pull him up and toward the bedroom. "To hell with the doctor."

Minutes later, I'm in Aidan's arms and, finally, all I can think about is Aidan.

Chapter 27

My latte is steaming hot and warms me up instantly. Jeff is quiet as he watches people go in and out of the coffee shop. It's crowded here today, but when I asked if he wanted to go to a quieter place, he plopped down at a table with a sigh and told me to order. I wonder if he simply wants to get this over with. I try to read his face. It's pale and blotchy, his misery clear to the world. I wonder what my face shows to him.

"Why are you doing this, Jeff?" I can't help asking. "Why are you protecting Shannon? I thought you and she were…"

"Splitting up?" He takes a sip of his espresso and flinches.

"Yes."

"It's not for her. It's for Ben."

"But I thought…"

"That he wasn't mine?" He smiles when he registers the surprise in my eyes at his acknowledgment. "He is not. But I still love him. I know it's hard to explain. I raised him. I held him in my arms when he was born. I was there when he took his first steps. I took care of him when Shannon wanted nothing to do with him and went to all her parties. No matter what she says, he's my kid, and I don't want him to get hurt because of her mistakes."

"I'm sorry."

"It's all right. It's my burden to carry."

I wonder what it's like to know you are raising a child from your wife's affair. When do I tell him it's Richard's?

"I will divorce Shannon shortly. I just want to get him to college safely and know he is set. I didn't expect things to get so…contentious. I should've expected it with her."

"I understand." Deep inside, I know I don't have the heart to tell him Ben is Richard's kid. I guess, somehow, in the last few days, I forgave Jeff. I never thought I'd be able to.

"All right, what do you want to know? I have all kinds of files here." He places his briefcase on the wooden table, unzips it, and takes out a stack of manila folders.

"We've got this drug going through approvals—Parozex. What do you know about it?"

"Well, I am very much involved in this one. It's going through the NDA, and it's a priority. Should be approved in a few weeks. The paperwork is just a formality at this point."

"But our scientists are telling me there are some significant cardiovascular side effects from phase three."

"Double the risk of heart attacks," he confirms.

"How can the FDA approve a drug that kills people at double the rates?"

"Wait a minute," he says. "No one has died yet. Or at least, not as far as I've been informed." He narrows his eyes at me.

"Are you waiting for someone to die?"

"Hey, don't blame me for this. This happens all the time. You pay some of us—we let the drug get approved. Extra money—you get fast-track and priority review."

I gape at him with my mouth open as he looks through the folders. "Here," he says, picking up the files one at a time and handing them to me. "Intestinal rupture, suicidal thoughts, risk of tuberculosis. These drugs were all approved."

I lift my arms off the table, afraid to touch the files, as if they are contaminated. "What the fuck, Jeff? You are not the person I knew," I can't help saying.

"Yeah, well, all of us have changed, right? Don't be so mighty. You were just trying to frame my kid for drunk driving."

"Touché. Fine, I know you are trying to help." I look at some of the files. Pages and pages of printed reports on side effects and then—approvals. Some with black labels.

"Look, you have to understand. It's not negligent. It's just that there is a lot of pressure on us. Everyone wants these drugs out faster. We have politicians breathing down our necks, patient groups, families of patients' groups, scientists. If we take time, everyone will say we don't care about people dying."

"Why are the politicians involved?"

"They get bribes from the drug companies."

"Of course they do." I read random pages from the files, trying to absorb the information. "What about the regulators? Do you take bribes too?"

"If we don't and we say anything against the drug approval, we just get removed from the advisory committee. So we might as well get paid, be quiet, and follow the protocol."

"But the minutes from the advisory committee have to be public, right? What if someone reads about the side effects?"

"Who is going to read those minutes? And good luck finding them on the government website." Jeff laughs, but his laugh is pained.

"How much do you get paid to cover up the data?"

"I'm not discussing that with you," he snaps.

"How can a federal employee get paid like that, though? Nothing personal." I touch his hand. "Only wondering how it's possible to get extra money and still be a regulator and not get fired."

"Those of us doing this—we call it a consulting fee. By the FDA rules, members of the advisory committee aren't required to declare receipt of amounts less than 50K per year from a drug company, if the payment is for work not related to the drug being discussed. The receipts will say it's for a different drug. So what you do is you work for several companies or on several drugs, and you can afford a boat and a lovely vacation home or two."

"Everyone at the FDA is doing this?"

"Well, not everyone. Just those of us who want to make money. I need another coffee." Jeff stands up and walks away as I cover my face and think fast. I must convince Jeff to stop the approval for Parozex. But how on earth do I do that? And does he have the power?

"Look," Jeff says, sitting back down, "you also have to consider that, sometimes, a drug can have serious side effects yet be useful to someone in a small population. You can have the case of a drug that causes GI bleeding, but it will save the life of a kid who is dying of cancer. Those GI side effects are not important at that point. We can't really reveal those to the doctors, or they won't use the drug to save that kid's life."

"So this is how you justify to yourself what you are doing? Perhaps you will save someone's life, and never mind that hundreds or thousands will die in the process because you got paid to approve a dangerous drug and hide its side effects?" I'm disgusted.

"We don't hide anything." Jeff looks hurt. "We don't highlight the side effects data in the final reports. Although to be completely honest, sometimes the drug company withholds data from us, too. When phase three and four side effect data comes in, we wait a while before releasing that data. We see if the benefits outweigh the risks. That's what the drug company pays us to do. If we started reporting the side effects in the first month, all drugs would be pulled. I mean, seriously, you know as well as I do that patients report all kinds of side effects not at all related to the drug."

"What if the drug causes deaths? How do you feel about that?"

He shrugs. "We can require you issue a strong warning about the use of a drug in a certain group of patients. And make you say that the drug increases the risk of stroke or whatever, but you will then phrase it carefully to make it seem this would only happen if you have all these other medical conditions."

"And often the black box warning is too late for those people who thought the side effects didn't apply to them."

"Right."

"So what you are telling me is that the purpose of the FDA is to protect the drug companies rather than the consumers." I sit back and give him a direct stare.

He wipes his hands with a napkin. "No, what I'm telling you is that the FDA is a typical governmental political organization which functions on deals and political pressure. There is more in play than simple ethics."

"Isn't there anyone at the FDA who doesn't play by the rules?"

"Depends. We had this honest doc—he worked with the FDA for twenty years. He tended to go with the flow, but then he reviewed a drug from Avias that he was really uncomfortable recommending." Jeff hands me a thick folder. "This one. So he wrote that the drug appeared to offer no significant advantage over other drugs already on the market and it caused stroke. Avias's board complained about him to his boss at the FDA. He was then simply removed from the approval process. When the advisory committee met, they weren't even told that he had concerns. The FDA cleared the drug."

"Is it still on the market?"

"It is. And continues to cause side effects. We still haven't put a black label on it. Avias pays well."

"I think I get how all this works, but what can we do about my particular issue?" I feel a headache coming on. I wonder exactly how to explain this to Jeff. "I need for Parozex to be denied the approval."

"Why this drug?"

"Because Richard thinks it's a huge moneymaker for the company. And also because it's a dangerous drug and D&P has had nothing to do with it. Avias brought us this drug and our R&D thinks it shouldn't be approved. So two birds with one stone."

"You hope to hit Richard with this? But will it hurt him? He's rich, and he has many other drugs keeping him rich. What will this do?"

"I want him to leave D&P alone. He only came here because…" I stop myself. He doesn't know about Richard and Shannon. "He wants to destroy my company, and I want him to leave it alone. I want him gone, and if I could make him lose some money and some credibility, I'd be really happy."

"I don't know, Katie. I can try to slow down the approval, for sure. I can also talk to a few other docs on the advisory committee and see if I can swing them to say no on the approval, but I'm sure they've been paid by Avias as well."

"Just do it, Jeff. A friend of mine is the head of R&D, and she's putting together a document with all the correct data on the side effects. You didn't get that with our NDA. The statisticians fudged it. I'll overnight it to you."

"I can't promise anything."

"You came to me asking for a favor, remember?" I narrow my eyes at him.

"I know. Take these folders. These are copies. Oh, one more thing we may be able to do if the drug is approved. Technically, it is possible to call a Senate Finance Committee hearing to investigate whether the FDA and the drug company adequately monitored the safety of the drug. Keep in mind that it never happens, though, as Avias pays some of the senators as well."

"Of course it does."

"Very large amounts. I can give you some names."

He gives me a stack of folders and a list of names, and I go back to the office, armed with information. I know Jeff is smart and can figure out how to stop the approval, but I hope he has enough courage and ethics to do it. I also hope stopping Parozex's approval will hurt Richard in the way I plan. I want him to go away with his tail between his legs, and then we can think about bringing Avias down for all the dangerous drugs they have brought to the market. What will it take to call a Senate Finance Committee hearing?

Chapter 28

I came in early to work on a marketing proposal for Parozex. I'm surrounded by charts, marketing plans, and empty coffee cups in the still-empty building, but my ideas are not flowing as fast as I'd like. I hate this drug and everything it represents. I want to stop working on it, but I must pretend nothing has changed, or Richard will suspect something. I'm pacing around my office, forming a marketing pitch in my mind, when I see Eric's patrol car pull up to the building. I don't wait for his call before I rush downstairs, throwing a coat on my shoulders. He never comes to my work.

"What's the matter?" I ask, opening the passenger door.

He turns his head. His eyes are red and swollen.

"Say something," I plead, a thousand worry thoughts running through my mind.

"It's Jenny. She checked herself into a psychiatric hospital."

"Oh, honey, I'm so sorry. It's that bad?"

"She said it was. It all seems the same to me, but I guess it's worse. She hasn't been able to cook. She was sure she'd burn down the deli. She's been afraid to drive the kids to school—worried about getting into a car crash. She had all these nightmares." His fingers run up and down the steering wheel as he speaks.

"Poor Jenny. I thought she was seeing a good

psychiatrist."

"She said the meds weren't helping, and she asked me to drive her to the ER. We waited and waited, and I thought I'd talked her out of it, but the doc there said she should go to a psych hospital to change her meds. So they took her in an ambulance an hour ago."

I take his hand off the steering wheel and rub it gently. "How long will she stay?"

"They said most people stay about a week, but because it's OCD, they thought she may need longer." He wipes a tear from his cheek. "What am I going to tell the kids?"

"You'll tell them their mom is getting help and will be back when she is all better. They are old enough to understand that. If you want, they can come to our house after school, so you don't have to worry about taking care of them and running back and forth to visit her."

"Thank you. That might be good. I don't think I can handle it all right now."

"No problem. Sophie and I will come pick them up this evening. Which hospital is Jenny at?"

"Winslow Psychiatric. I should go home and pack her some clothes. She'll want her books, too. Can you have books in there?" He looks at me in dismay.

"I don't know." Winslow Psychiatric rings a bell. I don't know why. I know this name. Was it a test site for us in the past? "I'm sure they'll let her have books. Maybe just happy books. Something she finds calming, not stressful."

"All right. I'll think about it." Eric taps my hand. "Thanks for taking the kids."

"Go to the school, talk to the kids, tell them to

come to my house after school. They can ride with Sophie. You can pack up whatever they need and drop it off later. Give Jenny my love."

I get out of the car and walk back to the building. As I wait for the elevator, I grow more sure of the fact that I know Winslow Psychiatric. I must find out how. The guilt of not helping Jenny and Eric sooner hangs heavy in my stomach. I should've asked more questions. I should've found her a better psychiatrist. I know so many through my marketing. I could've given her better drug samples. I could've helped somehow.

When I get up to my office, I search through my emails for Winslow Psychiatric. A long list comes up. How many have I missed? I should've paid better attention. I scroll through them as quickly as I can. Winslow was a phase three research site for Parozex.

"Janet, I'll be busy for a while. Cancel my afternoon meetings," I call out to my assistant. I add, "And let me know if Richard is in the vicinity." She is used to it by now. She knows he is not allowed anywhere near my office without a warning.

I open the files Jeff gave me and search for Winslow. It takes some time, but I find it. Avias owns two psychiatric hospitals, Winslow in Maryland and Morrow in Pennsylvania. They serve as testing sites for their drugs. The psychiatrists typically write up the articles on the drugs' effectiveness. Dr. Joseph Litvak runs Winslow Psychiatric. Dr. Adam Pansley is the head of Morrow.

I google both doctors and recognize quickly that they are on payroll with several pharmaceutical companies, not just Avias. Monthly CME presentations, keynote speakers at psychiatric meetings in Hawaii and

Europe, conference attendances at luxury resorts. Litvak owns several properties, one of them in the Caribbean.

So Jenny is in Richard's hospital with a shady doctor. I realize something else suddenly. It's a testing site for Parozex, and Jenny needs new medication. OCD is treated with antipsychotics when it's severe. It wasn't tested for OCD. Surely, they wouldn't… She won't consent to an antipsychotic, would she? The reality is—I have no idea what she would or would not consent to, or if they would provide her with enough information. I pick up the phone to call Eric, but I can't come up with the right words to even begin to explain all this.

I need to know more about the hospital. Are there lawsuits against it? Involuntary commitment violations? History of treatment complaints? It doesn't take long for me to find pages of records from various investigations of Winslow by the Department of Health and Human Services. But then—every hospital gets cited these days for some sort of violation. No citations against the psychiatrist, or lawsuits. Darn. I research hundreds of pages of records, but some are classified, and I end up nowhere.

I look through the staff list. No one I know. Leadership next. And my heart nearly stops. Julianna Barrow, Chief Operating Officer. The Victim Services' person who told me twenty-one years ago that I should be hospitalized for making false assault claims against Richard.

"Eric," I say in a shaky voice as he answers. "We have to get Jenny discharged. She needs to go to a different hospital."

"Why?"

"This Winslow hospital is not good. It's owned by Avias, and they use it as a testing site for some of their dangerous drugs. The head psychiatrist is shady. And the COO is the person who told me back at Westview that I was crazy."

He swears loudly. "You couldn't have told me this earlier when I was there to tell you where she is?"

"I had to look all this up. I'm sorry."

"How am I going to get her out? She signed all her paperwork for the voluntary stay. She's not going to want to leave."

"They can't hold her against her will."

"They can if she tells them she is afraid she'll kill the kids. Which is what she did."

"Oh, crap." I sit down. "But it's voluntary, right? Your kids are not even little. She can't be dangerous to them."

"I don't know how any of this works."

"Go in there with your cop car and get her out. Get a warrant or something."

"I can't get a warrant to bust someone out of a psych hospital. I just know how to get them in."

I take a deep breath and concentrate on explaining. "Listen very carefully. They are testing a new drug in that hospital, and it's very dangerous. She might have a heart attack if you don't bust her out."

"Jesus, Emma. What kind of company are you working for? You are telling me these doctors are going to try to kill my wife?"

"Look, I'm going to call Lori, and she'll arrange for Jenny to be transferred to another hospital, and then we can all go over there and transfer her. They can't say anything to a doctor's order." I get up and begin to put on my coat.

"I'm coming right over."

"No, wait for me to call you back. Lori needs some time to arrange this."

I hang up and call Lori's office, but I'm placed on hold. I pack up the markups I am working on, grab my purse, and run to my car.

The drive is an agony, but I take side streets and make it in no time. I pace outside of an exam room until Lori comes out. She looks tired, and I feel momentarily guilty for barging in on her, but I have no choice.

She pulls me into her office and closes the door. "What's going on?"

"Eric's wife's been hospitalized for her OCD at Winslow Psychiatric. I need you to help me get her out, because Winslow is owned by Avias, and it's a shady hospital."

"I have a full day of patients. How do you know it's shady?"

"They were a testing site for Parozex. One of the docs wrote articles stating Parozex was a great drug."

She frowns. "All right, it's shady. What do you want me to do?"

"She went to the ER and was transferred to Winslow by an ambulance. She is admitted voluntarily, but she said she's had thoughts of killing her kids. I think that if you and Eric go there and let them know she's been admitted to another hospital, maybe they'd let you transfer her in his car."

"You mean, because we are a cop and a physician?"

"Yes."

"Let's say I cancel my patients. How long is this going to take? My kid has an art fair tonight, Emma."

"It's Jenny's life at stake." I pace around the tiny room, my heart beating frantically. "You have to help her."

"Yeah, guilt-trip me. Fine. Do you have a new hospital in mind?"

"No, I wanted your opinion."

"I'll have my PA make some calls. Let me finish with my patients. My afternoon will need to be moved to another day." She points a finger at me. "You so owe me."

"I owe you for many things."

While I wait for her, I remind myself about my new honesty policy with Aidan, and I leave him a message telling him all I'm doing. I take out my markups and make notes. I think I have an idea about something new to do with the goddamn drug.

Janet texts me.

—Richard is looking for you. Something about marketing for Parozex—

—Tell him I've started the new campaign and it's looking great. I'm out in the field visiting some phase four sites—

—OK, I did. He looks happy—

He'll need proof soon. I can't keep blowing him off forever.

"You're ready to go?" Lori asks. She stares at my paperwork spread on her office desk. "Feel free to use my office." She smirks.

"Sorry, I seriously need to catch up on work."

"You and me both."

I call Eric on the way. "Lori and I are coming. Let's

meet somewhere on the way. Lori needs to go with you in your car, so it looks all legit."

"I may have screwed things up," he says quietly.

"What do you mean?" I look at Lori in confusion.

"I called over there and told them I don't want them to give her any drugs without my approval. So they got a court order and put her in an involuntary status."

"Oh, shit, Eric! Why did you do that? Lori, she is now involuntary."

"Is she committed or just in a seventy-two-hour hold?" Lori asks.

"Is she committed or in a hold?" I ask.

"In a hold. It has to be a hold first in Maryland."

"Hold," I tell Lori.

She takes the phone out of my hand. "Drive," she tells me. "Listen," she tells Eric, "we need to get an attorney, quickly. We can challenge the court. You'll need witnesses, which is fine, because Emma and I are coming. Get her a regular psychiatrist, too. Anyone who can vouch for her not being a danger to herself or others. They can't hold her involuntarily unless she is a danger." She nods. "Yes, I understand that's what she said, but a good attorney can spin these words. It's your only chance, man."

"Tell him I'll get him an attorney. He only needs to get hold of her psychiatrist."

"Emma will get you an attorney. You get hold of her psychiatrist. We'll be right over to your deli. Meet us there."

"You have an attorney?" Lori asks.

"Yes."

I ask the Bluetooth to call Abby, explain the

situation, and ask her to call her husband for advice. We are not even over the bridge to Maryland when Ryan calls me with two names.

"You have some good connections," Lori remarks.

"Yeah, I can bust someone out of a psychiatric hospital." I laugh.

"Hey, you never know when that can come in handy."

The deli is dark and empty, and my heart sinks. Eric looks worse than before. "I'm such an idiot," he says.

"Don't worry. I think we can fix it." I sit down next to him at a table and rub his back.

"If we don't, it will be entirely my fault she's there. I can't stand the thought of her being there for seventy-two hours. I don't want her there for twenty-four hours."

"She might still need to be in a hospital for a while," Lori says gently.

"I know. But it will be a safe place."

"Have you eaten today?" Lori asks him.

"No. I can't think of food."

"You need to eat. Let me see what you guys still have in there."

Lori busies herself making eggs a few minutes later. I'm ashamed to admit it, but I'm suddenly very hungry.

The clock ticks the minutes very slowly until the attorney calls. "I think we have a chance with this," he says. "The paperwork was done incorrectly. And if we could get two expert witnesses to state she is not a danger to self or others, I can get her out, hopefully today. Tomorrow at the latest. Sometimes the court order takes a while to process."

"It's already past three o'clock. You think there's enough time?"

"Oh, sure. I called for an emergency hearing, and there's a special judge that deals with these. The faster we get to the court, the better, though. So hurry. We want that order today."

The attorney is good at what he does. Jenny is released within two hours and sits, bewildered, in Eric's car for transport. We try not to worry her with the details of her transfer. Lori is talking to her in a hushed tone, explaining that she found a better hospital.

"Does she look sedated to you?" Eric asks.

"I don't know," I admit. "Could just be confused about what's going on. Relax. She'll be fine. She needs good help, and she'll be all better."

Lori comes out of the car. "Take her to this address, Eric. It's a lovely private hospital. I was in residency with the medical director. She'll take great care of Jenny."

"I can't thank you enough." He envelops her in a hug.

"Not at all. Just take care of yourself."

"Come on, I'll drive you back," I say. "And I have lots of kids and a neglected husband at home."

"You need to really look into this place," Lori suggests as we drive back.

"Believe me, I will."

"I spoke with the attorney. He can file a civil suit on their behalf for the wrongful commitment. I can report fraud and patient abuse. It will help the case."

"I can't believe it's the first time someone has challenged them."

"They likely settled in the past."

I drop Lori off and spend time with family. I assure Eric's kids that their mother is perfectly fine. But I can't stop thinking of Julianna Barrow and what I can do to her.

Chapter 29

It's one of those blustery February evenings when the wind howls all night and even the fireplace can't take the chill out of the house. Thankfully, the house is full of smells of a freshly cooked chicken, the leftovers of which Aidan is kind enough to clean up now as Lori, Dana, and I sit around the oak dining room table and look through the files Jeff gave me.

"Here is something," Lori says, as she holds up some papers. "FDA investigation of a suicide from another antipsychotic Avias developed a few years ago. It was approved but there were several kidney failures and a suicide. The suicide led to a lawsuit and—let me see." She pulls out another piece of paper. "A settlement by Avias."

"Was one of the sites Winslow?" I ask.

"The suicide was at Winslow, yes."

"What did the FDA say about the suicide?" Dana asks.

"No evidence of misconduct, significant violation of the protocol, or regulations governing clinical investigators or IRBs. Typical bullshit." Lori shakes her head, making notes on a legal pad.

"Who was the lead on the investigation?" Dana asks.

"Let me check. Jeffrey Rawley."

"Of course." I sigh.

"The patient who died was just released by the Winslow Psychiatric Hospital, and the lawsuit was then filed by the family, but the judge dismissed it since the FDA found no wrongdoing. Oh, check this out. Litvak cosigned on the original safety study for the drug." Lori hands me the file.

I read frantically through the paperwork. "The main argument by the family seemed to be that the patient was too altered to be able to give consent. Mom denied consent, but the patient was still given medication."

"Yes, that would be an issue if he didn't understand what the medication was doing," Lori confirms.

"Well, Winslow Psychiatric argued that he did. That they gave him a psychiatric examination and he was perfectly capable of consent. Yet a few weeks later, he killed himself. Interesting."

I look through the records. "An admission interview and consent for research co-signed by one Ms. Julianna Barrow, and a psychiatric evaluation by Dr. Litvak."

"Here is another antipsychotic Avias got approved a few years ago. It was taken off the market because it caused diabetes in large numbers of patients, yet they continued to market it for use in Bipolar Disorder. And…" Lori makes a dramatic pause. "You might find it interesting that several of the research articles lauding its effectiveness were co-authored by Dr. Litvak."

"This guy is something, isn't he? How can this be legal?" I ask.

"What you want to be asking is how much does Avias pay Winslow per patient in their studies," Lori says. "Winslow accepts Medicaid, so they can hardly make enough money just with their admissions, but with a nice supplement from Avias, they can make sure that Litvak can afford a house in the Caribbean."

"And the pay is per patient," Dana points out. "That means the more they sign up, the more they make. What I hear is that Big Pharma will pay 15K a head these days. Avias is not quite that rich, but I can see 10K a head easily."

"Wait a minute. Let me see something." I search Winslow's website and find Julianna Barrow's job description.

I read out loud, "'Julianna Barrow, Chief Operating Officer, assisting families with admissions, ensuring compliance with federal, state, and local requirements, and Joint Commission standards.' Admissions—wouldn't that mean she oversees the involuntary admissions as well?"

"Yes, it would. Between the study enrollment fees and the CME fees, Barrow and Litvak can do very well." Lori whistles. "I'm in the wrong business."

"Everyone at that hospital would be getting a kickback of some sort," Dana says.

"We need proof of that." I get up and refill our water glasses.

"Mental health records are sealed; you can't get copies of them," Lori says.

"Research records are sealed, too. They would be stored at Winslow." Dana takes a sip of her water.

"What about court orders of involuntary commitments? What if we looked at how many people they kept over the past few years and if the number was much higher than at other hospitals?" I propose.

"That actually might work. Those are public record. I'll get on those." Dana's fingers begin typing.

"Any other ideas? What if we don't find enough there?"

"All right," Lori says. "Here is what we'll do. I'll call over there and pretend I want a tour of the facility so I can send patients to them. Maybe I'll mention I like for patients to be in experimental research. While I am there, maybe I can ask to meet that Barrow person and assess how big a part she plays in the entire charade."

"I don't feel comfortable with you going by yourself." I shake my head.

"Well, you definitely can't come with me. She'll recognize you."

"She saw me once, twenty-one years ago, and trust me—I meant nothing to her."

"Fine. Come with me. You do work with Winslow, technically. You can pretend to be on the official visit. You can be the one giving me a tour. That might work even better."

****

Lori and I proceed on the highway toward Spring River to visit Winslow before it gets too dark. The road is dark and slippery all the way there. After about half an hour, the icy mist turns suddenly into snowflakes, which first gently fall on the windshield but then almost completely block the view.

"Sorry, I should've checked the weather forecast, Lori."

"Yeah, we'll be lucky if we get to Spring River in one piece."

I turn on the radio, and the announcer blasts, "Warning to drivers in Maryland at this time. A sloppy mix of rain, sleet, snow, and gusting wind is pummeling the area, causing public transportation delays and slick surfaces on roadways around the region."

Lori and I exchange hopeless looks as we crawl our way through the unfamiliar icy roads.

"We'll have to stay in Spring River tonight, I guess," Lori says. "Dana won't be happy."

"Neither will Aidan."

I find the first hotel near the highway and slide my car to it. After we check in, the temptation to climb into bed is strong, but Lori forces me to venture out to dinner at a small diner across the street. A small town works the same way anywhere in America. We need information, and we don't have much time. We must talk to the locals.

Pat's Diner is badly in need of updating. The '80s decor doesn't look like it was done in retro style. The counter is peeling, its grimy underlayer showing in several places.

"This place hasn't been cleaned since the '80s," I say as my pants get stuck to the vinyl padding.

"Maybe the '70s."

I look at the cheeseburger being served at the next table, and I lose my appetite. I'm pretty sure I saw a vending machine at the hotel, and a candy bar will do later.

"What can I get you?" A tired waitress stops by.

"What do you have for dessert?" Lori asks.

"We only got the cheesecake today. Blueberry or no topping?"

"No topping, thank you," Lori orders and looks up at me.

I shake my head. "Can I ask you a question,

please?"

"Go ahead."

"Are you familiar with the Winslow Psychiatric Hospital?"

"And what's it to you?" The waitress narrows her eyes, putting her notepad down.

I think for a moment. I must ask more carefully, apparently. "I'm looking for a place for my brother. And Winslow was suggested to me. I'm here to visit them with my friend. Was just wondering what people think about it."

"Well, it all depends on how much you care for your brother. I wouldn't let them take care of my dog, let alone my brother." She huffs angrily, turns, and is about to walk away.

"Wait, what do you mean? Can you please tell us more?" Lori calls out.

"And why are you in here asking me questions? Shouldn't you be visiting the place and asking them questions?" the woman asks, her eyes narrowed in suspicion.

"We were planning to. But we got here too late, got lost on the way. And then the weather." I point to the snow falling heavier outside now. "We'll go first thing tomorrow. Nothing beats asking for reviews from the locals, though, right?" I smile.

"I see. And why aren't you looking for some fancy city place? No one comes all the way out here."

"My brother is more of a country person. He…wouldn't do well in Baltimore."

She walks over to the counter and takes a plate with something resembling a cheesecake out. Lori and I exchange looks. The waitress obviously knows something about Winslow. We need to keep asking and stay here longer.

"Can I have a cup of coffee, please?" I ask as she sets the plate in front of Lori.

"This cheesecake looks fabulous," Lori says.

"My daughter-in-law bakes these."

"Does she have a bakery in town?" I jump in.

"No, she bakes them back in the kitchen." She points. "She does the breads also. She's always been into baking."

"Oh, I envy that," I say, taking a sip of the coffee she poured me. The coffee is surprisingly good. "I can never bake a cheesecake. Don't have any baking talent whatsoever."

"Ain't easy. You gotta have a talent for these things. And that she does, my Rose."

"That's a pretty name, Rose," Lori says.

"It is, isn't it? I'm lucky she wants to be by me and I can see my grandson." She pours herself a cup of coffee as well. "It's my son Sammy who's at Winslow."

"He's there right now?"

"He's in and out of there, but he's more in than out these days."

"That must be very hard on you and Rose."

"You got no idea. Although Rose is used to it by now. We do have his Social Security coming in, so that's nice."

"So he doesn't get better?" I ask.

"His doctors say he ain't ever getting better, honey. The disease he's got—it's all in his brain. There are these chemicals there that are all messed up or something. No matter what drug they try on him, it just makes him worse. All of them drugs, I'm not even sure he should be taking them. Rose wants them to try, but I be telling her that's enough of that nonsense."

"May I ask—what is his illness?" Lori asks, her voice gentle.

"Oh, sure, it's no secret around here. He sees spirits everywhere he goes. Of course, in this town, we have lots of folks who see spirits in these old homes, but he doesn't seem too happy to see these spirits. He can't sleep. And then he cries all day and talks to himself and these spirits a whole lot."

"I'm so sorry." I touch her hand.

"I knew something was off with him back in high school, but I figured it was all that teenage nonsense. Rose loved him and wanted to marry him. He had a job at the auto parts store. Then they got married, and it was all good for about a year. But then things went downhill from there."

"And you are not happy with the care he receives at Winslow?" Lori asks. She takes a small bite of her cheesecake, makes a face, and pushes it away.

"It's a nasty place. Every time Sammy goes there, he gets worse, not better. And I hate that I don't know what drugs they're giving him. They got him signed up for some sort of research, but they won't tell us what."

"What do you mean?"

"They made him sign a paper that he is all right to be in a study, but he won't know what drug he'd be taking. So it could be just one of them sugar pills or any drug they might care to give him. So he ain't getting any better. And he keeps forgetting things. Every time he forgets more. Last time he was home, he couldn't remember his son. He kept calling for his dog he had as a child. And there are other things, too."

"Like what?" I ask.

"He seems real afraid of the head doctor there. The Litvak guy. When Sammy sees him, he pees himself sometimes. And last time, they wouldn't discharge him home. They said it would be Friday, then it was next Wednesday, then they said he attacked a staff member and it would be the Thursday after. And when he came home, there were bruises on his wrists and ankles from where he was in restraints."

"That's awful! Did you make a complaint?"

"And what would happen if I made a complaint? If they shut the place down, where will I take him the next time he decides to have another breakdown? I gotta protect his kid and his wife. And Medicaid only pays for this one hospital. They do pick up the phone every time I call to tell them he stopped taking his meds again or he's seeing them spirits again."

I finish my coffee. "It doesn't sound like the place I'd want my brother to go to."

"No, go someplace else. Far away from this town. And listen—don't tell no one I said bad things about Winslow. The head doctors—they're friends with other shrinks around. I don't want trouble for me or my son."

"Of course not. I won't tell anyone."

"And we all around here do need Winslow's money. The head doctor's wife, she's on the city council, in charge of all the improvements around here. The city does whatever the doctors want."

I look around me. I have a feeling this town is being run into the ground by Litvak.

"Who is the head doctor's wife?"

"Barrow is her name. The skinny blonde lady with those high heels. I don't know how she walks in those."

Julianna Barrow is not just the admissions person, she is also Litvak's wife? Lori and I exchange looks. Should be an interesting visit tomorrow.

****

We look out the window in the morning, and all we see is white. The highway is empty. There is a strange hush in the air, as if the world has been silenced by someone. I can't believe it. I'm trapped in rural Maryland.

I check the news on my phone. Two feet of snow has fallen overnight. I don't have time for this. I run downstairs.

"When will the snowplows get here?" I ask the front desk clerk.

"Who knows? They have to do the highway first, then the police station and the hospitals. Then probably whoever else is more important than us." He looks at the clock behind him. "Should be here by noon, though."

"Noon? Are you kidding me? I can't wait until noon. I have to visit a hospital and then drive back to D.C."

"You may want to extend your stay here for another night, then," he suggests. "Noon is my best estimate. There is no telling when the plow gets here, though. They are not quite in a hurry this morning, as most businesses were closed, and the highway just reopened about an hour ago."

This is a nightmare. Lori is going to hate me forever.

Chapter 30

The snowplow arrives at noon as predicted, at about the time Lori and I resolve ourselves to walking all the way to Winslow. Aidan is beside himself lying to Richard all morning about my whereabouts, as we had a meeting scheduled at nine. Another thing for me to feel guilty about. But he knows I must finish this business with Winslow, for the company's sake, as well as mine. We need to find out what Avias's dealings are with Litvak.

We wipe the snow off the car and scrape the windshield as the path from the hotel is slowly cleared. The drive on the slippery roads is much slower than yesterday when we came to get Jenny. The traffic doesn't help my mounting frustration at all.

"I honestly don't understand why all these people decided to leave their houses after the snowstorm," Lori complains. "We've been standing still for over half an hour."

"Maybe there's an accident or something. You know people are such idiots when there's snow on the roads." I open the window and poke my head out but see nothing out of the ordinary.

Our heads turn as we hear sirens, and two fire engines promptly pass on our left.

"Yep, accident." I nod.

A police car and several ambulances follow.

"How large was this accident?" Lori turns her head, trying to see around the line of cars.

I pull up a traffic map on my phone. "All I can see is traffic. No accident."

"That thing is always behind."

It takes another half an hour for the cars to begin to move, and the first pangs of lunch hunger arrive in my stomach. "Should we grab some fast food on the way?" I ask.

"No, let's get this over with and then treat ourselves to something nice," Lori suggests.

"Here? Did you forget the diner?" I shudder at the memory.

"We have to be able to find something better than that."

As GPS directs me closer to the hospital, the traffic again increases, and we begin to see news vans and police cars. I'm forced to drive at turtle speed on a crowded street, and I regret my decision to forgo fast food.

"What's going on?" I wonder.

"My guess is another suicide," Lori says.

But as we turn yet another street corner, the smell of smoke hits us even through the closed car windows. It's unmistakable—something is on fire.

Lori and I look at each other, the same realization coming to us at the same time. "You don't think…" I start.

I park the car, and we run until we reach the police barricade, from where we can watch the Winslow Psychiatric Hospital's massive white building going up in flames. I can't watch. Lori stands with her hands over her mouth, her face pale, fire reflected in her pupils. I take shallow breaths, fearful of smelling the smoke, fearful of exploding with rage and questions.

"Are there any victims?" Lori asks the policeman nearest to us.

"No, ma'am. Everyone evacuated in time."

"What about any hospital belongings or records?"

"I can't answer that, ma'am. That would be something their spokesperson will likely discuss. Are you media?"

"Yes, we are." She flashes her hospital badge quickly.

"You may want to go to the media area, then. They'll answer some questions there in a few minutes."

Lori pulls me behind her, and we join the group of agitated cameramen and women with their perfect hair and cheap polyester suits.

"We don't look like media," I whisper to Lori.

"I don't care," she says. "We need to hear this."

A few minutes later, a woman with long blonde hair, impeccably dressed in a blue sleeveless dress with a pashmina scarf tossed around her shoulders, comes forward, a fake expression of grief on her face. I don't need the introduction. I'd recognize Julianna Barrow anywhere.

"I'll answer questions for ten minutes," she says as the cameras begin to flash in her face.

"Were you able to save your research records?" Lori yells out. I turn away, hiding my face.

"I'm afraid it wasn't possible to carry those out. We were only concerned with patient safety and evacuation. We'll know the full extent of the damage when the fire is extinguished."

"Where did the fire originate?"

"Is there any news on what started the fire?"

Questions keep flying at Ms. Barrow. She answers them quickly as I watch her face and judge the degree of her lies.

"How do you think we'll find out who actually set the fire?" I whisper to Lori.

"There will be a fire marshal report eventually."

"We need to get our hands on that. Do you realize we may never have the information from that hospital now? I may never be able to get back at this woman, even though she stands right in front of me, probably lying to this entire group of people."

"I'm sure we'll be able to find something. There's no way all the records are burned. It won't be today, but we didn't expect it today."

As we drive back, I'm so horribly disappointed that I start looking up my next target on my tablet, while Lori takes the driver's seat. Steven Moss, the pre-med advisor. Who apparently moved on to be the school counselor at Horace Lane Preparatory Academy, Charlotte, North Carolina. He moved way south, didn't he? I look up his tax records. He's clean. He makes decent money at the school. No children, but he's on his second wife. The wife is a history teacher at the same school. He has a nice quiet life. Probably a lovely cabin somewhere in the mountains. Doesn't that sound just perfect?

Obituary from a month ago? What? I look through the posting and the photograph. Yes, it's him. Died in a motor vehicle accident. I google the date and the location and read the newspaper article.

"A three-car fatal crash Thursday evening at Hawkins Avenue and Tillery Street was caused by a

drunk driver, Charlotte Police Department Capt. Reynolds said. The driver has been identified as Steven D. Moss, a resident of Charlotte, most recently a counselor at a private school. He was pronounced deceased at the scene of the accident."

Another disappointment. Another name I can't cross off my list. The day he told me the rape would go into my pre-med file and taint my medical school admission is clear in my mind. As is his face when he ordered me to write an essay from the perspective of my rapist. And the memories of my dad's dreams of wanting to see me as a doctor. I promised him I'd make it into medical school. I failed him. No, I didn't fail him. I was set up to fail. I wasn't given a fair chance.

And neither were the people he killed on the day he got drunk and got in his car. I need to have perspective. At least I'm not dead. I'm still here, fighting. There are people dead because of this man. I don't read the rest of the article. I don't have the heart to learn who his other victims were.

When I get home, I collapse on the couch in exhaustion. It hasn't been a good day at all. Nothing has gone my way. The two people who convinced me the sexual assault was my fault are either dead or with the evidence against them now burned up.

Sophie is out again. I'm starting to worry who she keeps going out with. She's never been this secretive before about her boyfriends. We've always met them, and she's preferred to spend time with them at the house, playing video games, eating pizza. Maybe it's just that she is older? What would I know about an almost eighteen-year-old dating? When I was her age, I worked all the time.

Aidan comes in, takes off his coat, and sits next to me. He listens to my day of failures, wraps me in his arms, and rubs my shoulders. "I'm sorry it's been so unsuccessful today. Would you like a glass of wine?"

"Yes, I think it might help. I feel so wound up, yet so tired."

"You've been going without sleep and rest for days. You need to try to relax a bit, sweetheart. I know you're upset about this, but we still need to finish what we started here with Avias."

"You know what stinks, Aidan? Richard is not the main person I'm angry with. Yes, he was the main one who hurt me physically. But the thing is, when he hurt me—he didn't even care who I was. I was a nameless victim to him. But everyone else I went to for help at the college—they knew my name, they heard my story, they knew exactly who I was and what kind of high-achieving student I was. And they still chose to blame me for what happened rather than him, and they chose to force me to leave rather than help me. All because they wanted money for their stadium. I was disposable. And that makes them worse than him, don't you think?"

"They hurt you mentally. And sometimes that's worse than physically. I get you."

"Right." I take a glass of wine from him.

"It's like when I was bullied at school," Aidan says, sitting down next to me. "I didn't mind the guys who pushed me, but I really minded the ones who said stuff to me every day. That's what really got under my skin."

"Absolutely. The physical stuff I recovered from. It's the other things that come with rape: blaming yourself, feeling worthless, helpless. And Julianna Barrow was the counselor who could have helped take it all away, but she didn't. She made it worse, on purpose. She chose money over ethics. That's why I'm so angry with her."

The doorbell rings, and Aidan goes to answer the door while I sip more of the wine. "Hey!" I hear him exclaim.

"Dana." I give her a hug. "So sorry I got Lori stuck in the snowstorm."

"No worries. I need a break from her once in a while. The girls and I had a lovely time." She sits down on a bar stool. "I come bearing gifts."

I laugh. "All right. Let's see."

She digs around in her purse, pulls out an envelope, and hands it to me.

I feel something hard inside and open it. It's a flash drive. My heart beats fast in excited anticipation.

Her smile is infectious. "Plug it in."

Aidan and Dana follow me to my office as I plug it in. "How did you get this?" I exclaim.

"Turns out I knew a researcher over at Winslow. He was just part time with them. But he had access to the files, and that's all we needed. This arrived today. He called me this afternoon to make sure I got it. He said he's convinced someone from the administration started the fire. And he was darn sure it was started in the research storage. He went to lunch and, when he returned, it was all filled with smoke in the basement, but there was no smoke yet anywhere else."

"Dana, this is incredible. We are so grateful to you," Aidan says.

"Happy to help. We're all working together on exposing these people, aren't we? Listen, Lori knows someone at the Joint Commission. We can also file a complaint with the FDA and the Department of Health and Human Services."

"I think we may also want to find an attorney who might take on the cases of the involuntary commitments."

"You can't release the names to him, though, can you?"

"No, but I can find every one of these names and pay the families a visit and tell them what's going on. Still a violation of their privacy, but I have a feeling that, once they learn of a lawsuit, they might not mind so much."

Aidan rubs his forehead. "Is it a privacy violation that we have a list of their names?"

"No, because it's a research study our company runs with them. We technically have authorization to look at the names," Dana says. "Just not hunt them down at their homes."

"I'll ask the attorney," I say.

****

A week later, I drive back to Pat's Diner, give the waitress the attorney's name, and explain the lawsuit that she and her son Sammy can join. She cries as she hugs me and gives me five addresses of people who have been forced into research participation just like her Sammy. I drive house to house and provide phone numbers they can call for help.

When I finally arrive home, I'm exhausted, but my heart feels lighter.

Chapter 31

I return to my office from an R&D meeting to hushed whispers. Janet tiptoes to me. Her face is flushed.

"What's the matter in here?" Not a fan of surprises at the moment.

She points at the closed door of my office. "She's in there," she whispers.

"Who is in there?" I'm about to lose my patience.

"Abigail Davis." She giggles. "I'm making her a latte. Vicky ran out for soy milk."

Oh, no. Not the best idea, Abby. This isn't D.C. You showing up is a big deal.

I lunge for the door as I glare at Janet. "Don't tell anyone else, and hurry with the coffee. One for me as well."

"Abby, how did you find me?" I ask.

"You are not exactly a secret person." Abby laughs. She's in a bright pink sleeveless dress, completely inappropriate for the frigid weather outside. She is typing away on her laptop on one side of my desk, her shoes kicked off. "Sorry, I just have to finish this email."

I stand awkwardly at my end of the desk. Do I give her a hug? Then she closes her laptop, runs over to me, and hugs me tightly.

"So good to see you in person again after all these

phone calls! I was on location just a few minutes away from here, so I thought I'd pop in."

"Of course. That makes sense," I say. Like she has nothing else to do.

Janet comes in with two coffees and sets them down. "Anything else I can get for you?"

"This will be all." I lock the door as she leaves and turn to Abby.

"So you are filming your show here? For how long?"

"Filming an interview today and tomorrow morning. But I only had free time today. And barely. More like half an hour. My car is waiting outside. I need to tell you something important."

"Oh, yeah?" I sip the hot coffee and wince. Soy milk is terrible.

"I have a friend at the *Pennsylvania Times*. He found me the phone number for the assistant coach who worked at Westview with Coach Turner. This guy was fired when he tried to talk to the media a few years ago about some of the allegations against the football team, the Westview Wolves. Apparently he was, at the time, very eager to tell his story to someone."

"And he is willing to tell it to us?"

"I don't know. He was, back then. According to Mike, this guy will talk to anyone. So here is the plan. We will talk to him. I am media. I represent KIPT, after all. We'll see if he has a good story for us. And then Mike will interview him in more detail and will decide if the story is good enough for print."

"Why don't we let Mike handle it?" I don't want to admit it, but I'm nervous.

"I want to hear what this man has to say first. I've

had him verified, so I know he's a good source. But I want to make sure the story is what we're looking for. I want this to blow up. Some of these MeToo stories haven't been large enough."

I sit down. "That's some great work on your part, Abby."

"That's what I do. So you want to call him?"

"What, now?"

"I only have a few minutes." She punches his number into my speaker phone before I have a chance to say anything.

I grab a notepad and pen. My heart is bursting out of my rib cage as the phone rings. Did I know this assistant coach? Not possible. It's been too long.

"Hello," a male voice comes in.

"Mr. Kenner, this is Ms. Davis with KIPT News. I was given your number by a reporter at the *Pennsylvania Times*. He said you might be willing to talk to me about some things that have been going on with the Westview football program."

I hold my breath. There is silence on the phone. It lasts so long I wonder if he hung up. Abby and I look at each other. She opens her mouth and is about to say something, when his voice comes back.

"I don't know if I want to ever talk about this again."

Abby breathes a sigh of relief and I wipe the sweat off my forehead. "Look, Mr. Kenner," Abby says. "I absolutely understand how difficult it must be for you that this topic is brought up again. I assure you, this time we are not just loosely talking about this. We mean to bring this out into the media for certain. And not for a day. For forever. We are going to make you look like a hero, and you'll have a choice of jobs. You will be bringing light to an important issue, and Turner will be fired."

"I don't want to be in the center of a media circus," he says gruffly.

"That's fine. But maybe the reason you came to the media in the first place was because you wanted some justice, some fairness for what you saw was happening. How about we make sure that happens this time around?"

"How do you know that it will?"

"I assure you I have the power to make it happen now."

I look at Abby's face, and I believe her. I know she will make this happen. And I can feel very strongly that Mr. Kenner on the other end of the line believes her too. My heart glows with hope.

"Fine, what do you want to know?" he asks.

Abby opens her laptop again. I hear the clicking of the keyboard. "Thank you so much, Mr. Kenner. Can we begin by you telling us what were your concerns with Head Coach Turner's handling of the football program at Westview?"

Does she have questions typed up? I peek around the screen, and she does. I put down my yellow pad and pen and just listen.

"Well, you have to understand that when Turner was hired, he inherited a football program that was failing. The Wolves didn't have a winning season since the '80s, not even a mention of going to the playoffs or any of the Bowls. Then we get Turner, and the year after he arrives he recruits this star quarterback, Richard Stolar."

I raise my head, and Abby puts her index finger to her lips. I bite on my fingernails.

He continues, "We begin to win, and the Wolves set records that the school has never seen before. Then we have one of the best seasons in Westview's history."

"Was it all because of the quarterback, or were there other talented players as well?" Abby asks.

"It had something to do with Ed Turner being a good coach and something to do with the money we paid to the kids we recruited to the team. Turner went around the country and picked out the best players. He gave them money—good money—to come to Westview."

"You mean scholarships? Tuition, books, dorms, that sort of thing?"

"Oh, no. I mean actual cash. We kept a ledger back then. Two thousand, four thousand, five thousand. Called them travel expenses for the kids to come visit. But it was straight cash. He'd hand it to them in an envelope. All of this approved by the administration. They wanted the best team."

"But"—Abby looks at me—"this is illegal, right?"

"Of course it is. No one cared. The kids took the money and came to the school. The trustees got their team."

"Is that all it took? Just the right team, then?"

"That and the steroids."

My head pops up again. Abby gives me the two thumbs up. I begin to pace the office. My body vibrates with nervous energy. This is exactly the information we've been looking for.

"Can you tell me more about the steroids? Who knew about the steroid use?"

"All the coaches did. And the administration. A few of our offensive linemen were underweight, so Turner brought in Stanozolol injections. We tried to bulk them up with food and training, but it wasn't working. The injections got them those extra thirty pounds in no time. Then some of the other players asked for it. And Turner would inject them. Mainly right before the big games."

"Wait, isn't there drug testing? Didn't anyone notice they were gaining weight rapidly?"

"Yeah, they noticed, but that's what everyone wanted them to do. And drug testing is done when the coach doesn't want the players to use steroids."

"Oh, I see, this was coach sanctioned, so no need to test. Do you think the Wolves are still using steroids now?"

"I'm sure they are. They continue to win. And if you watch these players all season as I do, you can see them grow at least twenty pounds in a few months. All muscle, too. The leagues do require doping tests now, but the student is not always suspended if he's found using. Sometimes they just have to miss a game. Also, colleges will test for marijuana and then report that they drug-tested the kids. You don't have to report that you specifically tested for steroids."

"Thank you, Mr. Kenner. I got all this down. Anything else you were concerned about when you were with the team?"

He is quiet for a bit. Then he starts again, his voice quiet. "The trustees held a campaign for a new football stadium, and we raised, like, several hundred million dollars, and it drew all these people to the school who were so proud to go to this place now, because of its stadium and the athletics." He pauses.

I feel ill. I can feel the blood draining from my face. Abby doesn't notice. She keeps clicking away.

"So we hire more coaches, and we are all instructed to build a recruitment program. And Turner tells us to do whatever it takes to get these kids in. If they have the skills, we must have them. So we bring alcohol and…drugs. And then Turner—he tells the freshman football guys to bring freshman girls, and he says that if they want to stay on the team…they have to let the new recruits have sex with them. We get these girls liquored up, we close the doors, and we pretend not to hear what happens."

Abby stops typing and looks at me. I nod to her. I hold my throat to stop myself from vomiting, but I won't stop him from talking. We must continue.

"Sometimes the girl would pass out and then two, three guys would go at her. I would just let her sleep it off then. Better for her not to know what happened right away. Many of them didn't remember much of it."

"But some did," Abby interrupts.

"Yes, they did," he confirms. "Some would try to go to the police. One of the detectives was married to Turner's sister," he says. "He took the girls' statements and shredded the files or wrote that there was no evidence. When he retired, a few girls managed to get charges filed, but the university just settled with them."

"Anything else?" Abby asks.

"No, that's it. When will you run this story?"

"I have to verify all this information, Mr. Kenner, and then I will give you a call and let you know when it will run and where."

"All right."

"Goodbye."

Abby hangs up, and we look at each other. I try to smile, but it's difficult. She stands up, comes around the desk, and gives me a hug. "We have some good information."

"What are you talking about? It's great information. Just really difficult to hear it from him."

"Steroid use. I should've suspected."

"Me too. Richard was huge. He's half the size now. Why didn't I think of that?"

"There is a lot to this story. I'll get people working on it."

"So you think your guy at the *Times* will print it?"

"I'm sure he will. How will he not? We got steroid use, recruitment bribes, gang rapes. And I'm throwing all this into his lap, with a verified source."

"I don't want my name in the newspaper."

"No need. We have many others." She packs up her laptop. "Sorry, I have to run."

I hug her goodbye and watch her leave. I hear excited whispers outside my office after she leaves.

Did all this just happen?

Chapter 32

The story about the Westview Wolves' recruitment practices, steroid abuse, and endorsement of sexual abuse by the coaches runs in the *Pennsylvania Times* two weeks later. Richard is not named in the article. I asked them to keep his name out; we don't need him on alert. Mike also kept his word and didn't mention my name. Abigail Davis is mentioned several times, however.

At first, the rest of the media takes no notice. It's silent for about a week. And then a parallel story appears in the *Philadelphia Inquirer*. The major outlets pick it up shortly. Before long, Abby does a report on her show, and all the major news shows are blasting it 24/7. I cry as I hear her speak for the victims. And I am so happy for her.

Turner is fired by Westview. He gives a newspaper interview saying, "The fuss will pass, and I'll be promptly reinstated." When this doesn't happen, he sues Westview for libel and conspiracy. He claims he's been used as a scapegoat and names Dean Scott as one of his accomplices. Dean Scott is suspended by the trustees, pending an investigation. I read in the Sunday paper that the proceedings for stripping him of his tenure have begun. It will take some time, however.

Several lawsuits are filed by major law firms against Turner, the university, and the police department. Multiple victims join the lawsuits. I don't. My name can't be out there. I'm satisfied with what has happened, but I must finish what I started.

It's not enough. Richard hasn't yet paid for what he's done.

****

"Are you avoiding me?" Richard asks as we enter the conference room for the quarterly meeting.

I straighten up and face the enemy. "Not at all, Richard. Were you looking for me?"

"You've been blowing me off for several days now. Your secretary keeps canceling our meetings."

His face looks irritated, and his eyes are baggy. His hair is no longer nicely sleeked back. He is tired, worn out. He hasn't been sleeping well, I deduce. We are finally getting to him. Is it the news from Westview? Or something with Parozex? Or maybe he finally discovered that Shannon is a lying bitch.

I shake away my thoughts. "Sorry, it's been one crisis after another. What do you need?"

"Obviously, we need your marketing plans for Parozex."

"I have those all ready. I'll present a preliminary plan and budget at today's meeting, and we can go over the details whenever you'd like." My voice is sickeningly sweet. I'm honestly impressed with myself. I don't have a good marketing strategy. I have a piss of a marketing strategy. It will give us no profit whatsoever. But that's the plan.

"Do you know anyone at the FDA besides Rawley?" Richard asks as people begin to enter the conference room and sit down.

"What? No, I don't think so. We had one contact at

the FDA before, but I think she's left."

"I don't think he has our best interests at heart."

"Jeffrey Rawley has never been known for having anyone's best interests at heart but his own."

Richard looks at me with narrowed eyes. I stare straight back at him. It's the truth. He knows it. Jeff is a weasel.

"We are having a problem with Parozex. There's a CDER committee member speaking out against the drug and its fast-track approval. I need to deal with him."

"What do you mean 'deal with him'?"

"Have a talk with him. His boss. See if I can change his mind. See if we can offer him some consulting fees. Maybe sponsor a trip overseas. I checked him out, and he hasn't been to an international conference in a while. Can you help me arrange for that through the CME marketing budget?"

I think through this for a while. Why is he telling me all this? Doesn't he worry about me knowing the truth about his bribery? Maybe he's so far into this lying he doesn't even care.

"Yes, I can add this to the CME budget."

My mind works furiously through this. I write down different ideas during the meeting, trying to figure this out. Aidan makes faces at me, and I give him looks to leave me alone. Richard nods during my marketing presentation, and I ignore him.

I pull Aidan and Dana into my office. "Richard told me he's having FDA trouble with Parozex, and he wants me to help him bribe someone else at the FDA to get the drug approved."

"He told you that?" Dana's eyes are large as

teacups.

"What kind of games is he playing now?" Aidan sets his laptop down with a bang.

"I don't know. I need your opinion. Why would he admit to this? To me of all people. He knows I hate him. He knows I've sabotaged the drug before. Why tell me?"

"He's testing you," Aidan says. "To see if you'll sabotage the drug again. Then he'll know for sure to get rid of you."

"That has to be it."

"You'll have to play along," Dana says.

"I can't just do that."

"You have no choice, sweetheart."

"We can't simply let him have whatever he wants. I'm not letting him win."

"We'll find a way to make this work. Don't worry." Aidan opens his laptop. "I'm making a note to look into his spending. Maybe I can find records of any other bribes he's made recently."

"Fine. I'll go along with it." I huff. "God knows, fighting him openly has never worked for me."

"Just hold on for a little while longer." Aidan gives me a kiss and takes off.

"I'm so sorry." Dana gives me a hug and leaves as well.

I open my laptop and think through this. So Richard wants to test me, does he? How can I make him think I'm on Avias' side, yet keep Parozex from getting on the market? I can talk to Jeff again and see what his thoughts are about this. My guess is Richard already knows Jeff is useless to him and that's why he is playing me like this. Son of a bitch! He wants me to bribe someone else. I look through the FDA open records and find the list of CDER committee members.

Against my better judgment, I call Jeff.

"Oh, good," he says. "I was planning to get in touch. My boss is pulling me off the approvals. I think Richard knows."

"He knows. He talked to me this morning and said he doesn't quite trust you."

"Well, not much I can do about that, can I?"

"You could've done a lot about that. How did he figure out that you didn't want the drug to be approved?"

"I wrote a recommendation against it."

"You have to be more clever than that." I groan. "Talk to other committee members. Point out the side effects data. Point out that the drug doesn't work any better than the other antipsychotics on the market. You ruined this, Jeff."

I shouldn't be mad at him. Why did I expect anything of him in the first place? I knew he was useless.

"Look, I tried, all right? I did talk to other committee members, and Dr. Thomas also wrote a recommendation against the drug. There are a few other people who are on the fence. I did all I could. You don't understand how things work here."

"Well, Richard wants me to bribe your Dr. Thomas now."

Jeff whistles. "He doesn't give up, does he? I'm not sure Thomas can be bribed that easily. He has that whole integrity thing that the rest of us don't."

"If I chose to bribe him, how would I do it?"

"You'll do what Richard asked? Why?"

"Because if I don't, he'll know I'm working against him."

"Oh, I get you." He is silent for a moment. "Well, Thomas has never been to Hawaii and he has teens. I bet they'd like to go surfing. Send him to Hawaii for spring break. He's been talking about how his wife resents the weather here."

"Who else on the committee is on the side of writing against Parozex?"

"Simonsen, Martin, and Gale are somewhat on the fence."

"All right. That's helpful. Thanks."

I'm about to hang up, when Jeff calls out, "Wait, are you okay with our kids dating?"

"What?" I pop out of my chair.

"You didn't know? Ben's been talking about your daughter quite a bit. I thought you knew."

"You must be mistaken. Sophie isn't dating anyone." I suddenly remember, however, Aidan telling me about seeing Sophie with a new boy. How could she? What the hell is she thinking?

"I assure you they are dating. They've gone out three or four times, at least. I'm sorry you didn't know. I'll talk to Benjamin about that."

"It's not your fault. My daughter didn't say anything. I have to go."

"I understand."

I leave the office and hurry to Sophie's school. Fear and anger are churning violently in my stomach. I park and find her car. It's not locked. I search through the glove compartment, all the door pockets, then come out and get in the trunk. I'm not sure what I'm looking for. Evidence? I find nothing.

I pace outside the car, hoping to calm the storm inside me, but it's useless. I'm so frustrated that she would betray me like this. As I see groups of kids begin to leave the school, I brace myself for our conversation. I must not snap at her. This must be productive. I have to get her to see reason in what I'm saying.

"What are you doing?" She sets her backpack on the ground as she approaches.

"I'd like to ask you the same question."

"I don't know what you mean." She looks around nervously, worried I'm about to embarrass her as her classmates approach the parking lot.

I can't play games. I don't want to play games. "You've been dating Benjamin Rawley."

The panic in her eyes is rewarding. For a second. I want to shake her, make her understand.

"What are you doing, Sophie? He's a bad kid."

"He is not a bad kid, Mom. I knew you'd be like this. That's why I didn't tell you. He is kind and sweet and romantic."

"What is wrong with you?" I gasp. "He is the child of two of my dire enemies. People who betrayed me." I bite my tongue. I can't tell her exactly whose child he is.

"He had nothing to do with it. He is not his parents. Whatever you have going on between you and his parents, leave him out of it!" she yells as she paces between the cars. "You have no idea how much damage you've done to him with those pictures at the police station."

"You took those pictures. It was your idea."

"I know. But he can never know this. Promise me," she pleads, coming closer.

"Oh, God, Sophie, what is happening with you? One minute you're on my side, helping me. The next minute you pick up a kid who's drinking and doing drugs and getting in trouble. His parents are a mess. His family life is a nightmare. What are you thinking?"

"You don't know him like I do. His parents may be a mess, but he is nothing like his parents. And he is very hurt by his father's rejection of him. He loves his dad. It's not his fault his mom slept with someone else. He doesn't even know who his real father is."

I'm so tempted to tell her. But it's wrong. I know it's wrong to pull Sophie into this mess I've created. I need time to untangle all this. I think fast. She's leaving for NYU soon. She'll forget all about him. If I tell her to stop seeing him, she'll never listen. She'll do it more. But—Richard's son. The pain of this hits me so hard, I nearly double over.

"What's wrong? You're very pale, Mom." Sophie touches my shoulder.

"It's worry, Sophie. When you are a mother, you'll understand."

"Who says I'll be a mother?"

"You will be. But I hope it's not anytime soon." Oh, God, Richard's grandchildren… "Are you having sex with him?" I gasp in horror.

"Stop looking at me like that! No, I'm not. And I wouldn't tell you if I did."

"You can't have sex with him, baby. Please don't." My face is wet now. The tears keep rolling.

"Okay, Mom, just relax. You're making a scene." She looks around. "My friends will see you. I have a reputation here."

"Get in the car."

"Fine."

I take out tissues from my purse and blow my nose. I have to tell her. There is no other choice.

"Are you better now? I'm not like in love with him or anything. But I have the right to date whoever I want," Sophie begins.

"Listen to me very carefully." I turn to her. "Ben's real father is Richard Stolar, the man you helped me look up. The man I've tried to get revenge against. The man having an affair with Ben's mother. The reason I want revenge against him is that he raped me when we were in college together. Brutally. I nearly died. He was never punished for what he did to me. And neither was Ben's mother, who set me up to get attacked by him. This is who you are dating."

Sophie is quiet. It's dead silent in the car until I blow my nose again.

"Does Ben know any of this?" she asks.

"How would he know? He doesn't even know Richard is his father."

"He is not his parents," she whispers.

"I know. I also need you to know what kind of family you are dealing with. They are not good people. You've grown up around kind people. These are evil people."

"I'm sorry this happened to you, Mom." She turns her face to me. Her eyes are watery. "I will think about it. I don't know what I want to do yet."

"Come here." I pull her in for a hug.

It feels good to hold her after a fight. I can't remember the last time we fought. But I can't get all mushy. I will keep my anger to go after Richard. Especially now that I know his son tried to go after my daughter. I want all of this done with. I need to keep Sophie away from these people. Enough of all this. We need to move. And soon.

Before anything else happens.

Chapter 33

I head to Dana's office with a new plan. I must convince her. It's urgent now.

"We got the FDA approval this morning." Dana looks up from the papers on her desk.

"I read the email."

"Did you hear?" Aidan walks in behind me.

"Yes," I say. "We knew it was coming. Avias paid Thomas well. He should arrive in Hawaii this afternoon."

"I have the information on how much we paid him. And how much we paid everyone else. We should be able to do something with that."

"I want to wrap this up quickly," I say. "We can't keep dragging this out. Enough. This has taken much longer than I anticipated. I want it over with, Aidan." I stand by the window and look out at the busy highway below.

"I'm not happy with it simply being over. I want the drug taken off the market," Dana says.

"I'll get it off the market, Dana. And then Aidan and I will get out of here."

"What are you talking about?" Dana asks and walks over to me.

"I know how we can wrap this up quickly." I look at both. I hope they can see the certainty and resolve in my face. "I will do a marketing campaign, but not the one Richard wants or thinks I am doing. A slightly altered one. It will violate the FDA rules and it will flag the drug to the FDA for investigation. It will go to the Office of Prescription Drug Promotion. I checked, and Richard doesn't know anyone there. He can't bribe his way through."

"You are going to do what?" Aidan says, his mouth gaping.

"FDA has all these rules with which advertising has to comply. If you violate these, the OPDP has a Bad Ad Program, and our marketing will get filed with them. They issue us warning letters, then make us send letters to physicians admitting we are advertising falsely."

"But mainly, FDA will be forced to look closely at the drug this time," Dana says.

"Maybe the OPDP will even send it to the Advisory Committee and they'll notice the previous data on the side effects," I say.

"Sometimes they issue a request for an independent panel of researchers to review the data." Dana sits back in her chair and makes notes.

"Now you see it?" I ask Aidan.

"But your career will take a fall if you produce a false marketing campaign," Aidan says. "Everyone in the industry will know it was you."

"It will be worth it to see Richard and Avias fail."

"Maybe there's another way," Dana says.

"I don't see one. Do you really think I mind?"

"What if Richard or someone from Avias's marketing notices you are advertising incorrectly?"

"I know how to do this cleverly. I've been doing this for over ten years. And I'll make sure that only some of the ads are in violation, not all of them. Especially not the ones that Richard sees."

"I need to think about this," Aidan says. "It seems like such a drastic solution."

I wrap my arms around his neck and kiss him. "I know what I'm doing. For the first time since I started this, I know exactly what I'm doing. Trust me. Let's get this over with and move on with our lives. I need to."

"Why don't you put some ideas together and run them by me? Then I'll think if I am on board with this," Aidan says, taking my arms off his neck.

It takes me the rest of the day to finalize the sample advertising portfolio for this failing campaign. It's harder than I expected to plan ads that break rules just slightly, just enough to raise a red flag. We need to be in violation of all the FDA rules, though. First, we'll fail to send the required marketing form and sample promotional materials. Forget to include Form FDA-2253. That should get us an immediate warning, and we'll get flagged to be closely monitored.

I will need to ensure the visibility of the ads. Maybe some billboards. Public transportation. TV stations. All the conferences coming up in March. CME talks. This will take some time. I'll get my entire marketing team on it. Tell them it's a priority. Richard will surely approve, because he believes the drug will make him super wealthy.

How to craft the ads is a challenge. Off-label marketing would be the easiest. I can put a kid on a few ads. It's against the FDA rules to market the drug to the population it wasn't studied on. This will be a major violation, and we'll get in trouble for this.

I draw a prototype of an ad—a teen riding on a

skateboard, smiling. Another group of teens watching him. I have the wrong pitch all ready for the campaign. *"Return to the fun of life, forget you ever had hallucinations. Parozex is the only drug to help you fully enjoy your life again."* Risks in tiny invisible letters on the bottom. Minimize risks and overstate benefits. Breaking three rules in one ad.

This is a good start, and it will be enough to get us the Dear Doctor letter which will make the drug's stock plummet. No one will want to prescribe it after that. More importantly, these types of deceptive ads are done all the time by other pharmaceutical companies. My reputation won't suffer if I do this. I'll get a slap on the back from my colleagues, if anything.

I show these ideas to Aidan in the evening, as Sophie helps with the dishes. He is quiet for a while.

"What about the *US v. Caronia*?"

"How do you know about that?"

"Everyone in pharma knows about that. It was huge when it happened."

"It hasn't made the FDA change its advertising rules. It was one case, and the free speech argument will not always hold up."

"The fact is, since that case, it's been possible to get away with promoting off-label use of an FDA-approved drug."

"Fine. So maybe this ad won't get us into trouble. Although I think you are totally wrong."

Aidan rolls his eyes. I try to pull my portfolio out of his hands, but he pulls it back, and I fall on top of him.

"Stop it." I laugh as he tickles me. "We have to finish discussing this."

"There is nothing to discuss," he says, placing the portfolio on the coffee table. "Go for it. I already called the headhunters and told them I need a new job. We'll get the house ready for the market, Sophie will graduate in June, and we could be out of Great Falls and off to a new life."

"I so badly want us to have a fresh start." I place my head on his chest.

He strokes my hair. "So do I. So do I."

****

The first letter from the FDA arrives about two weeks later. Janet runs into my office. "A Warning Letter from the FDA just got faxed over."

"Let me see."

The letter is addressed to me and cc'd to Richard. Crap!

"Janet, can you call Richard's assistant and make sure she doesn't show him the letter? I need to fix this before he sees it."

"No problem."

I scan the contents of the three-page letter.

"We have received a report of your promotional materials misbranding a drug... Both your product webpage and the exhibit panels fail to communicate information about the drug's side effects...potentially life-threatening risks associated with the drug. OPDP requests that Avias immediately cease misbranding Parozex... You must cease introducing the misbranded drug into interstate commerce. Please submit a written response stating your intent to comply... The violations above are serious...volatile promotional materials."

Okay, then. "*Volatile promotional materials.*" I can screw up an advertising campaign quite well.

My desk phone rings, and I stare at it in surprise. No one ever calls this phone. I touch the speaker button.

"Emma," I answer.

"I assume you got the letter?" Richard's voice is a shock.

"What letter?" Damn it, Janet.

"The FDA Warning Letter about Parozex."

"No, I didn't get it. What do they have a problem with, exactly?"

"Failure to submit under Form FDA-2253, it says here."

"What?" I look through the faxes on my desk. Was there another letter?

"It says the FDA regulations require each marketing submission to be accompanied by a completed Form FDA-2253. This form has to include a copy of the promotional materials."

"Oh, yes. It's the Transmittal of Advertisements and Promotional Labeling for Drugs for Human Use form. I did submit it to them," I lie. "They probably lost it. Usual government bureaucracy. I will send them another set of materials. Don't worry."

"Don't worry? Don't worry?" He gets louder. "We are to shut down the drug sales until we fix this."

"It's a very easy fix. Won't take me more than a day." I make my voice light and convincing.

"Fine. But this is highly negligent of you. Send them extra information this time. A comprehensive plan of action on how you'll do truthful marketing."

"No problem."

"The fate of this company depends on you."

Your fate depends on me, Richard. I want to say this so badly, but, of course, I don't.

I hang up and look through the paperwork on my desk. Did I miss the fax about the 2253? I can't find it anywhere. They wouldn't have sent it just to Richard. Then I find it. I need to pay more attention to these. I can't let Richard get his hands on them.

I walk over to Janet. "We are in a bit of trouble with the FDA over some ads. I need you to do me a huge favor."

"Sure, anything."

"If there are any faxes or any other communication from the FDA, please immediately get my attention. Also, please make sure they don't get to Richard's eyes."

She smiles. "No problem."

I'm lucky to have Janet. She's been with me for ten years.

Another letter arrives in two days, explaining our TV ad was in violation of the law and we are required to immediately remove the ad from all the TV channels until it's fixed. That was fast—I'll give it to them.

But they are still allowing me to get away with these ads. I will need to come up with a final strike against us.

Against myself.

Chapter 34

Dana and I eat lunch in my office and discuss the next step.

"It needs to be something really awful," I say.

"Can we just put down all the side effects in really big letters and have that be the focus of the campaign?" Dana asks.

"That does nothing to the drug's reputation. You know there are all these huge moneymakers on TV that say they will cause death or suicidal ideation, and docs are still prescribing them to their patients every day. Patients ignore side effects information. So does the FDA."

"What if we get a speaker to talk about the side effects at CMEs?"

"Possibly, but that will not get us into trouble with the FDA."

"Okay, another idea. Parozex is a third-generation antipsychotic. It does have some promise. It has no extrapyramidal or anticholinergic side effects that are so typical of first and second-generation antipsychotics. Normally, you'd want someone with a great reputation to talk about it at CMEs. What if you get someone who has a poor reputation?"

"A spokesperson who is a fake."

"Exactly."

"We call them KOLs. Key Opinion Leaders. Like a

psychiatrist, who'd go to conferences and tell all his buddies that this is the best antipsychotic for patients."

"Yes. But get someone no one would trust."

I sit still, almost paralyzed with the thought. "What if—this is so wild—what if we use Litvak, the Winslow guy, if he still hasn't been arrested? He's being sued for all these involuntary commitments. If his colleagues know and find him generally despicable, wouldn't he be a perfect spokesperson right now for this purpose? And it's likely he's badly in want of money."

"He's perfect for this."

I search Litvak to make sure he hasn't been arrested yet, and I see that his license has been placed on probation. Even better. A doctor who is not even allowed to practice medicine. Maybe we could place him on one of the TV ads. In his lab coat. And then have an anonymous report to the Bad Ad Program at the OPDP.

I feel outright devious as I write down his name on an email. I feel a smile form on my face, and there is true joy spreading through my chest. For the first time in a long while I feel I'm close to ending all of this and going on with my life.

A week later, I read the next FDA letter, smiling, relishing the words inside. Someone at the Psychiatry for Primary Care Physicians Conference in Punta Cana raised a concern that our spokesperson showed slides with questionable data and discussed off-label use. The FDA has also become aware that our spokesperson has had his license revoked. We are to replace Dr. Litvak and pull our marketing materials until they are corrected.

I write an email to get Litvak fired as the

spokesperson and sit back in my chair. Now I need to come up with one more strike against us. My insides are knotted painfully as I go on to the next step in ruining my reputation. I will come up with something that will get the FDA guys to schedule an emergency hearing.

It takes all night, but I put together a new portfolio. False advertising claims. The markups look great.

"When you live with symptoms of psychosis, it's not easy to find a drug that works as well as Parozex."

"Parozex helped 75% of patients in a recent clinical study."

"Five out of six patients with hallucinations agree Parozex is the best drug they've ever tried!"

"Parozex is the first drug to finally control your symptoms of schizophrenia."

Each of these should work. I'll put them up on the web, do posters at a conference. Early in the morning I email my team to go ahead with the new promotional materials. The new materials will not have any side-effects data on them at all. I hope my team members don't question me. If they do, I'll say we are trying a new aggressive strategy to stay competitive, Richard's orders.

I'm barely able to work for the next few days. I have a TV ad running in three states in the evenings, with side effects listed in tiny font and false advertising claims.

Jeff calls three days after the new ads run. "What are you doing?"

"Drinking my coffee?"

"You know what I mean."

"I don't, actually."

"Emma, I heard about your ads. You are about to receive notice to issue a Dear Doctor letter."

I nearly jump up with glee. "Well, that's unfortunate," I say. "Are you sure about that?"

"I saw the notice. You know he'll fire you for this."

"I expect he will. I didn't see any other way, Jeff."

"I was trying to find another way. I just needed more time."

"I'm out of time. I want to finish this. And this seems to be the fastest way."

"For your career to take the fall? You are so good at what you do."

"There's no other choice." I realize something. "How do you know what I do?"

He is quiet for a few seconds. "I've looked up some of your ad campaigns. They are well done. Not the Parozex one, though." He clears his throat.

"Let it fall. All right?"

"What if it doesn't fall? What if you have thousands of patients requesting this drug now from their doctors, and then they get ill or die, all because of your marketing claims? Have you thought of that?"

Worry invades my body. What if he's right? What if people fall for my claims? I haven't thought of this at all.

"What if a child is given your medication?" he pushes.

I stumble through what to say. He is right, of course. "Help me get the black box warning, then."

"That never stops anything. We've had the black box on arthritis drugs and on antidepressants and patients still beg for them."

"Then what do I need to do? I want this drug to be

pulled. You know I do. I don't want anyone to get hurt from it. That's the point."

"Is it? Or are you so blinded by your hatred of Richard that you don't care about the cost in human lives?" he asks.

"How can you say that? You were the one who got the application for it approved in the first place."

"I know a woman at OPDP. I'll see what I can do." He hangs up.

The Warning Letter arrives quickly. I scan for the Dear Doctor language, but it's not there. What will it take? Do I have to say the drug cures cancer in 100% of people? At least the letter is stronger in language. It mentions us ignoring "significant health and safety concerns," minimizing "crucial risk information," and promoting Parozex for "unapproved new uses." My favorite paragraph, though, is this one:

"In previous letters we objected to your dissemination of promotional materials for Parozex which made unsubstantiated claims and lacked fair balance. Despite our prior written notification and despite your assurances, you have continued to engage in false or misleading promotion of Parozex. Your TV ads misbrand Parozex within the meaning of the Federal Food, Drug and Cosmetic Act (FD&C Act), and make its distribution a violation. This product is associated with several serious risks. The promotional materials fail to include important risk information associated with the drug. OPDP requests that you immediately cease violating the FD&C Act, as discussed above."

If that's not a threat, I don't know what is. So I'm close. One more thing, I think. I need to mess up one more thing. And then it will be enough for them. I have to hurry. Before Richard makes his money and before someone dies from this goddamn drug.

In the end, I decide to simply run the same ads they told me to pull. I send them to two major CME conferences and run more TV ads. And then I brace myself for what's to come next. And it comes. Jeff calls to tell me he spoke to someone.

"*Your product misrepresentation poses a serious threat to public health... You must immediately issue letters to physicians correcting the statements in your promotional materials and informing them of the risks associated with your product... Failure to correct the violations discussed above may result in FDA regulatory action, including seizure or injunction, without further notice.*"

Seizure or injunction. The most beautiful words I could read. That will work. So all I should do is *not* send the Dear Doctor letters. Or not send them to everyone.

"You are going to get named in a lawsuit," Aidan says, reviewing the letter for the second time. "You are required to send these to everyone. You have to comply with the FDA."

"It's the company that will get sued, not me. This happens all the time. Eli Lilly has been sued like this. Pfizer has been sued. It's not a big deal. I won't be named, and I'll probably be lauded for my aggressive marketing strategy."

"That's despicable."

"That's Big Pharma for you."

****

Richard storms into my office the day the Dear

Doctor letters are scheduled to go out. Or not go out. Because only some will. And the ones that will—the information will still not be quite accurate.

"This is highly disappointing, Emma. I'm pulling you off this project, and I'm having my old team at Avias handle the marketing from now on. When I came here, I thought you knew what you were doing, but clearly I was wrong. This is a major stain on our reputation. And yours. And it will cost the company thousands of dollars."

"These issues with marketing are very much anticipated with every new drug, Richard. Thousands of dollars is nothing for our budget. We will make millions with my aggressive marketing."

I can see he is thinking this through. Calculating. Wondering if I may be right.

"Avias's Senior Director of Marketing will be in touch with you. You will discuss your plans with him from now on. I'll check with Aidan on the profits, and then we'll see." He walks out of my office.

I breathe out in relief. Did he buy it? Well, of course he did. He hasn't seen the warning letters. I need to hurry and finish this.

Dana walks in as soon as he leaves.

"What did he want?"

"He knows about the Dear Doctor letters. He is pulling me off the promotions. Has someone from Avias supervising me now. But that's all right, because I am sabotaging the letters. That should get FDA pissed off enough."

"No need," she says.

"What do you mean?"

She sits down. "I've been thinking and thinking for

days about how to speed this up. What you've been doing—it's great, but it's too slow. There are people out there taking this drug. And more will take it watching your ads. I can't let this happen."

"I don't want it to happen either. I'm going as fast as I can, Dana."

"I was sitting in a meeting this morning when I realized we needed a whistleblower."

My blood runs frozen suddenly. "What?"

"When AstraZeneca got sued for Seroquel, it was because of a whistleblower. Same with Pfizer and Bextra. And Eli Lilly and Zyprexa."

"Dana…" I can't continue.

"I called it in. I told them everything. And I called a few newspapers."

"You will be fired!" I gasp.

"I have no desire to work here. I will take some time off. I have no need for money. I can't let this be on my conscience. Now you can move on."

"So you sacrificed yourself for me?"

"No, I did what my ethics told me to do. Helping you was a bonus."

"I love you, Dana. And your ethics." I hug her for a long time and a warm glow of hope lights up in my stomach. It's done. Parozex will fail. Avias will leave our lives. Richard will leave our lives. We can all finally move on.

Chapter 35

The first article about Avias came out this morning. It's not so much about Avias but more about several drug companies and their attempts, under the new regulations, to bring out "breakthrough" drugs that have significant side effects and no clear advantages over the older and safer drugs. I'm certain media frenzy will follow. Richard will have no choice but to disappear. Dana quit last night. I expect to be fired sometime this week. Aidan has a phone interview this afternoon.

I'm on edge for most of the morning. I scan the web for news articles repeatedly and wait. Richard is out of the office, in New York. But he won't be gone for long, I'm sure. Not once he hears.

I keep trying to focus on something else: What do I pick up for dinner tonight, what time did Aidan say his interview was, when are Dana and family coming for dinner? But I feel a constant sensation of a prickle on the back of my neck. That sensation of something awful that's about to happen. If only I knew what it was.

A text from Sophie arrives after lunch.

—Can you come home now? I am sick. XOXO—

I'm relieved to have an excuse to go home. Maybe this was the source of my anxiety. I can always tell when Sophie is sick. Even though I doubt she is really sick. She likely just wants to skip yet another pointless senior test. I quickly pack up my bag and grab my coat.

And then I stop and look at my phone again.

I read the message again.

She's never had to use it before, but "XOXO" is our code word for danger.

Fear spreads through my veins, freezing my body in terror. What does this mean? Come home. Is something terribly wrong at home? Has something horrific happened to her? To Cookie?

Then it hits me, and my heart begins to pound a million jolts a second. Sophie is trying to send me a message. But that means…

I don't finish the thought. I bolt out of my office, coat forgotten.

I call Aidan, but the call goes to voicemail. I leave a message. I call again. And leave another message.

The ride is agonizingly slow, even though I speed through every intersection. The cops better not stop me. I'll run them over.

I dial Eric, but he doesn't pick up either. The one time I need everyone to answer their goddamn phones… I leave him a message as well.

I arrive at home ten minutes later and park my car away from the house. It's likely futile. Whoever it is probably is watching my arrival through the window. I contemplate waiting a second, but then I change my mind. Every second might be important in saving my daughter's life. As I run up to the driveway, I stop and stare at the familiar black Jeep parked next to my house.

I'm going to kill Benjamin Rawley. And then Sophie. She swore to me she'd never see him again. I warned her. I pry the garage open just enough for me to sneak through. I stand on tiptoes to reach the box labeled "old paperwork, discard this year" from the top storage shelf. Inside is a gun case. I load the gun and place it in my pants pocket, then cover it with my sweater and jacket. I'm going to kill him if he's anything like his father. I don't give a damn that he's a child. If he's laid even a finger on my daughter, he is dead.

I rush to open the door, but when I enter the house, I'm struck by silence. It hurts my ears. I can't understand what's so disturbing about it until I see the body of my dog, prostrate in front of the couch, her tongue hanging out of her mouth. I fall to my knees in front of her and feel my heart bursting in sorrow.

"Don't make a spectacle," a voice says behind me.

I spin around, and I can't see for a moment through my tears. I rub my eyes, and then I see—Shannon.

"What have you done to my dog?" I rise and lunge for her, but she points a gun at me, and I step back, almost tripping over Cookie's body. I can feel the dog's suffering suddenly, and I nearly throw up. "And where is Sophie?" I whisper.

Terror icicles begin to grow in my chest. What was I thinking? How did I believe I could stop anyone on my own? But Aidan knows where we are. He'll come, surely. I sit down slowly on the couch and pretend to be calm. But there is a storm of fear inside me. Where is Aidan? Where is Sophie? Is she drugged? Is she alive?

"I promised Ben I wouldn't hurt her. My idiot son has feelings for her, apparently," she says, twisting her lips at the word "feelings." Shannon walks over to me, the gun still pointed in my direction. "I need your phone."

"Why?" I need to stretch time, so Aidan can trace

my location. If he got my message.

"Hand it over."

"Oh, I don't remember where it is." I begin to search through my purse. I do it slowly, checking every pocket, one by one, meticulously. "You have a really great kid. Why do you want to ruin his future?" I need to draw her into a conversation. Stretch time.

"Leave my kid out of this. Worry about yours."

I begin to regain my ability to think. Sophie is alive. And she may be all right. What does Shannon want, then? And where is Ben? His car is here. I need to keep talking to her until the police arrive.

"So did you recognize me when you met me that day, at the police station? I wasn't sure…"

"Would I have invited you to my house for a party if I remembered who you were?" She paces a bit, and I watch the gun point to the floor. "I thought we got rid of you for good twenty years ago. Richard should have. God knows I paid him enough to do it. I had no idea you'd be so much effort."

"You paid him?"

"Jeff was mine, you idiot. You weren't the one to date a Rawley, a nobody like you. You should've stayed where you belonged. I grew up with Jeff. We were supposed to get married. I had no plans to lose him to you."

"Don't you love Richard?"

"Richard had no prospects when I met him. Another nobody. People like me don't marry football players. He was a son of Croatian janitors. Do you think my parents would've allowed that? He was the joke of our high school. Did you know that? People used to leave mops in his seat and ask him to clean up their garbage."

"You went to high school with Richard? But how could he afford…" My head begins to spin.

"The school let him go for free, a charity case because of football and his parents cleaning for the school. He only got into Westview because of a football offer. He followed me like a puppy." Her face contorts in disgust.

"What have I ever done to you? Why have you always been after me? You're rich, everyone loves you, you got Jeff. You got Richard. What else do you want?"

"Jeff? I never had Jeff. He was supposed to be mine, but you stole him from me. Ever since he met you, he's always been in love with you, you bitch."

"What?"

"He's never loved me. Do you know what it's like to live day after day with a man who looks at you like you are vermin? Who keeps pictures of someone else in his books? His stupid Shakespeare sonnet book has one of you from just last year."

Jeff has been following me? All these years… I remember giving him that book. Our one-month anniversary. But she is a raving lunatic. I shouldn't listen to her.

"Get that phone now!" The gun is shoved at the side of my neck rather painfully.

"I can't search for it with that thing in my neck."

"You'll have to."

I get the phone out of my coat pocket. Aidan should've had enough time to get the location. Unless he is not worried at all. Unless he thinks I'm making up the entire thing. Unless he is out to lunch, having a burger, and not even thinking about me and Sophie.

"Why are you with Richard if you care so much about Jeff and couldn't care less about Richard?"

"I am with Richard because he is the only one who ever understood me. I do care about him, you know. He's not like Jeff. He does what I tell him, and he's the only one who's ever understood what I deserve. But you couldn't leave the past alone, could you? You had to ruin everything Richard and I planned."

"Just like you and he ruined my life when we were in college." *Stop it, Emma. You have to save your daughter.*

"That was over twenty years ago. Why can't you let it go?" she screams. "Everything was perfect until you screwed it all up!"

You pathetic thing. There's pity growing in me as I stare at the barrel of her gun.

"Did Richard come here to take over my company just so he could be with you?" I ask.

"Yes, but he fucked it up. Just like he fucks up everything. I should never have trusted a man to do things right. Richard found this failure of a business that your tiny pharmaceutical was. He tried to rescue it, and you and your husband pay him back by ruining his reputation and any job prospects he might ever have. How can I marry him now?"

"But you're still married to Jeff."

"Not for long. The only person who matters to me now is Ben. And then you and your daughter had to come after me and my son."

I shake my head in protest.

"Be quiet!" she yells, and the hand holding the gun shakes and raises back up to my chest.

I freeze. *This is it. Aidan, where are you?*

"You just had to crawl out of wherever you were and come after me and my son, didn't you?" she says, her eyes red with anger. "You couldn't leave us alone. None of my friends will speak to me now, with my son a criminal. Did you think I wouldn't realize it was you spreading those pictures on Facebook? You were the only one there with us that night."

Darn it. Sophie and I didn't think this through.

"And then your daughter had to come after my son? How could you let her? What is wrong with you both?"

I stare at the barrel and think of everything that's dear to me and of any possible way I've ever heard to talk a psychopath out of shooting someone. I need to stall more. Aidan is coming. Any second.

The back door slams, and we both jump a little.

"Everything all right, Shan?" Richard's voice booms as he bursts into the room.

"Yeah, you ready for us?"

I have no time to ask what's going on as I feel the sharp barrel of a gun pushed into my ribs and I'm forced to move toward the back yard. I glance at my dog's body once more. I don't allow myself to feel pain. Later. I will fall apart about Cookie later. And they are going to pay for it. As soon as I find my daughter.

Shannon moves ahead and motions Richard to walk beside me. We move quickly toward the woods, and then I know where we are going. There is a house for sale about a mile down the road. The owners moved to California a year ago, but the house is overpriced and there have been few buyers to see it. It stands dark and empty, and I can feel my daughter there.

What is their plan? I need to let Aidan know where

I am, so I'm careful to step hard into the mud to leave footprints. I wonder why Richard only makes a mild effort to cover them up.

"Hurry up," Shannon says. "She could've called the cops."

I don't increase my pace and neither does Richard. I shiver from the freezing cold, and I think of Sophie. Is she cold? Did she have a coat as they walked her there? As my fingers turn icy, I feel my wedding band slip off my finger, and, as we pass by a tree, I pretend to trip and let it slide off on a branch. I look at Richard and see him staring at me and then at the ring on the tree.

My heart stops for a second but he does…nothing. He pushes me roughly to walk on, and we both stay silent for a few minutes while I try to gather my thoughts. What does this mean?

"What have you done to my dog?" I finally whisper.

"It's ketamine spray," he whispers back.

It rings a bell, but my adrenaline-filled mind can't make sense of this right away. And then it does. Ketamine is an anesthetic. A tranquilizer. Cookie is only asleep. But why is he telling me that? I need a moment to be alone and think, but we are already in the front driveway of the house.

Fuck! What do I do? How long will it take Aidan and the police to get here?

Richard pushes me in behind Shannon, and then he sharply turns me around, even though Shannon is already past the front doors. "Is that gun loaded?"

"What gun?" I make my face blank. He can probably see the gun sticking out of my pocket. It's too late to hide it.

"There's no time for this." His eyes flame in anger.

"Yes," I say and regret it immediately. I should've shot him when I had a chance. Then it would've been just me and Shannon. I need to think faster. There is no time for logic.

"Don't use it unless I tell you," he says sharply and pushes me through the door.

Chapter 36

I enter the house, bewildered. What is happening? Did Richard decide to use me to get rid of his lover? Maybe he expects me to help.

"Where is my daughter?" I call out to Shannon.

It's dark, and I squint to try to distinguish any shapes in the empty spaces. I hear the door slamming, then steps, and someone runs into the room.

"Sophie?" I call out.

"Stand over here." Richard points to the window.

The shape I thought was Sophie approaches, and I see now it's Shannon.

"Richard, she doesn't even love you," I say with as much disgust as I can manage.

"Don't talk to her, Richard."

"It's fine, Shan. Why don't you go check on the girl?"

Shannon storms off. I walk to the window, while Richard hides in the dark kitchen.

I don't let him stay hidden. "You are successful at your company. You have a future to look forward to. Why are you throwing it all away?"

He comes out of the darkness a little, his face contorted with frustration. "I have a future to look forward to? You just ruined my future. I've lost any chance of making Chairman of the Board at Avias, due to your efforts. Jennifer's father will never forgive me for the loss on Parozex. Do you know that the FDA is looking into several of our other drugs now? The board must go testify in the Senate. They are blaming it all on me. And as if that's not enough, the media is hounding me with phone calls to ask me how many girls I raped when I was a quarterback at Westview."

"You left me for dead on that staircase. You deserve all of it," I throw at him.

"I did not leave you for dead." He suddenly walks fast toward me and comes so close I can feel the heat of his breath. "I called Jeffrey. I told him you'd been hurt and where you were. He was supposed to come pick you up."

"Liar!" I accuse, staring back at him. "Jeff never said you called him. And why will I believe any words coming out of a rapist's mouth?"

"You want to know how many girls I raped at Westview?"

"I don't fucking care."

"One." He lifts a finger. "Just one. And I know you won't believe me, but I felt awful about it."

"My heart is breaking for you. You only raped one, so that makes you a saint. You beat me! I was covered in bruises for weeks!"

"I was defending myself. You kept hitting me. I just didn't know my strength. I only pushed back."

"You punched me in my jaw and beat me all over."

"I told you. I didn't know my strength. I didn't mean to hit you."

"You just meant to rape me. I should be grateful to you, right?" The anger begins to boil inside me, and I want to reach for my gun so badly I'm sure it shows on my face.

"Look..." He turns away. "The coach was pumping us all full of steroids. I was just a kid. I felt out of control when I was on them. And Shannon—she said you were easy. That you were one of those girls who wanted a football player. I had a few drinks. And then you started hitting on me. I lost control, okay?"

"None of it is an excuse." I walk around and force him to look at my face. "I never hit on you. We had a conversation. I told you 'No' over and over. When I started hitting you, what did you think it meant?"

"I was an asshole, all right? But this was a long time ago, and you had no right to destroy my life."

"You shouldn't have come back into mine!"

"I could've fired you the day I recognized you." He straightens up and looks at me, his eyes angry again. "You and your husband. But I let you stay and work on a project that was important to me. A project that should've been important to you as well, given how badly your company was failing before I arrived. I wanted to give you a second chance."

"Give me a second chance? Are you serious? You raped me and tried to ruin my life."

"One night of sex doesn't ruin your life. But you are sure trying to ruin mine." He shakes his head.

I hear steps down the stairs, and I know I have to hurry. "Look, you should never have done this to me. But here we are. The damage is done. No one can undo it. You worry about your shattered reputation, but I lost my life twenty-one years ago. Now we both have a choice. You can go to jail for this. Or you can be a bigger person," I whisper as I hear the steps approaching. "Help me and Sophie get out of this."

"All right," Shannon says loudly, walking into the

room. She flips the light switch on and I rub my eyes, blinded by the lights. “Let’s all have a talk about what’s going to happen now.”

“Yes, I’d love to know,” I say sarcastically. “Do you have a plan, or are you just showing off?”

“I don’t know, Emma/Katie. Maybe I shouldn’t have a plan. Maybe I should just act on pure emotion.” Shannon points the gun at me, and my right hand automatically goes to my pants pocket, feeling my gun.

“What is it you’ve got in there?” Shannon zeroes in on my pocket. “Richard, take a look.”

I give Richard a defiant look as he approaches me. He narrows his eyes at me, pats my pockets, then turns back to Shannon. “Nothing. She’s empty.”

“Keep an eye on her, will you? We don’t want any surprises. So…” She hops up to sit on the kitchen island and pulls out a laptop from her bag. “Here is what we are going to do. You are going to call the newspaper that ran that story this morning, and you will discredit Dana Kapur. I wrote what you need to say—you just need to read it off. Then you will send an email to the FDA and tell them that you designed this false marketing campaign because of the pressure from Dana Kapur, as she threatened your life. I also have a resignation letter for you to sign. As soon as that’s all done, Richard and I will get on our way, and you and your darling daughter can wait for whoever it is that you called to come and rescue you.”

“So…blackmail. That’s what you wanted to add to your list.”

“Add? You think it’s my first time?” She throws her head back and laughs loudly.

Her laughter echoes through the house, and I

shudder. Can Sophie hear it? Is she frightened? How can I send her a message that I am here?

"I'm sure it's not your first time!" I say as loudly as I can. "I'll bet you blackmail whenever you get a chance." I hope Sophie can hear my voice.

"What I do and how I do it is none of your business. And don't think I don't know what you are doing." Shannon hops off the counter, takes a few steps toward me, and slaps me across the face.

The slap echoes through the kitchen, and my tense nerve endings send the pain through my entire body. I vibrate from the pain, but I no longer fear her. What I do fear is that she's hurt my daughter somehow. Or that she will. My fingers curl involuntarily into a fist, and I raise my arm to hit her, but I feel a sharp grab on my arm, and then it's twisted painfully behind me.

"Fuck!" I yell out, this time not on purpose.

"Yes, Richard, show her she needs to listen and keep her hands to herself," Shannon says with glee.

"Yes, Richard, do what your puppet master says," I mimic.

I try to wrestle out of his grasp, but he has iron strength. I should have remembered. A moment later, I feel him tying a rope around my wrists. It hurts, but I bite my lip and tolerate the pain. Better they are occupied with me than hurting Sophie.

"You are right. He does do what I say." Shannon's smile stretches on her lips. "He did a nice job beating you up after I gave you the drugs. I told him you'd be easy."

"So it was you who drugged me?" My voice is calm, but I feel myself trembling in fury.

"Of course it was her," Richard says, relaxing his

grip on my arm a bit.

"Did Shannon tell you she was in love with Jeff and that's why she wanted you to attack me? So she could tell Jeff I cheated on him?" I can't help but injure him, somehow.

He pales, and I can tell Shannon didn't say anything about that.

"Shannon, why didn't Jeff come to pick her up that night?" he asks.

Shannon doesn't answer. I answer for her, "Maybe because Shannon told him to ignore that message."

"Did you, Shannon?"

Shannon remains quiet.

"What the fuck, Shannon? She could've died. I would've gotten a murder charge!"

Of course. They only think of themselves.

"Hey," I yell. "Can we finish this kidnapping thing you are trying to pull off, and can I finally get to see my daughter?"

Shannon hands me her phone. "I dialed the number."

But before I get a chance to say anything into the phone, we hear steps outside, and the front door swings wide open.

"Jeff!" I exclaim. "You're in with them too?"

"Good grief, no. Ben called me. Cops are on the way."

I watch Ben enter behind him, his head down.

Shannon points her gun at Jeff. "Don't even think about it."

"What are you going to do? Shoot me and your son? Give it up, Shannon. This is over for you. Hand me the gun. Cops will be here in a moment." Jeff makes himself busy cutting the rope on my wrists.

"Why did you get involved in this, Ben?" Shannon asks.

"He didn't. You took his car to trap Sophie, and he came and told me right away," Jeff says.

"Mom, put down the gun," Ben pleads. "Let them go. Please don't do this. I don't want you to go to prison."

"I won't, baby. It will all be all right. Your dad and I will go to a safe place where no one will find us."

"My dad doesn't want to be involved in this."

"She means your real dad," Jeff says.

"This is your father, baby." Shannon points at Richard.

"What? This is how I find out? As you and my father are kidnapping a girl I love and her mother?"

"You love Sophie?" Jeff and I ask in unison.

Richard laughs. "How is that for irony?"

"Shut up," Shannon yells and moves her gun from Jeff to me to Richard. "All of you are missing the point of what's happening here. No one is leaving until she fixes what she's done." She points at me.

"She is raving," I tell Richard. "Do something about her."

He shrugs. I free my hands from the rope and run upstairs to Sophie. Finally, I get to see my child. "Stop," I hear Shannon yell behind me. A gunshot rings out right after that, and I fall on the hallway floor.

"Mom!" I hear Sophie screaming.

"Mom!" Ben echoes.

Sophie's hands scan my body. I'm terrified to move and feel where the pain may be. I can't feel anything. I try to make my mind blank. I know I've been shot. I just don't know where.

"I'm so happy you're okay," I whisper to Sophie.

"Mom, I don't see a shot on you. I think you're okay."

"What?" I try to sit up, and I can. I touch all over my body and allow myself to feel. There is no bullet in me. Then where is it?

We both run downstairs as the back door slams. Jeff stands by the kitchen island, the gun in his hands. The smell of gunpowder still hangs in the air.

"What happened?" Sophie asks.

"Mom was going to shoot your mother. So Dad shot her." Ben's voice is shaking badly, and Sophie runs to him and holds him in her arms.

"How hurt is she?" I ask. "Where is she?"

"Her leg," Jeff says. He looks bewildered but not frightened.

"I didn't think you had it in you, Rawley." Richard runs his hand through his hair. "Well, I better go find her. She won't get far with that leg."

"Police will find her in a moment. But I guess you want to run off," I say.

"I don't," he says. "I texted Aidan earlier. He's on his way," Richard says.

"What?"

"I don't wish you ill, Emma. I just wanted to put our past behind. Taking your daughter, threatening you—none of this was my idea. It's not my style. I didn't get to where I was by kidnapping and shoving guns in people's faces."

"Just lying and bribing and insider trading, right?"

"Whatever. No one is clean. Look what you've been doing to me and Shannon." He walks out, slamming the door behind him.

"We can't just let them leave, Mom," Sophie says.

"What are we going to do? Go after them?"

"I do have a gun," Jeff points out.

Chapter 37

"Yes, we are all very aware of that. How did you even know how to fire that thing?" I ask.

"I didn't. Shannon collects guns. I just borrowed one from her."

"Great hobby for a society woman." I smirk. "Let's wait for the police, all right?"

We hear the sirens a minute later.

"They're here. Let's go." Jeff opens the door.

I look back at Sophie. Ben is stroking her hair and whispering something to her. She smiles, as she tucks her head into his shoulder. She'll be all right. She's stronger than me. "Stay here, guys. Wait for the police. We'll be right back."

They don't even look at me, wrapped up in their…*love*, I realize.

Jeff is already outside, calling for Shannon. "She must have fainted somewhere. She's not answering." He turns to me.

I couldn't care less if she bled to death.

"Is there any place to hide near here?" Jeff asks, covering his eyes from raindrops.

"I don't think so. The trees are so bare, we'd see her. And there are no sheds or other empty houses, as far as I know. Just logs, trees, and the river."

He begins to walk toward the river, still calling for her.

"Why don't you just wait for the cops to find her?"

"Maybe she needs help."

She is his wife. Was his wife. I guess no matter how awful she is, he cares about her a little. I follow him—not because I care, but because I want to make sure she doesn't get away from the police somehow.

I listen for the sirens. They've stopped. There are flashing lights away in the distance, by our house. Darn it. They went to the wrong house. Hopefully, the kids will figure it out and walk over there. So probably another ten, fifteen minutes.

It's getting dark now. The sun is hiding somewhere over the river, gently going down. I see less in front of me and rely more on my hearing. The winter trees all seem to look the same, but the mud is increasing as we approach the river. It's been a wet winter and a soggy spring. The smell of moss is everywhere.

I wish I had my phone with me, to use the flashlight. My foot hits a puddle, and I fall rather painfully on the stump of a tree. This will be a nasty bruise. I feel for the gun, and it's still in my pocket. I'll just be filthy when the cops see me.

I slowly stand, brushing some of the dead brown leaves off me, and suddenly a heavy weight crushes me from behind, causing me to fall face first in the mud again. I fight to get up, but the weight is pushing me harder, crushing my ribs. I hear heavy breathing in my ear. I know it's Shannon, even though she doesn't say anything. The weight is not heavy enough to be Richard, or any other man. I won't allow her to frighten me. I won't ever let anyone frighten me again. She hits the side of my jaw with her gun. The pain radiates all the way to my skull.

"Get off me, you bitch," I manage to say, my face still partially squished in the mud.

"You don't expect you can actually get out of this, do you?" Shannon says, sitting on top of me and holding her gun to my head. "All I have to do is squeeze the trigger now, and I'm not clear on what's to stop me at this point."

I'll have to fight her harder. I force myself to think, and I remember that self-defense class I took years ago, way before Sophie was born. We practiced this move over and over. I squeeze my abs and throw my knees suddenly forward underneath me. Shannon's head and shoulders jerk forward and her body hangs on top of me. Good. One of her legs is weak. It's likely she can't even use it. I grab her right arm firmly, wrap my right leg around her right leg, and roll. As I land on top of her, I hit her face as hard as I can with my elbow. There is a crunch.

"What's going on?" I see Richard running toward us, out of breath.

"Are you all right?" Jeff follows behind him. He has his phone light on.

"Now you show up," I say, still gasping for breath.

Shannon lies on the ground, blood spurting out of her nose.

"Did you break her nose?" Richard yells.

"She jumped me from behind. I had to defend myself." I get off Shannon and try to clean some of the mud from my clothes with leaves. It's useless.

"Are you okay, Shannon?" Richard shakes her shoulder. "Get up, come on. The cops will be here any second. You need to get away."

Shannon moans and moves her head. Richard tries

to help her stand up.

"Richard, leave her alone. The police are here. It's too late for her. Her leg is bleeding. Her nose… She needs medical attention," Jeff says.

"She is not your concern."

"She is my fucking wife." Jeff stands close enough to Richard that I can almost see the charged air between them.

"You never wanted her."

"She never wanted me. I was just a way into society for her." Jeff's voice is sad.

"If you'd showed her more kindness, maybe your marriage could've had a chance." Richard kneels by Shannon.

"You are a fucking rapist, so who are you to give lessons in kindness?" Jeff's fingers curl into a fist.

"You've been taking bribes from a rapist for over ten years. What does that make you?" Richard scowls as he stands up to face Jeff.

The blow from Jeff's fist comes so suddenly I scream. The sound echoes through the empty gray forest and all the way to the riverbank.

"Mom!" Sophie calls from the direction of our house.

"We're here!" I answer.

Richard stands still, rubbing his jaw. I'm surprised he doesn't hit Jeff back. Jeff is kicking the dry branches on the ground. There is nothing else for either of them to say, I guess. Trapped by the same woman. Hurt by the same woman.

"Wait." I begin to look around. "Where the fuck is Shannon?"

She's gone. For all the heavy weight of her I just

felt on my back, she has managed to disappear like a firefly.

"How did you not see her go?" Jeff yells at Richard.

"I was too busy getting hit by you."

The three of us run to the river. I follow the men with their flashlights and try to watch for soggy spots and logs. I can hear voices behind us, and flashlights begin to light up the forest. I know the kids are all right, and this happy thought propels me, even though I'm muddy, hurt, and exhausted.

I'm trying to remember if Shannon still had a gun with her, but I can't. Jeff stops and doubles over.

"What's the matter?"

He gasps, then answers, "I'm old. I can't run like this anymore."

"Come this way," Richard calls. He points to the side, where another road leads to the riverbank. I think he's trying to intercept her. I hesitate a moment. He is her accomplice, after all. I can't possibly go along with him. But then gut instinct takes over, and I run behind him, frustration and fury giving me super speed.

"Shannon, what on earth are you doing?" I hear Richard screaming a minute later.

I arrive at the riverbank and see Shannon attempting to climb a pile of logs.

"Where is she trying to go?" I ask.

"I don't know."

"She's lost her mind. She'll fall into the freezing water." I put my hands to my mouth and yell as loudly as I can, "You're going to fall in!"

I can see her there, trying her footing on the logs, climbing onto one unsteadily, losing her balance. She is probably feeling faint; she must be losing blood from the gunshot wound.

"Shannon, come back!" Richard shouts. "Shan, just come back here, all right? You have no place to go. You'll fall and hurt yourself. Come here. We have money to get a good lawyer. We'll be fine," Richard begs.

"Fine, but get her away from me, because I swear…"

She doesn't finish the sentence as she tries to jump, from where she stands, over the log next to her. As she does, though, we see her foot land between two logs, and the impact sets the large pile of them rolling and moving. For the next few horrifying moments, as the police finally arrive and begin to shout at us, all we can hear are the earsplitting sounds of large logs scraping against each other as they fall into the river, taking Shannon with them.

Then, silence.

Even the cops are quiet, searching with their flashlights in the direction of our frozen stares.

I feel Aidan's arms around me. "I'm okay." I point at the river. "Shannon is under those."

Richard runs to the bank.

"Stop!" a policeman shouts.

Aidan walks over and says something to the officer, and they leave Richard be. He's gone a while.

I finally begin to shake from the cold. I'm still wearing just the thin sweater.

Aidan puts his coat around me.

"Let's go home," he says.

"I want to know if she's…"

"Probably not."

“Where are Sophie and Ben?”

“At our house.”

“We need to know what to tell him.”

“I think we should let the police tell him, don’t you think?”

As we walk toward our house, I glance back and see Richard walking slowly behind us.

“Aren’t the cops going to arrest him?” I ask.

“No, I told them he was the one who called me about Sophie being kidnapped.”

“He did? Hold on.” I wait a minute for Richard to catch up with us.

“Why did you kidnap Sophie? I don’t understand.”

“I told you I wasn’t involved in this. I wanted—and still want—to put the past behind us. I just hope we can be amicable now. Maybe you can forgive me. We can all move on, then.”

Aidan’s fist comes out so fast I don’t comprehend what’s happening until Richard is doubled over on the ground.

“She will never forgive you. I will never forgive you. What you’ve done you can never repay—do you understand?”

His fists are still clenched, and he is in position to strike Richard again if he gets up. But Richard makes no attempt to get up. He lies on the ground, staring at the dark sky, pathetic.

I grab Aidan’s arm. “Enough. Let’s go. I need this night to be over. Leave him. You’ve made your point.”

As we approach our house, Richard trailing slowly behind us, Ben and Sophie come out to meet us.

“Cookie is all better now, Mom,” Sophie says.

The dog bolts through the open door and comes to

lick my face. I stroke her soft fur and check her all over. She really is all fine. I glare at Richard. He shrugs.

"Where is my mother?" Ben asks.

I look at Richard, who now looks as muddy and disheveled as I do.

"She fell in the river, Ben," Richard says. It's gratifying to see him look so distraught.

"Is she all right?"

"She is not. She drowned. Her husband is giving a statement to the police now. If you want to go talk to them as well, I will join you in a moment."

Sophie gasps and covers her mouth.

Ben stands still and silent, then says, "Did someone throw her in the river?"

"She fell in. It was an accident, son."

"Who are you again?" Ben asks. "My father? The rapist? Why don't you shut the fuck up?"

"Look, I know you are upset. Maybe we should postpone this conversation," Richard says wearily. "We don't want to ruin this any further."

"I always ruin everything, don't I?" Ben seems to have grown a few inches taller as he looms over his father, his face dark with anger. "My mother's marriage, her social life, your kidnapping plans, apparently. What else am I ruining right now? Were the two of you planning to murder Mrs. Shephard? Should I feel lucky to have such wonderful parents?"

"Ben, just go back to the house. I'm sorry we dragged you into this," Richard says. "You weren't supposed to—"

"I wasn't supposed to what? Find out you were my father? Or find out you rape women for fun? Or spend your time kidnapping and holding women at gunpoint?

Or is that what my mother does and you just get off on it?"

I watch Richard's face, and I think he is genuinely heartbroken. I finally feel I've gotten my revenge.

I pull Sophie and Aidan inside.

I guess it's over.

Epilogue

New York City in August is hotter than Washington, D.C. The heat radiates from the pavement and bounces off the buildings and then settles right on top of people. The weight of it is heavy on my head and face, and the sweat trickles in little rivers down my sides and my chest. I want to sit down, but we need to finish getting Sophie moved into her dorm today or she won't be ready for her classes on Monday.

I bend down to pick up one of the boxes, but Ben swoops in before I even reach it.

"I got it."

"I can still lift a box, you know." I straighten up and look accusingly at Aidan. The look he gave Ben still lingers on his face.

"We got it," he says.

"I'm not on bed rest until next week. And maybe not even then," I point out.

"Better safe than sorry."

"I hate that expression." I pout and sit down.

He opens a cooler and gives me a cold water bottle. "Now this I like." I drink the cool liquid with pleasure, allowing some of it to run over my swollen belly. The wet spots form all around my popped belly button, and I smile as I notice a little motion around one of the spots. She is kicking. She doesn't mind the heat.

I catch Aidan looking too. He smiles, but there is a

hint of tears in his eyes. Is it worry? Or grief for the child we lost last winter? I don't want to ask. I want to enjoy watching my healthy baby. A few weeks ago, the doctor put in the stitch to keep her safe. I go for my appointments weekly. No more surprises. This is the most overprotected baby ever.

The last box is in by five o'clock. I face my daughter, and I try to look brave. So does Aidan. He clears his throat a few times to cover his distress. I don't bother covering. Sophie and I cry on each other's shoulders.

"Take care of my sister, all right, Mom?"

"Take care of my Sophie."

"I'll miss you so much."

"I'll miss you more. We'll be back to see you next weekend."

"What if I have plans?"

"You'll have to cancel them."

"Fine." She laughs.

Aidan pulls me away, and I let her fingers slip through mine slowly. She is gone just like that. All those years raising her. All those times I put her in danger last winter. All gone and forgotten in this moment. Now she has her own path, and I'm just a support person.

I blow her a kiss from the car, but she is no longer looking in our direction.

Aidan takes my hand in his, before he starts the car. "We'll get through this. It will be okay."

"I know. And I have my therapy session with Dr. Schnyder tomorrow. I'll be fine."

I look back as we drive away, but Sophie is gone now.

"We have to decorate the baby's room, don't we?"

"The baby's room? I haven't even thought of that."

"Well, that'll give you something to think about between visits to New York."

"Yes, it will." I laugh.

"We have to get used to having two children now."

I sleep on the way back home, but, as we pull into our neighborhood and I hear the river rushing in the back, I realize what Aidan said.

Two children. I will be a mother of two.

I will have a new life.

A word about the author…

Elena Mikalsen was born in Ukraine and came to New York City as a refugee with her family at age 17. She is somewhat obsessive about travel but when at home in San Antonio can be found browsing through bookstores or antique shops with her family and two adopted pups.

When not writing stories, she is a pediatric psychologist, working at a children's hospital, helping children cope with chronic medical illness. She actively blogs and gives interviews on issues related to child and adolescent mental health.

ALL THE SILENT VOICES is her third novel.

You can visit her at:

https://www.elenamikalsen.com